Library of Congress
Catalogue Card Number
72—95—234

SECOND EDITION

First Edition Published 1969 by Davidson Publishing Company.

Second Edition Copyright © 2000 by Dr. J. B. Davidson

All rights reserved.

Distributed by Unlimited Publishing.

www.unlimitedpublishing.com

Cover Design by Charles King.

ISBN 0-9677649-2-0

AMELIA EARHART RETURNS FROM SAIPAN

Joe Davidson

Unlimited Publishing
Bloomington, Indiana

DEDICATED TO
DREAMS
AND THOSE THAT MAKE THEM REALITIES

Fred Noonan was an outstanding celestial navigator making the trip around the world with Amelia. Anna Diaz Magoofna witnessed their execution on her way home from school.

Amelia Earhart with one of the early aiplanes she flew. Chamorro eyewitnesses told of how she and navigator, Fred Noonan survived a crash landing on the beach near Tanapag Seaplane Base. While a captive of the Japanese she was seen by many natives, known to have dysentery, was executed, cremated and buried with Noonan.

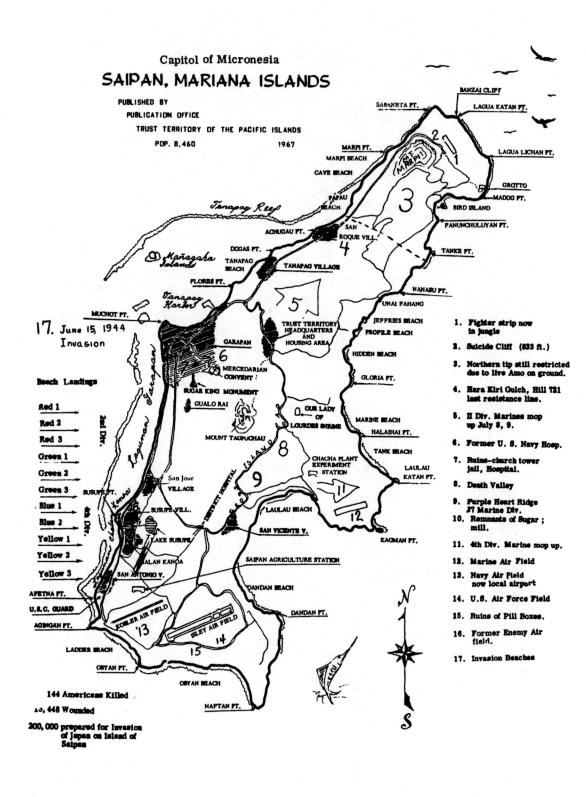

FOREWORD

Breathes there a soul so dead who has never said, "I wish I could participate in a real life adventure." It is much easier than you might think. All you have to do is look around a little and accept the challenge, then hang on with bulldog tenacity. The results will be gratifying.

This book is about five men with diverse backgrounds and occupations that made them least likely candidates for high adventure. Yet they were pulled together by a common interest and have succeeded in changing the history books to be written. Don Kothera, Ken Matonis, John Gacek, Jack Geschke, and Marty Fiorillo made personal financial sacrifices, endured personal discomforts and often lived with the barest necessities of life to set the record straight on Amelia Earhart. They succeeded where others had failed because they had a burning desire to right an injustice, as they saw it, and each possessed a compassion for their fellowmen who have been needlessly relegated to unfortunate living situations that caused a lot of investigators to take a less than adequate look.

It would be impossible to single out all who should have credits that made this book possible. We shall be eternally grateful for all who contributed. A special brand of thanks must be accorded to Florence Kothera and the rest of the wives who inspired, pushed and suffered through the agonies of two typhoons with no way to communicate with their husbands.

Marty Fiorillo must be given a special vote of gratitude for the exceptional pictures. Conditions on Saipan are less than ideal for movies and still pictures. Hopefully, a color album will follow to share the beauty and detail he has captured on film. Marty shares his bouquet with Ed Paulina who was most helpful.

I extend my personal thanks to Mac and her secretarial staff at Cuyahoga Falls, Ohio for reading the manuscript and putting it in shape for Carpenter Lithographing Company, Inc. Special thanks to them for beating an impossible deadline.

Orchids to my lovely wife, Lucile and my daughters Pam and Deb for their endurance and encouragement that really made it possible for me to write this book. If it enjoys any success, they and all who contributed deserve the credit.

Dr. J. B. Davidson
June 6, 1969

Don Kothera—He saw an airplane on Saipan in 1946. Twenty years later he saw a picture of Amelia Earhart's airplane and reported the similarity to the Cleveland Press. The resulting story prompted Ken Matonis to suggest they go to Saipan to see if it was the same plane.

Ken Matonis—The real sparkplug who started the adventure by telling Don Kothera, "Let's go to Saipan and find that airplane you saw in 1946."

John Gacek—A chance member of the first trip to find Amelia's plane when he went as a substitute for Jack Geschke. His warm personality and interrogating ability made him a valuable member of the adventure team.

Jack Geschke—A World War II veteran who had been on Saipan and wanted to return. He sent John Gacek in his place on the first trip. He made the second trip to help excavate the remains of Amelia Earhart and Fred Noonan.

Marty Fiorillo—Selected as the official photographer because he had previous archeological experience.

Letter cover from Dick Earhart's collection. This relative of Amelia lives in Cleveland. He has spent 30 years collecting material concerning his famous namesake.

The Earhart home where Amelia was born July 24, 1898.

Don visiting with Mrs. Albert Morrissey, Amelia's sister who lives in Medford, Massachusetts.

CHAPTER I

SOS KHAQQ   SOS KHAQQ   This signal was picked up July 2, 1937 by a powerful amateur radio set near Los Angeles. The operator, Walter MacMenamy was very excited and delcared, "It was Miss Earhart all right! I know her voice very well!"

To review our history a bit, Amelia Earhart was born in Atchison, Kansas in 1898. Her father was a lawyer and railway claim agent who had an alcohol problem. This had a profound effect on Amelia because she truly loved her father and was driven to great achievement because of his weakness.

She went East to study at Columbia University, then West to be with her parents, who had moved to Los Angeles. In California Amelia saw many airplanes and was intrigued by them. She had her first flight with the famous Captain Frank Hawks. In 1918 she made her first solo, after ten hours of instruction. Two years later she set a woman's altitude record of 14,000 feet. She would have continued flying, but finances were a bit of a problem.

Amelia Earhart and her mother went East again by automobile, which was a major operation at that time. She enrolled again at Columbia and studied at Harvard Summer School.

She got into social work at South Boston's old Denison House and her work at the settlement house was outstanding. Her willingness to endure long hours of hard work, and the warmth she projected made her a favorite of everyone she came into contact with at this establishment. Marion Perkins, Head Worker at Denison House, wrote the introduction to Amelia Earhart's book, "20 Hours and 40 Minutes". She said, "A tall slender, boyish-looking young woman walked into my office in the early fall of 1926." Several witnesses who saw her on Saipan referred to her as looking like a man. She was often called "Lady Lindy" because she resembled Charles Lindberg.

We are getting ahead of our story so we will back up. While at Denison House she was asked to go along as a passenger on a transatlantic airplane flight. The sponsor of the project thought it would be good publicity to take a woman along. She had established herself as a flyer and this would add interest. Without hesitation Amelia said she would go. This was prior to the establishment of commercial aviation and her ready acceptance indicated her complete lack of fear that many regarded as daring or fool-hardy. She would have regarded it as just another positive move to prove human weakness should not limit anyone, and especially women.

Amelia Earhart thus made national headlines as the first woman to fly across the Atlantic. She had star billing along with Wilmer Stultz and Louis Gordon in the *Friendship*. After that she settled down to learn flying as well as she could, with her inborn determination. She always felt that any job worth doing was worth doing well. She flew for fun, flew for publicity, and flew without any good reasons at times. While flying for Beechnut Products she made headlines by cracking up an autogiro—about the nearest thing to a foolproof aircraft. However, nothing could stop her and she learned to fly so well that she became the world's number one woman flyer and rolled up an impressive list of "firsts":

*First woman to fly the Atlantic.
*First woman to fly the Atlantic alone.
*First person to fly the Atlantic alone twice.
*First woman to fly an autogiro.
*First person to cross the United States in an autogiro.
*First woman to fly from Mexico to the United States.
*First woman to receive the Distinguished Flying Cross.
*First woman to fly non-stop across the United States.
*First woman to fly from Hawaii to the United States.

Amelia Earhart became a good friend of Eleanor Roosevelt who shared her belief that women should not stand in the shadow of men. In 1931 she married a publicity minded publisher named George Palmer Putnam. He never dissuaded her from flying wherever she wanted to go.

She wrote a book entitled *"The Fun of It"*, which best fitted her career, but she still regarded flying a serious business and professed interest in the scientific aspect of flying. She became a consulting member of Purdue University's faculty, specializing in aeronautics and careers for women, and while there acquired a Wasp-motored Lockheed Electra 10 which was supposed to be a 'flying laboratory' equipped with up-to-the-minute flying and navigating devices. Its $80,000 cost was mostly provided by anonymous members of the Purdue Research Foundation. This drew a few barbs at the time since it was specified that the plane should be her personal property to do with as she saw fit.

One thing Amelia Earhart Putnam still wanted to do—for the fun of it—was to fly around the world. Amelia had flown alone across the Atlantic and a good part of the Pacific. It was natural enough that such an adventure would be selected to add to her many aviation firsts. This trip would require some expert celestial navigation. There were few navigational aids around the world during this era of flying and going from coast to coast was a major hazardous project. Going around the world required a working knowledge of fixing one's position by the sun, moon and stars. Any miscalculation could put the entire mission in disastrous jeopardy. Someone, perhaps Miss Earhart, selected two outstanding celestial navigators to make the trip, which was to go from West to East starting in California. Fred Noonan was outstanding in the field of navigation, having been the ace navigator for Pan American Airways until John

Amelia in California showing mannish appearance many witnesses mentioned.

Don with native boys in 1946.

Unused shells on Saipan in 1946.

Barleycorn got the best of him and he was relieved of his duties. However, he had been the navigator on Pan American's first survey flights across the Pacific and needed the job, so Amelia agreed that he should go along. Captain Manning of the U.S. Navy was well qualified as a navigator, and accompanied Amelia Earhart and Fred Noonan on the first leg of the first attempt. They made it safely to Hawaii, but blew a tire and crashed on take-off for the second leg of the trip. No one was seriously hurt and the plane was repairable, so the trio and the airplane went back to California by ship. Captain Manning's leave ran out while the airplane was being repaired at the Lockheed factory in California. For some strange reason he was not given permission to go along on the second attempt some two months later.

The plane came out of the factory May 19th with some modifications. It had a gasoline capacity of 1150 gallons which gave it a cruising radius in excess of 4,000 miles. Two Wasp H engines developed 1100 horsepower with top speeds of over 200 miles per hour.

With the airplane thus rigged Amelia took off June 1, 1937 with Fred Noonan, after she confided to close friends that this would be her last flight of this type. That is, she was through with so-called stunt flying and would concentrate on the scientific aspects of flying when she returned. When asked if she was worried, she philosophically stated, "The time to worry is three months before a flight. Decide then whether or not the goal is worth the risks involved. If it is, stop worrying. To worry is to add another hazard. It retards reactions, makes one unfit." Then with a smile added, "Hamlet would have been a bad aviator. He worried too much."

They made mostly back page news as they flew leisurely to South America, Africa, India and Australia. There was little publicity or public interest until on July 1 when they left Lae, New Guinea

Don and Mac on Saipan in 1946.   *Robert Green and Don on Saipan 1946.*

Don clowning in 1946.

on the 2,556 miles over the ocean to Howland Island and failed to reach it. Howland Island is only one mile wide and two miles long, which makes it a pretty small target out in the vast Pacific. However, they figured they had four means of locating it:

1. Dead reckoning (which is simply the estimate of position based on speed in a given direction for a definite time while taking on consideration wind drift and all variables).
2. Radio bearings from ships at sea and shore stations.
3. A radio direction-finder in the cockpit.
4. Celestial navigation.

With all of these aids they failed to reach Howland Island.

For reasons known only to them, Miss Earhart and Mr. Noonan did not bother to reveal their position along the way after leaving Lae, New Guinea for the "worst section" of the 2,556 miles of open ocean for the tiny Howland Island. The Coast Guard cutter *Itasca* heard from them approximately once every hour. Amelia's final message said she had only half-an-hour's gas left and could not see land. They were flying a line position of 157-337 but did not indicate the direction on this line. She still gave no position and the *Itasca's* direction finder could not get a bearing because she failed to adjust her radio to its frequency.

Several facts made it clear that much more than simple bad luck was involved. Before the take-off, the capable Navigator Noonan inspected what he supposed was an ultramodern "flying laboratory." He was dismayed to discover that there was nothing with which to take celestial bearings except an ordinary ship sextant. He remedied that by borrowing a modern bubble octant designed especially for airplane navigation. For estimating wind drift over the sea, he obtained two dozen aluminum powder bombs. For reasons unknown these bombs were left behind in a storehouse. The Coast

Don took this picture of a dental assistant on Saipan, 1946.
(PHOTO BY DON KOTHERA)

Guard cutter *Itasca*, which had been dispatched from San Diego to Howland Island solely as a help to the flyers, would have been able to take directional bearings on the Earhart plane if she could have tuned its signals to a 500-kilocycle frequency. The airplane's transmitter would have been able to send such signals if it had been equipped with a trailing antenna. Miss Earhart considered all this too much bother to keep reeling in a trailing antenna, so none was taken along. Finally, the *Itasca's* commander would have had a better idea where to look if the airplane had radioed its position at regular intervals. But not one position report was received after the plane left Lae, New Guinea. In fact only seven position reports are known to have been radioed by the flyers during their entire trip. This may have been planned if they originally planned to go to Saipan without anyone suspecting that to be their mission. When it became apparent that the plane was down, the *Itasca* steamed around hopelessly to search without the slightest idea where to look. Experts believed the airplane would float a long time if undamaged in landing and if the weather was good.

A Navy flying boat that set out from Hawaii was turned back by a severe, freakish ice storm. Then came the first faint radio signals, S O S KHAQQ, which were reported by amateurs in Cincinnati, Wyoming, San Francisco and Seattle, by the British cruiser *Achilles* in the South Pacific, by Pan American Airways in Hawaii and others. Though all that could be distinguished was a faint voice saying S O S KHAQQ (the plane's call letters) over and over. There was no indication whether the plane had landed on land or sea, south or north of Howland.

George Palmer Putnam clung to hope believing Amelia had come down on land, which we now know she did, because the radio batteries, located under the ship's wings, would have been put out

A close-up of the hotel where Amelia was held prisoner. Matilde San Nicholas lived next door. Amelia helped her with a geograph map and gave her a ring just before she died.

An official Japanese photo of pre-war Garapan City which had 52 Japanese business establishments including the Kobayoshi Royokan Hotel indicated by the arrow.

of commission in the water and that S O S KHAQQ would not have come through.

According to one report, when Husband Putnam got word that her plane was lost he wired an appeal for a Navy search to President Roosevelt. But even before the message reached Washington, Secretary of the Navy Swanson had ordered the Navy to start hunting. The greatest rescue expedition in flying history speedily got under way at huge expense. The battleship *Colorado* raced at forced draft from Hawaii. Four destroyers and the aircraft carrier *Lexington* with 62 planes left San Diego. Japanese vessels of the Japanese fishing fleet joined in the search. At week's end no one knew whether Miss Earhart was another Kingsford-Smith, who was lost forever in the Bay of Bengal, or another Ellsworth, who was found snug and happy in Antarctica after a two-month search—which gave him more publicity than he had ever received before.

Anyway, it seemed a bit strange to mobilize a full naval task force which, by the end of the week, was costing $250,000 a day just to hunt for two people on a stunt flying mission. Could it have been, as has been often suggested, that they were indeed on a spying mission for the Navy? It likely does not make much difference, at this point, except the public has a right to know the truth, especially when tax dollars are spent.

At first the *Colorado* catapulted three planes from its deck upon reaching the Phoenix Island. The flyers skimmed over Gardner and McKean Islands and Carondelet Reef. They eventually scanned 100,000 square miles without sighting anything significant except birds that were menacing to their propellers. The *Itasca* continued a futile patrol around the area until fuel ran short. The mine-sweeper *Swan* put a searching party on Canton Island. The aircraft carrier *Lexington,* with its 62 planes aboard and an escort of four destroyers stopped in Hawaii to refuel and arrived on the scene by the week of July 19th. Rear Admiral Orin G. Murfin was co-ordinator of the search. When the *Lexington's* great fleet of planes failed to turn up a clue the search was abandoned.

It had been a pretty hairy experience. Sixty of the *Lexington's* sixty-two planes took to the air near the International Date Line while commanders prayed and hoped fervently for no mishaps. Later this searching complement was cut to forty-two planes. The weather, was sheer torture. Some days everyone was burned to a crisp by the equatorial sun, and the aviators had to cover their faces with protective grease. The next day would bring tropical squalls that sent planes scurrying back to the ship hoping to be able to land. Although they had found nothing, there was a big sigh of relief when this nerve-wrecking torture ended and the fleet headed back home.

There was much criticism in Washington about using the Navy to search for 'stunt' flyers. The House Naval Affairs Committee prepared to take up legislation which would prohibit the Navy from undertaking costly service or on missions of "unquestionable scientific value." Here, again, it might be well to mention that if, indeed, Amelia Earhart and Fred Noonan were on a mission for their country, someone at the top should have stood up and been counted. From all appearances now, these two courageous people sacrificed their lives. They may have become the first two casualties of World War II without an official recognition. This situation might have remained in this sorry state if it had not been for the efforts of five men from Garfield Heights that will go a long ways beyond the call of duty to right a wrong. Their dedication to purpose developed into one of the greatest adventures of modern times.

This group succeeded in solving the mystery of Amelia Earhart and Fred Noonan. As their uncanny adventure unfolds, it is obvious that Lady Luck was in their corner at all times. Their avowed goal of finding out what really did happen to Amelia and Fred some thirty years ago became an obstinate task that required much personal sacrifice. With all of their dedication, however, it is doubtful that this attempt to bring Amelia home would have been successful and, certainly their adventure would never have gotten in book form, if they had been deprived of any one of several strategic strokes of luck or fate.

This portion of a church is all that remains as a reminder of the total devastation of Garapan City by U.S. forces prior to the invasion of Saipan June 15, 1944.

Awaiting customs clearance at the Saipan Airport.

The pink Datsun that transported the group around during their adventure on Saipan.

Oxen cart is still used by some natives.

CHAPTER II

THE FIRST TRIP TO SAIPAN TO FIND AMELIA'S PLANE

Before we get into their great adventure, a little more background material will help set the stage for better understanding.

Amelia Earhart and Fred Noonan's ill-fated trip around the world in 1937, with their mysterious disappearance, touched off a wave of speculation that brought up theories involving them in all kinds of intrigue. Some said they were on a super secret spy mission for the United States government to photograph the illegal build-up of fortifications in the Marianas and, more specifically, Saipan. Japan had moved into Saipan early in World War I without Germany's permission. Japan sought and obtained the League of Nations' permission to hold the Marianas as a trust territory with the definite understanding that no part of the territory would be fortified. The United States government was sure this agreement was being violated, but since they did not belong to the League of Nations they could not bring it up. Positive tangible proof would have been required to get any action from the League of Nations.

We now know that Saipan was the center of much Japanese intelligence and planning for World War II. The highest ranking intelligence officer captured during the whole war was captured on Saipan. That is another interesting story that someday may be told.

The fact remains, at the time Amelia Earhart attempted her trip the United States was on friendly (but somewhat suspicious) terms with Japan. Any suggestion that her trip was anything other than an adventure to add to her many flying accomplishments brought vehement denials from official Washington. That was in the good old days when no one dreamed public officials in a great democracy would stray from the truth, even for political purposes.

A native family that lives off the sea. Head of the family holds a harpoon used to spear fish.

Beach at Magician Bay. Natives are fishing with detonators that stun the fish.

Four hundred years before that, Shakespeare said: "What fools we mortals be........"

If we are dedicated to the prime virtue of truth, having brought up the past does obligate us to pursue those events of the past in the light of more recent knowledge concerning the facts. It seems increasingly apparent that our trusted political servants perform less and less like trusted political servants should. They have mislead us to the point of having to coin the phrase, "credibility gap". We seem to be willing to accept "credibility gaps" from our politicians and "communication gaps" from our children with wreckless abandon. Such understanding permits us to proceed with charity, but very little dignity. If all facets of this one little episode were probed in depth, this credibility gap would be a new rival for the giant yawn of the Grand Canyon. We never seem to learn that little white lies have a way of growing into great, monstrous, hairy, black desecrations of lovely Madam Truth.

This still leaves us without a firm start on a trip that will help close the gap on Amelia Earhart and Fred Noonan's whereabouts. I am only trying to set the stage to tell it like it is. Whether it hurts or not, most people want to know the truth. There are people who will sacrifice a great deal to provide the truth for their fellow men.

There have been some new discoveries about the Amelia Earhart flight that could have been known long ago, but would likely never have been known if some dedicated men had not become involved over thirty years after the flight's tragic end July 2, 1937.

Now that the historical events of the Amelia Earhart flight have been sketched and we have alluded to another adventure, a point of beginning has been established to pursue that adventure of some very adventurous men. Their almost unbelievable fascinating life episode must be told the way it happened in sequence to be appreciated.

The logical order of this chain of events takes us back to the invasion of Saipan during World War II. This island was a command station for the Japanese for the Marianas group. This stronghold was defended by nearly 30,000 well-armed Japanese that were dug into caves which covered the mountainsides. The Marines landed June 15, 1944. Saipan fell to the United States July 9, 1944 with very few Japanese soldiers being taken captive. Cost to the United States was 4,442 dead and nearly 13,000 wounded. General Tojo was relieved of his duties over this loss and the emperor's naval adviser, Fleet Admiral Nagano exclaimed, "This is terrible! Hell is on us!" He was so right. This was really the beginning of the end for Japan. With little effort, comparatively speaking, Tinian was taken and airstrips built that soon launched the airplanes which dropped the first atomic bombs on Japan. The second atomic bomb jolted the emperor into complete submission.

In the ensuring years of occupation following victory thousands of military personnel spent varied stints of duty on Saipan. Among these thousands was an 18 year old Navy man who hailed from Cleveland, Ohio. Like most men who were not in service by choice, he answered when called (and there was no place to hide), to the name of Don Kothera. Don left his West Coast Port of Embarkation June 4, 1946. As he started up the loading ramp a Chief Petty Officer asked him if he would help him with his extra bags. Since this was a superior and they were going to be on the same crowded ship for several days, Don grabbed a couple of bags that he was sure were loaded with pure lead and struggled up the ramp and on into what could be loosely referred to as a stateroom. With a feeling of being very lucky to get into the room first, Don picked out a bottom bunk that he felt would be easy to get in and out of and put his bag there to claim it. The Chief followed him in and said, "I am in charge here. Move your things to a top bunk". Respecting that rank again, Don did not say what he thought at that moment (and we could not print it even if he had), but it boiled down to the understatement that he did not think this was very much gratitude on the Chief's part for Don's help. They were not out to sea very long when he realized the Chief had been on a crowded ship before and had done Don a big favor by ordering him to a top bunk. As Don explained it, "He had not realized there would be so much sea-sickness and with 3500 on the boat the first few hundred took up all of the available rail room for tossing their cookies. The rest had to stay in their bunks. With all of that vomiting and the law of grav-ity being what it is, it was much more desirable to be on the top bunk even though it was not quite as handy to get into." He appre-ciated the Chief more every day for the next fifteen days of that rough crossing.

June 19, 1946 this floating mass of unwell humanity docked at Guam. After stretching their legs they were told to line up on a bunch of marked squares. From the 3500 men 400 were selected to go to Saipan as a skeleton occupation force to run the Island. They were given strict orders that there would be absolutely no fraterni-zation with the natives and no one was allowed to leave his area.

Don lost no time in hunting down the personnel officer to find out what would be available in the way of duty. He had learned that sometimes those in command can be helpful. Lt. Hunt put Don in charge of service records, after he recovered from the shock of having him volunteer. Part of his duties was keeping fresh coffee available. He liked the job fine, but this was to be short lived. After being there two weeks an Admiral came in and asked for his service record which he said would be easy to find as it had been following

The horseshoe bay gives a good panoramic view of the beautiful beach.

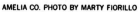

Roadway into a Saipan jungle.

him for forty years and would be the thickest one there. Don's inability to produce that record got him an immediate transfer to Ensign Regan who was in charge of communications. Don was very happy to go, after the wrath of the admiral had subsided and he was assured of his shortcomings in ungentlemanly phrases that forty years in the navy can teach a man. Don was sure he had not lost any records, but just knew he had set one by bringing out the best tongue-lashing that admiral had ever handed out. In fact after Don was sure he would not have to walk the plank or be shot at sunrise, he began to appreciate the admiral's great performance. Few people he had known had even half the range in volume changes and no one he ever knew could change from bright red to white with a patriotic blue in between. Had the admiral taken up acting as a career, he would have clinched an Oscar in any horror movie for the facial changes alone.

Don's job with Ensign Regan was working in the code room. This meant being locked up in a concrete building most of the time. While there he learned a little about running a typewriter and was told one day to report to a Captain Sherman. He went over to the Captain's quarters, a quonset hut with a banana tree growing through the screen into the small room. Don rapped on the door and was greeted with a very audible, "What the hell are you trying to do? Do you want to knock all the bananas off the tree?" The next request was for him to come on in. Cautiously opening the door, Don found himself eyeballing a big four striper. His automatic salute brought absolutely no response from the Captain except to tell him to relax. That banana tree running through the window was informal enough, but there was more to come to convince Don this was the place he had been looking for. Captain Sherman asked Don if he had met Vince DeCarlo and shouted, "Hey Vince". From

Saipan Mission Church. The building to the left is all that remains of the once flourishing Japanese sugar industry.

Don takes a lonely look towards home 9,000 miles away.

the back room came the response, "Yeh, what do you want?" Don cringed a little and waited for the old respect lecture that most officers like to give with their own individual embellishment. There were no lectures; informality was the password here and Vince came out smiling to meet Don. After about six weeks of code work the Captain asked Don about his journalism qualifications. Don admitted he had none, so in typical military fashion he was put in charge of getting out a newspaper for Saipan. Fortunately he could type a little by the hunt and peck method. Armed with a typewriter, a mimeograph, and news that came into Guam on the AP and UP wires, Don started putting this remote place back in touch with the world. The first issue offered five dollars to the person that provided the best name. A nurse named it SAIPANARAMA and claimed the five bucks for her contribution.

This turned out to be a night project as the Captain wanted the papers on all of the officers' desks by six o'clock every morning. Don found this much to his liking. Once the paper was delivered, he had the rest of the day to look around for contraband and search the many caves on the mountainside where the Japanese had holed up. He found a buddy, Gilbert H. Smith who was in a similar situation as far as time was concerned. Together they spent day after day looking for souvenirs. They were primarily interested in guns, swords, and knives. All of this effort could be justified since they reported anything they found pertaining to American soldiers to grave registration. Sending back personal momentos to families that had lost loved ones in the war was much appreciated. It was a violation of the rules to keep any Japanese material, but these rules were not enforced very rigidly. It was pretty much finders keepers, especially if you did not report what you had found.

One day while going through the jungle up to the caves from a little different route, Don came across a non-military airplane that was stripped of engines and seats. It seemed strange to him that the plane had no damage to the fusilage and was in the jungle in a box canyon. He realized it could not have landed there without extreme damage and the jungle was grown up around it so it would have had to have been there for some time. Being a bit curious he looked inside and was further baffled by the fact that the interior contained no seats, nets, or racks the military planes used for seats.

There were no souvenirs inside so Don closed the door and he remembers his buddy taking a couple of shots at the door handle just for target practice. Seeing the bullet holes in the door brought Don to the realization that there were no bullet holes in the plane other than these two and that the windows and windshields were also intact.

While Don was inspecting the plane further, Smitty climbed up the steep bank 15 to 20 feet above and yelled for Don to come on up. Knowing Smitty had found something more interesting, Don climbed up to see what it was. There, above the plane, were some very large coastal guns. They were about 12 inch guns taken from Singapore after the Japanese had captured the city by coming in the back way through the jungle and four were on permanent mountings. They sighted down the barrels to see what these guns were aimed to hit. This later became very important to find the location of the airplane. They realized these guns were never used for combat as there were no shell or bomb craters around them. If they had ever been fired at an American ship out in the bay the fire would have been returned. The city of Garapan, for instance, was completely destroyed during the invasion of Saipan.

After playing around with the guns for some time Smitty discovered a cave that had been carefully camouflaged about 30 feet from the guns. They broke open the cave and found it contained two Japanese bodies and a lot of booty. They took all of the guns, bayonets, swords, and decided to call it a day. Upon leaving, they remarked about the trees being planted carefully on ten foot centers to camouflage the guns. Their return trip took them by the plane again and Don still just could not quite figure how it was there so well preserved and this far away from everything.

Back at the base word leaked out that Don and Smitty had broken open a cave. They got orders to report to the officer of the day that evening. They reported to Chief Petty Officer Ryerson, who asked them about the cave and what they had found. They were scared and did not know what he might know about the guns, but decided not to tell him about them. They were sure these would have been confiscated. Instead they told about the maps, diaries, briefcases, cans of water and rice, etc. This was important enough that the Chief told them there would be some men from Guam the next morning to see them again.

When Don and Smitty reported to the officer of the day the next morning Don was introduced to an ensign and a Lt. J. G. who again insisted on knowing what they had seen in the cave. After telling them all they had remembered seeing, less the guns, a squad of marines was called and a personnel carrier requisitoned to take them to the cave. The carrier had to be stopped on the road and the party walked in much to their dislike. Don and Smitty took fiendish delight in leading the unconditioned desk officers up the mountain. It was a very hot trip to the plane and on up to the cave. The contents of the case were removed—including maps, 8 briefcases, diaries, 2 G.I. water cans containing water and rice, money, and pens. The detachment marched back down the hill the way they had come up, past the airplane again. Back at the base

One of the many unused beaches on Saipan.

Interior of the Japanese prison where an American prisoner was allegedly burned alive as reprisal for a U.S. bomb hitting the structure.

they were dismissed.

About two months later Don was asked to take Bob Green and a marine gunnery sergeant up to see the big guns. This was his third and last trip by the airplane that did not look as if it should be where it was without being torn completely apart. He and Smitty continued to hunt through the caves and help the grave registration teams.

Don came back to the States December 24, 1947 and was discharged from the service. He started a ceramic tile business, Crest Tile Company. He worked at that, getting married in 1950. The everyday problems of business and maintaining a home gradually eliminated most thoughts about Saipan, but from time to time Don mentioned the plane to his wife and they looked at the picture of the plane on various occasions.

At the beginning of 1959 different articles started appearing in Cleveland papers, tying Amelia Earhart to Saipan, which interested Don since he had been there. In 1962 Don called Fred Goerner at C.B.S. in San Francisco to tell him about the plane he had seen on Saipan. Mr. Goerner was doing intensive research into all facets of Amelia's trip at the time which he later put into a most interesting and informative book called the "Search for Amelia Earhart." Mr. Goerner told Don if there had been such a plane it would by this time have wound up as a hut or a belt buckle. Still having a very vivid picture of the plane in his mind, and knowing the inaccessibility of that plane, made Don wonder if the local situation on Saipan was bad enough that the natives would actually have removed the airplane. He rationalized that Mr. Goerner was plagued with so many leads, many of which had to be blind alleys, that anything this unlikely just had to be dismissed as "another person trying to get some publicity."

Female prison built by the Japanese.

The controversial NTTU looking north towards Suicide Cliff.

About a year later Don read another article by Fred Goerner and called him again. This time Don repeated his account of the airplane in the jungle and offered to go over to help find it if the proper financial arrangements could be made. That is, Don did not feel he could afford to pay for his trip, but was willing to take the time from his business to go. Mr. Goerner told him that some financial arrangements were pending for another trip and that he would call Don if he could be included on the next trip. By this time Don was getting keyed up over the possibilities and waited anxiously hoping every day to hear from Fred Goerner. No call ever came and again Don became lost in his routine of business.

July 2, 1967 Florence Kothera, Don's wife, pointed out a full page article in the Cleveland Plain Dealer written by the editor of a Columbus newspaper, Mr. Al Andrews. The article showed a picture of the Lockheed airplane that Amelia Earhart had used for her last trip. Don said to Florence, "That sure looks like the airplane I saw in the jungle on Saipan." Florence suggested that he should write a letter to the editor. His previous rebuffs from editors had left him somewhat bitter and as far as he was concerned this one likely would be no different. He had concluded that newspapermen write because that is their job and they are not greatly concerned about what they write about once it is in print. Florence kept bugging him about writing a letter because she knew that airplane would bother Don until it was checked out.

Wives can be very persistent when they think something is right and worthwhile, so Florence kept up her insistence that Don write the editor in Columbus. He finally gave in and very reluctantly scribbled a note to the editor on a pencil tablet without any idea who would see the note and certain he would not get an answer. He got an immediate reply encouraging him to continue his interest and report this information to a local reporter. The letter stated further that a Cleveland reporter would call on Don and any information would be appreciated. This last part appeared to Don that someone was passing the buck, and he doubted that anyone would contact him on this matter. He dismissed the whole thing from his mind and went to work, telling Florence he would be late as he had a tiling job to do that evening after his regular work was done. That day a reporter came to the job where Don was working. After an interview a story was published.

That story became a turning point in historical events and events that were about to take place. For one thing it changed Don's image of newspaper reporters. He found they really are interested in what they write about. He also found out that many people read the newspapers with more than casual interest.

Typhoon Rips Saipan

AGANA, Guam—(UPI)—The 175-mph winds of Typhoon Jean flattened most of Saipan's residential areas today but reports from the World War II battlefield island said no lives were lost.

Radio broadcasts said at least 90% of the U. S.-governed island was devastated, with homes crushed and most foliage stripped away. About 75% of the U. S. Government buildings were heavily damaged, the radio said.

The typhoon moved off to the north and its center later was spotted by weather planes near Pagan Island 175 miles from Saipan.

(Five Greater Clevelanders are on Saipan searching for traces of Amelia Earhart's plane, missing since 1937 They are Donald Kothera, 11315 Brunswick Rd.; Ken Matonis, 13901 Grove Dr., and Police Lt. John Gacek, all of Garfield Heights; and Jack Geschke, 3708 Walter Ave., Parma, and Martin Fiorillo, 4916 E. 84th St.)

CHAPTER III

THE TRIP TO SAIPAN

One of the people who read that article was Ken Matonis. Ken had been a very close friend of Don's for many years. Ken and Earl Herbold had gone into business as Cuyahoga Cleaning Contractors. From time to time they had discussed the airplane. Ken knew now that it had almost become an obsession with Don. Ken and his partner, Earl Herbold had done well in business and felt their company could justify an expenditure for a trip to Saipan. He knew Don was very positive about where the airplane was located and could find it if it was still there. He also knew Don would never rest comfortably until he was certain this one had been Amelia Earhart's plane or proved it had not.

It is impossible to have a friend who understands one's innermost feelings without knowing that person would do anything in the world for you. Such was the relationship between Don Kothera and Ken Matonis. Ken had decided he must do this for his friend. In spite of the bond between them, Don was overwhelmed when Ken called and said, "Hey, buddy I read your story in the paper and you are still telling it the way you have told me. Now would you like to return to Saipan and find that airplane or continue to wonder about it the rest of your life?"

"Boy, Ken, you know I would sure like to go back over there and find that (unusable descriptive adjective) airplane. People are starting to think I am a little squirrelly. In fact, if it were not for you and Florence I might decide that they could be right."

Ken was more convinced than ever now that they must go to Saipan and said again, "I am serious, Don, how about you and I going to Saipan?"

With a thoughtful pause that seemed like an hour to Ken, waiting on the other end of the line, Don finally came through with, "Ken, you know I would rather do that than most anything I know of, but I cannot afford any such trip."

Recognizing the futile tone of depression in his old friend's voice, Ken blurted out, "Let's go, I will finance the trip through my company. I have it all figured out how."

Don knew at that moment that he was going back to Saipan and an ethereal feeling came over him. That feeling was soon transformed into an expression that Ken could have enjoyed more if he had hung up the telephone and just gone to the window to listen to Don's screams of delight across Garfield Heights. Ken was sure Mother Nature would eventually restore his hearing. Anyway, it was worth having a ruptured eardrum to know Don was so happy about his plan to go to Saipan. They agreed to get together that evening to make plans for the trip.

Florence, always a delightful hostess, was at her best that evening. The first part of the evening was spent reminiscing about everything from the time Don went into service until the present moment. Everyone was completely ecstatic about what a wonderful trip this was going to be for Ken and Don. If the women had any reservations they did not let it be known.

Then like a bolt of lightning out of the blue came horrible reality. HOW DO YOU GET TO SAIPAN? All had read Fred Goerner's book and knew it was a trust territory administered by the United States and that it was possible to get there, but now they must find out how. It was like deciding to go to the moon. Who do you get permission from and after you have the permission to go, just how to get there becomes very important.

Florence called United Airlines first. They had heard of Saipan, but did not know how to get there. The clerk suggested they call Pan American when she was advised it was in the Pacific near Guam. The Pan American staff was not much more help. They could get them to Guam, but could not give them much information about how to go from there. By this time Ken and Don would have swam through the shark infested waters, if they had to, in order to make it from Guam to Saipan. Don knew it was not far from Guam to Saipan and there had to be a boat or charter plane over to Saipan. Several cups of coffee later they were down to the 'nitty gritty' of how to begin, as far as getting visas was concerned. Florence became the unanimous choice by conscription to handle those little details.

The next morning our new conscript called Washington. It was to be one of many calls to many people. None of them knew how to get to Saipan and all had to know why anyone would even consider going there even though they themselves had no real good idea where Saipan was located. After two weeks of completely negative results, Florence was ready to resign her commission and turn in her telephone. She was starting to get a feeling of hopelessness, when a bit of fate stepped in that was to occur time and again throughout their adventure.

Ken was talking to a business associate, Jack Geschke, and told him about the planned trip to Saipan except there seemed to be no one that could tell them how to get there. The whole affair intrigued Jack and he wanted to share the expense and participate. He had spent some time on Saipan while in the service and was a real fan of Amelia Earhart. He had seen her perform at the air shows prior to her fatal flight. Ken told Jack he would discuss the possibility of a third party going with Don. As far as Ken was concerned, he could see no reason why such an arrangement would not be most

NTTU looking west towards Tanapag Harbor.

One of the Japanese guns being removed from the jungle by Ex-Chief Aiken.

satisfactory, but Don's feelings on the matter would be the deciding factor. It was Jack's turn at anxiety. Just the thought of joining such an adventure and returning to Saipan put him in a nervous state that would have made the most keyed up expectant father a model of self-control.

Ken and Don had another of their many coffee and cookie meetings to decide about taking Jack along. Don agreed this would be fine. It turned out to be another one of those good fateful decisions. Florence was still running into blind alleys in trying to get visas and permits to go to Saipan. Jack being a very practical man, with some experience with the political approach to problems, got them an audience with Congressman Charles Vanik. It took him very little time to get them the proper forms and permission to go to Saipan, which the United States controls under a trust agreement with the United Nations. With permission granted they could get started with their preparations to go.

While the preparations were going on, including various immunizations, Jack became involved in the acquisition of the International Airport Inn. Negotiations were at a point where he could not leave and there was a great deal of uncertainty about when he would conclude the deal. In order not to delay them, Jack decided to drop out of this trip.

Another stroke of luck entered the picture. Police Lt. John Gacek was a friend of the group and had been at Don's house during many of the evening coffee sessions. He had talked about going if anyone dropped out. While discussing Jack's inability to go, John's name was mentioned as a possibility to fill out the party. The more Don and Ken talked about John going the more practical it seemed. He was a licensed pilot and they still did not know how they were going to get from Guam to Saipan. John knew several languages which could be helpful on Saipan to talk to the natives. Having been a policeman all of his life gave Don some added feeling of security. After all, they were going to be 9,000 miles away from home in a strange environment and there is no way to predict what will come up that might need some police ability. This assumption turned out to be almost prophetic later when they were being stalked in the jungle by a rifle carrying Chamorro intent on picking them off because he thought they were stealing his grandfather's betel nuts.

John's decision to go created some special problems within his own police department. He had to obtain leave from safety director Henry Trubiano and Chief Schieberl, and finally the Chief law enforcement officer of Garfield Heights, Mayor Frank Petrancek. A combination of John's enthusiastic determination to go, his infectious genial approach to everything, and understanding superiors, made these problems disappear in rapid order. He was issued the necessary permits and got his shots (which, by request, I must say were medical). With his immunizations completed, they assembled equipment they thought would be needed for a two week's stay on Saipan.

If the women had any notions of considering the trip these were completely squelched by Don's explanation of the jungle to those who had not been there. If his descriptions of leeches, scorpions, ants, and centipedes were not enough, the solid growth of vegetation and swatches of razor-like kunai grass that will cut clothes to ribbons made it sound like there were better places to take a vacation.

Their equipment included machetes, pistols, combat boots, old clothes, and jungle survival equipment. Just this collection of equipment would have been enough to jolt most reasonable thinking people back to reality and call the whole thing off. Not so with Don and his loyal companions; they were actually getting more excited with each step that would take them out of warm security to very inhospitable surroundings. There was never any doubt in any of their minds that Don would be able to walk right up to that airplane in the jungle. They were in for a surprise.

Finally the best jungle outfitted safari ever to assemble in the Cleveland area met at the International Inn to say their last goodbyes to families and a host of well-wishing friends. It was a very happy occasion with absolutely no obvious misgivings on anyone's part. There were, of course, the usual wisecracks said in fun on such a jovial occasion.

With the last farewell parting kisses firmly planted, the group climbed aboard a jet airliner and winged their way to Los Angeles, with eager anticipation to reach Saipan. Each had his individual thoughts about the future and was reliving the parting scene. There was very little conversation on the first leg of the trip and Don's mind was nearly exploding with all sorts of thoughts about this turn of events which was actually taking him back to a place he had not seen in over twenty years. Would the plane be there? Would it be as easy to find as he imagined? What if someone had really removed it as Goerner suggested and left no traces? Regardless of any negative thoughts about what might have been or could be, he was happy to be going to get it settled. His thoughts switched back to his family and business, wondering what he had left undone that should have been done. He thought of a few, but rationalized a few, and finally decided there was not much he could do about it at 30,000 feet and, anyway, most important was the fact that they were finally on the way. It was like a dream coming to life. He smiled at Ken, knowing they were thinking about the same thoughts and glanced across the aisle at John Gacek who was already sound asleep. They were to find out he could sleep anywhere any time,

The cave area where the Japanese made their last stand on Marpi Point. The caves are still black from the flame-throwers.

Tanapag Harbor shipping dock built by the Japanese and used to bring in war material.

which had come from years of training. Police work is not done on 8 to 4 shifts and policemen learn to grab their sleep when there is nothing else going on. Then, too, he may have looked at a map and checked their tickets and realized this was going to be a 20 hour ordeal so take advantage of every opportunity. John also had a little age advantage, or disadvantage, depending on whether the task at hand required experience or physical endeavor. This factor turned out to be a blessing in disguise in some very unsuspected places later on in the jungle. Anyway John slept all the way to Los Angeles while Ken and Don remained awake and pensive, with only occasional glances at each other to be sure they were communicating by extrasensory perception, generally reserved for very close and dear friends. Had either have had the slightest doubt; the other would have detected it immediately.

They had left Cleveland's Hopkins Airport at 5:30 October 30, 1967 and arrived in Los Angeles a little over four hours later. The next leg of the journey would be to Honolulu. As they left the coastline in the background, Don could not help but think that this was certainly a better way to go than in the upper bunk of his sea-going-vomit-comet that brought him to Saipan the first time. John stayed awake almost a whole hour but finally drifted into dreamland in true Gacek fashion, leaving Ken and Don to their thoughts and conversation.

They discussed Amelia Earhart's first trip which ended with the crash on take-off from Honolulu. It occurred to them that they likely were on the same path she had flown, but much higher up. This led into talk about how far aviation had advanced in such a short time and subsequently they discussed all kinds of irony about what might have been, and what they would find on Saipan that could help solve the mystery of Amelia's never having been found.

John woke up long enough to request that they wake him when they reached Honolulu so he could see it from the air. After assuring him they would do just that, both decided they had better try to get a little sleep also.

John was aroused in time to see Honolulu and stayed awake until they boarded the plane for Wake Island. By this time Don and Ken had learned to expect to find John asleep if they left him alone for a few minutes, so they left him to his peaceful pursuit while their jet whistled through the Pacific air. They spotted a few ships on the way to Wake Island that reminded Don of different experiences on his boat trip back in 1946. Most of them were not pleasant to think about so were promptly dropped.

Wake Island was little more than a fueling stop, and wake-up stop for John. Soon they were on their way to Guam, which would be their last leg on the scheduled airline. They had skipped a day by crossing the International Date Line and could not resist telling John he had completely missed October 31 as it was now November 1. Our modern Rip Van Winkle flashed one of his famous disarming smiles just as if it did not matter how many days he may have missed and went back to sleep. By this time Don and Ken were getting pretty weary and wished they could have slept more. Don remarked, "Father over there may be a lot smarter than we think," which was not intended to be disparaging about intellect, but a respectful jest about John's ability to adapt so quickly and conserve his energy, which he has an abundance of when in motion.

Everything had progressed as planned, when they touched down on Guam at 8:00 A.M. November 1. They had traveled 9,000 miles in 20 hours with 4 fuel stops. Don was quick to recall that it had taken his troopship 15 days to make the same trip and he was not smiling then as he was now.

They found out they would have to transfer all of their belongings to a Micronesian Airline which operated in the Trust Territory. This questionable looking craft was a converted C-54 that looked like a poor relative of something in the scrap yards. John, being an expert on planes, told Ken it was a converted C-54. Ken said, "It looked kinda like it had been converted to junk long ago." They soon found out it was operated by Micronesian personnel. They surveyed it with great skepticism concerning its ability to make one more trip. If they had considered the return trip and known this was the only plane that operated between Guam and Saipan they would never have gone. Since it was their only choice other than to swim to Saipan, they climbed into the tin goose. Going from their sleek high-flying jet to this bucket of bolts was going to be an experience and one they all agreed they could have done without, but in true adventuresome spirit they cast caution to the winds and climbed aboard. Knowing a little more about airplanes and what makes them fly, made John the last reluctant member to accept the challenge. This is one trip he did not sleep on.

John and Ken sat in one seat and Don seated himself beside a Micronesian passenger. After the airplane struggled into the air John stayed awake by helping Don and Ken keep track of the numerous coughs of the tired old engines trying desperately to keep them airborne. They really thought every cough might be the last. John and Ken continued to joke about the airplane and Don tried to talk to his Micronesian seat-mate who just kept on reading his newspaper as though he had been trained on the New York Subway.

Don is not one to give up easily anytime, so, he finally asked a direct question knowing his uncommunicative friend would have to answer if he could speak English and Don had already taken into account that he was reading English. Don began with, "Do you live on Saipan?" The Micronesian admitted he did, without any enthusiasm at being disturbed. Having established that this chap could speak English if he wanted to, Don added, "I was on Saipan twenty years ago." "I spent two years there."

Micronesian, "Do you have a child on the Island?"

"No, I am just coming back to visit. I was not able to talk to anyone before when I was there and besides I was very young." This newly found friend eyed Don with an expression he interpreted as meaning he was not THAT young. At any rate, saying he had lived on the Island prompted Joe Diaz to fold up his newspaper and become very conversational. He explained that he managed the Joe Ten grocery stores on Saipan and that if he could be of any help he would be glad to. Little did Don realize just how much help Joe Diaz would be from that moment on.

On the other side of the plane John commented, what he hoped

A Japanese pillbox.

Some grave decorations.

Some Saipanese boutique.   *A gun for the salvage crew.*

was in jest, "Even Amelia Earhart and Fred Noonan had a better airplane than this and they did not make it." That was good for a short laugh which ended abruptly when their plane coughed, pitched forward and started down. It was a little breath taking until they realized this was a short hop and the pilot was heading for the Saipan runway. Ken recovered his composure by saying, "It is because you have not been asleep, John, that I did not realize the trip was over."

Don was mentally photographing the Island, trying to get his bearings. Somehow it looked a great deal stranger to him than he had thought it would. It was as though he had never been here before, and he was anxious to get on the ground to dispel this feeling of being in a strange place. After all, he had lived here two years and it should seem a little like coming home.

Joe Diaz had taken a great liking to Don with his sincerity, and asked if he could help them find quarters and a car. They readily accepted his hospitality which was a fortunate move. He first took them to a hotel which could not accommodate them; that was another stroke of luck. By moving into a one room concrete house at the outskirts of Chalan Kanoa they met Vincente Camacho who was to play an interesting role in future developments. He owned their modest quarters. They noticed the better than average construction and commented about it. Camacho told them it was built with 'happy labor'. John decided to be the straight-man and asked, "What is happy labor?"

"Relatives who work for nothing?" This was a big joke to Vincente so they all joined in and helped him laugh, to his obvious pleasure. Without being much aware of it, Don, Ken, and John were making an invaluable contact. It is extremely doubtful if many groups could have been so readily accepted and taken into confidence the way these three were.

One possible explanation was that they had all gown up in a large city and lived through a depression which instilled a type of humility necessary for appealing to the perceptive nature of these less fortunate people as far as economics go. If everyone who traveled abroad were blessed with this trait "The Ugly American" would never have been written and "Yank Go Home" never would have been heard around the world. This important aspect of their nature turned out to be crucial in their destiny. It endeared them to everyone they met. Trust and respect of the Saipanese opened doors for them that had been bolted for over thirty years.

CHAPTER IV

THE SEARCH FOR AMELIA'S AIRPLANE

Joe Diaz took the trio to an auto rental place where they rented a Datsun automobile. Diaz had told them previously that his boss was Joe Tennario, better known as Joe Ten. This same Joe Ten leased the house they were living in from Vincente Camacho, and now the auto rental establishment turns up as a Joe Ten enterprise. They were too tired to worry much about who owned what and decided to get some sleep. John, of course, voted yes! The local mosquitos had different ideas. One thing the group had forgotten to pack was mosquito repellent. There were no screens on their house. They tried every way to fight the mosquitoes off, but finally gave up at three o'clock in the morning and had a board meeting to determine how they could keep from being eaten alive. The only answer was to get in the car and go for a drive. Drive they did until the next morning. They took turns driving and trying to sleep. Datsuns are not built like four-poster beds and they were glad when daylight ended the torture.

They found the nearest store to prepare for the next night. After equipping themselves with every available kind of mosquito repellent, eating seemed like a good idea.

While at the store, they inquired as to where a good place to eat might be located and were directed to an old enlisted men's club which enterprising Joe Ten had converted into a restaurant of sorts. They were rapidly finding out that payment for everything ate, drank, or used, wound up back in Joe Ten's wallet. They entered with some reservations, but were delighted when the waitress brought them a menu containing an assortment the Waldorf-Astoria would have been proud to offer. They ordered steak from page one.

MEDFORD DAILY MERCURY

ZERO GOVERNORS AVENUE

MEDFORD, MASS. 02155

ALPHONSE R. FREZZA
MANAGING EDITOR
ASSISTANT TO THE PUBLISHER

April 20, 1968

Mr. Robert C. Stafford
Editorial Department,
The Cleveland Press
Cleveland, Ohio

Dear Mr. Stafford:

Mrs. Albert Morrissey of this city has furnished me with clips from the Cleveland Press relative to the search for Amelia Earhart's plane in Saipan. Mrs. Morrissey is the surviving sister of Miss Earhart and has lived in Medford for many years.

We have, of course, been keenly interested in the continuing story of Miss Earhart's disappearance. The latest search, by Mr. Kothera, had not been known to us until Mrs. Morrissey received the clips of your stories from a friend in Cleveland.

Both she and myself are interested in learning what if anything has resulted from the latest trip to Saipan by Mr. Kothera and his associates. Any clips you may be able to supply will be appreciated.

Sincerely,

Alphonse R. Frezza

arf:s

"No steak."

"Oh, well, its breakfast time (by the sun anyway) so we will have bacon and eggs."

"No eggs—Also, no bacon."

When questioned about the chickens' (running around outside the door) ability to lay eggs, the waitress informed them that they only laid enough for their own family's use. After several long, unproductive negotiating sessions, they did finally get the only item available—the complete menu notwithstanding. The food they got was some sort of rice concoction, difficult to describe. According to John, "Any attempt to analyze it would have rendered it unfit for consumption." They just ate it and thanked the waitress. She assured them steak, eggs, bacon, and everything else on the menu was enroute and would arrive any day. This was good news and they remained hopeful until the day they left two weeks later.

They had made this long trip to find the airplane, and now seemed the time to start looking. Don found Marine Road without too much trouble, but everything else had changed completely. He was completely horrified at the way the jungle had taken over. The sugar cane fields he remembered were all over-grown, leaving him with no landmarks. He thought he knew the general area, and they would just have to start hunting. Metal salvage companies had come in during the '50's and changed everything. They had burned the sugar cane, allowing the jungle to take over, and bulldozed many landmarks under the coral.

Don picked the most likely looking jungle and they parked the car as close as they could. This would have been about 8:00 in the morning. Three hours later they had progressed about one thousand feet, getting cut by the sword grass. By noon they had arrived at the base of the jungle incline tired and bleeding. They spent the

Airplane parts found on the first trip.

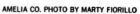
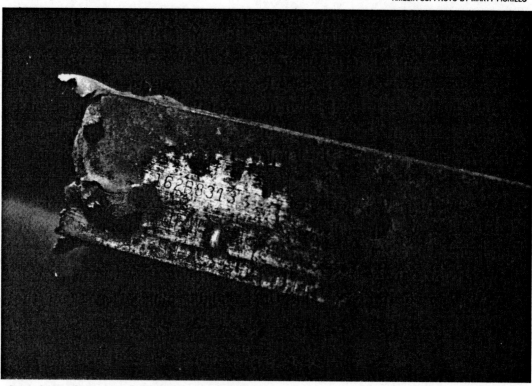

Serial number on one of the airplane parts.

rest of the day searching for the ravine where the airplane was supposed to be. Discouraged, they gave up and went back to their modest home away from home.

That evening they all sat down and recounted the entire day's activity and decided what they would do the following day. This set a pattern for their entire stay on Saipan. They planned their work and worked their plan.

The mosquito repellent was the greatest thing since the round wheel and enabled them to get a good night's sleep. They awoke early, ate their Waldorf rice, admonished the chickens to lay a little better, and drove back to the unfriendly jungle, feeling certain this day would bring them into contact with the airplane in the jungle.

The second day in the jungle proved very little other than just how impenetrable it really was, and how much out of condition they were for this sort of activity. They decided to cut the day's activities a little short and drive around the Island and see if any new ideas would miraculously pop into their heads. It was rapidly becoming apparent that they could spend a lifetime here and never find that airplane by just going out and hacking their way through the jungle which grows back nearly as fast as you can chop it down. As Ken put it, "You have to keep pushing ahead because the trail closes up behind you."

While they were driving around the Island, several stops were made to pick up what they thought to be empty seashells. These were tossed casually behind the back seat of their car and they had accumulated quite a good size pile before going back to their home base. These shells were forgotten about until several days later when they nearly broke up a long and beautiful friendship between Don and Ken.

Nothing new had occurred to them on the excursion, so the

third day found them back in the jungle hacking their way around trying to find the ravine where the airplane was. Don reassured them that it had to be in this particular area. The trio spread out and were continually losing contact. As it turned out they were spending more time looking for each other than they were for the ravine. To solve this problem it was agreed that at appointed times they would signal with their pistols. If any one of them wanted the others, a shot would be fired and the other two would work their way to that spot. In many instances it took more than one shot to get the other two there as the jungle was so dense; being just one hundred feet from the appointed spot gave no clue as to how near nor how far away they really were. Moving one hundred feet in that jungle was a very time consuming, and often painful, experience.

While hardship was not a new word to any of the three sturdy men, there were times when they were completely spent and on the verge of dispair. After struggling through the undergrowth of the jungle, being cut to ribbons by the sword grass, continually stung by wasps, bitten by mosquitoes and other insects, constantly slipping on the slimy up and downhill terrain with several drenching rains every day, tried the souls of these courageous men. They had been well grounded early in life that basic principles of love and dedication are useless without courage, or they would have quit after the first day in the jungle. Every day the comforts of home loomed mightily as there was no real reprieve for their discomforts when they returned to their four walls at night. They were always soaked to the skin, muddy, and without facilities to freshen up. It is a gross understatement to say they longed for the soul food of a good meal in a warm home with some love and affection. There must have been many moments of wondering just what they were doing here, but determination to complete the mission provided them with courage and new hope to conquer the jungle and find that airplane.

On the fourth day they got up a little slower than usual, pulled on their soiled clothing and boots, without much robust enthusiasm, and made their way to the Saipan Hotel for another one of those non-inspiring breakfasts of rice and something else. They each watched the other while they ate in almost complete silence and realized that they were all beat. One more day in the jungle right now would have been the straw that broke the Camel's back.

Ken finally broke the silence by suggesting that perhaps they had been pushing a little too hard for fellows out of condition, so why not go to the garbage dump and fish for sharks. Don pointed out the place that the Navy had built to dump garbage when they drove around the Island picking up seashells. This was built on the Southern end of the Island near Kobeler Field where they had landed upon their arrival. It consisted of a concrete ramp with a low retaining wall so trucks could back up and dump garbage into the ocean about thirty feet below. During the occupation in 1946 it was a favorite fishing spot for the forces based on Saipan. At that time, Don recalled tons of garbage being dumped every day. He said, "Very little is dumped there now, I suppose, with the poor natives barely getting enough to eat. They would not have much to throw away." He went on to tell Ken and John how rank meant absolutely nothing while fishing here during his previous tenure. When you walked out on Agingan Point with a fishing rod in your hand it made no difference whether you were a general or a buck private. You fished side by side and helped each other pull in large fish. They all agreed that fishing was the thing to do to get rested up before going back into the jungle.

It was necessary to gather up some fishing equipment, and they were reminded of their decision to go to Saipan before they considered how one would get there. They had to decide what to use for line, bait, etc. — Joe Ten was about to get some more of their money. John suggested that it might be a good idea to go take a closer look at the spot before investing in equipment. This met with Don and Ken's approval, so they were off to the dump.

Upon arrival they saw several sharks swimming in circles about one hundred feet from the shore. They watched them for awhile, wondering why the sharks did not come in closer to the shore to pick up the refuse instead of waiting for it to drift out to them. After watching this action for awhile, they decided it was time to go get some fishing gear and bait.

They found some four inch treble hooks and some fifty pound test line. They thought this should be strong enough to land a one hundred and fifty pound shark. They were soon to find out their information about sharks was woefully restricted. Their fellow airline passenger and friend, Joe Diaz sawed some large chuncks of frozen Australian beef with a hacksaw, telling them it would be ideal shark bait. They were all pretty skeptical as to how they would ever get it on the hook, but took it anyway and drove back to the dump to catch those sharks.

On the way back they decided that 'sure-shot' John should shoot a shark first and they would take pictures of the other sharks tearing him apart in true cannibalistic fashion. This plan was discarded after several shots failed to do no more than annoy a shark now and then. The guns and cameras were put away, to get down to serious fishing.

By the time they got the lines rigged and found some scraps of two by four lumber for bobbers the meat was completely thawed. Joe Diaz had been right, and this was the first of many instances where this group found out the natives had better ideas about things

ALUMINUM COMPANY OF AMERICA

ONE ERIEVIEW PLAZA · CLEVELAND, OHIO 44114

G. KEITH SHOOK, District Sales Manager

Area Code 216
522-1000

February 6, 1968

Dear Allen:

Following up on your request as to the chemical composition of aluminum alloy 24S in the 1930's, I hope you find the following information helpful:

	Alloy 24S	Nominal Composition
As of 2-12-34	Cu	4.15%
	Mn	0.5%
	Mg	1.5%
	Fe	Traces
	Si	Traces
9-28-36	Same as above	
10-8-36	Cu	4.40%
	Mn	0.65%
	Mg	1.5%
	Fe	Traces
	Si	Traces

It is our hope that you find this information helpful, and if we can be of further assistance, please do not hesitate to call us.

Very truly yours,

DELL W. FERGUSON

DWF:emf

Laboratory Report

CROBAUGH LABORATORIES

RESEARCH • ANALYSIS • TESTING

3800 PERKINS AVENUE
CLEVELAND, OHIO 44114
216 - 881-7320

To: Mr. John Gacek
12301 Sunset Blvd.
Garfield Heights 44125

Reporting Date February 13, 1968
No. B7-73
Date Received February 7, 1968
Material Aluminum
Marked --
P. O. No. Verbal

ANALYSIS:

Copper	4.00%
Magnesium	0.61%
Silicon	0.04%
Semiquantitative Analysis	Attached

Respectfully submitted,

CROBAUGH LABORATORIES

[signature: Morton L. Levy]

1r

CROBAUGH LABORATORIES

Report of
Spectrographic Examination

SAMPLE NO. B7-73					
SPEC. NO. S0331					
Aluminum	Major				
Antimony	ND				
Arsenic	ND				
Barium	ND				
Beryllium	ND				
Bismuth	ND				
Boron	0.001				
Cadmium	0.001				
Calcium	<0.0001				
Cerium					
Chromium	0.002				
Cobalt	<0.0001				
Copper					
Fluorine					
Gallium					
Germanium					
Gold					
Hafnium					
Indium					
Iron	0.57				
Lead	0.001				
Lithium					
Magnesium					
Manganese	0.20				
Mercury					

SAMPLE NO. B7-73					
SPEC. NO. S0331					
Molybdenum	ND				
Nickel	0.001				
Niobium					
Phosphorus					
Platinum					
Potassium	<0.001				
Silicon					
Silver	<0.0001				
Sodium	<0.001				
Strontium	ND				
Tantalum					
Tellurium					
Tin	0.001				
Titanium	0.0005				
Tungsten	0.0009				
Uranium					
Vanadium					
Zinc	0.10				
Zirconium	ND				

ND — Not Detected.
Values are semiquantitative estimations as percent in the samples as received.

they had been previously exposed to, than novices with more formal training in a country presumed to be more advanced.

They threw the baited hooks out as far as they could and let their makeshift bobbers drift on out to where the sharks were still making large circles. They had no trouble getting strikes, but the fifty pound lines snapped as fast as they hooked the sharks; Ken and Don both caught smaller fish and pulled them in, but it was obvious the sharks would require heavier line.

They were feeling much better now and determined to catch a shark so drove back to town and bought some one hundred pound test line that they felt sure would be strong enought to land any shark. Their shark adversaries broke the one hundred pound test line about as easily as they did the fifty pound line. Now the situation had become a challenge and you know by now how well this group responds to challenges.

They lost little time in driving back to town in their faithful little Datsun and this time bought one hundred and fifty pound test line. This was the heaviest line available from the store so it had to work. John drove back to the dump while Don and Ken rigged the heavy line. They all baited their hooks with the previously frozen beef and threw out their lines. In a very few minutes John hooked a big shark. Don and Ken pulled their lines in somewhat, so they would not be fighting two or three sharks at once, and helped John. They were pulling for dear life when the line snapped and cut John's arm to the bone. This unfortunate accident ended the fishing for the moment while they took John to the local hospital to get sewed up. The trip to the hospital was good training for a trip that they were to take later under some very adverse circumstances when time was really of the essence.

Like most hospitals that are overworked and understaffed, this one had a long waiting line at the outpatient section. It seemed like a good time for some small-talk, so Don started telling Ken about how he could be a real hero in the newsreels. He had a plan that would promote Ken as a World Famous Shark Killer and the idol of all small boys to say nothing of the attention he would get from the women of the world, besides making all of the men jealous.

"So far it sounds great," ventured Ken, "but how am I going to catapult into this new role when so far, our experience with the sharks has been pretty sad."

John eyed his traumatized arm, which had began to throb with pain, and told Don to hurry up and tell about this great plan before he had to see the doctor.

Don began by saying, "Now remember Ken, you will be famous throughout the free world (and maybe a few Communist countries) and here is the plan: We will rent two boats. John will take one with the camera equipment and you and I will take the other one. Together we will row out to where the sharks are. Once there, John will position himself about fifty feet to the starboard (a term I learned in the Navy when I took the first of my two rides on a ship). When he is all set with the cameras I will tie a rope (line in the Navy, I am told) around your waist using a square knot." At this point Don glanced at John to see how he was holding up and gave him a sly wink indicating the best was yet to come. Turning back to Ken with more instructions on how to be the world's greatest shark killer, Don continued, "You strip to the waist, take a machete in your teeth and jump into the water. I will throw some of our unused bait in the water to draw the sharks over to you. As the shark swims towards you John will be taking pictures of you hacking furiously at the shark with an appropriate sneer on your face. The meaner you look the better your public is going to like it. In fact, you can practice sneering while we row out to the shark-bed. At the last minute, just before the shark makes an attempt to grab you, I will haul you in with the rope. You can continue to hit the shark a few smart blows on the head with your machete as I pull you in, for extra drama." Don was a little surprised that Ken seemed genuinely interested in this wild scheme and glanced at John who, also, did not quite understand the gleam in Ken's eye. Don said, "Now that's the plan, Ken, what do you think of it?"

Ken said it was the greatest plan he had heard of in a long time. There was only one suggested change. "Don you be the matinee idol and fight the sharks while I pull you in." John really didn't care who was going to be the hero since he was to be the photographer. Don's response to Ken's suggestion startled a few waiting room patients. With the whole program a failure, John went in to get a few stitches in his arm. Ken was not ready to quit. He said, "Don, I will be the hero, but you must do a couple of practice runs to show me how." The waiting room was shocked again.

Anyone who thinks this was the end of the shark episode, just does not know these fellows' determination to accomplish whatever they set out to do. With John sewed up and bandaged, the shark obsession took them on a hunt for stronger line. Some natives directed them to a tuna fisherman.

A genuine interest in the native fisherman's way of life soon started the fisherman telling them how he could catch about four hundred pounds of tuna per day. When the boat was loaded with fish the Captain and owner of the boat would sell the fish to the natives who came to meet them at the dock when they came in. The Captain would keep fifty per cent of the proceeds and split the remaining fifty per cent among the crew. No one got rich, but it was a living. They were directed to the house of the head fisherman's brother. He had a two hundred fifty pound test monofilament nylon line that he said could pull a truck. He, also, told them they would need a ¼" steel cable for a leader. The group realized now that the reason the sharks were snapping their other lines was because they did not use any leader. The line came from Germany and was a prized possession. The native told them it belonged to his brother and they were welcomed to use if free, but if they lost it the price would be twenty-five dollars. They thanked him and assured him they would return the line just as soon as they landed one of those (censored) sharks.

Back at the dump, they found the natives had helped themselves to their bait and someone was going to have a good meal tonight. They made the fourth trip to the store for some more frozen Australian beef. They let it lay out in the sun while they rigged the line to the leader and found a piece of tree trunk for a bobber. Don got some towels out of the car to protect their hands just in case they hooked into another shark. The hook was baited with the partially thawed meat and thrown out as far as possible. The bobber drifted out slowly and the action started. A large shark got wind of the bait and came slowly in. When a few feet away, this easy-going monster, in their eyes, rolled over on its back exposing its light colored belly and grabbed the bait. John, Ken, and Don counted to ten and with towels wrapped around their hands, six hundred pounds of human flesh set the hook.

The fight was on. They had five hundred feet of line and were running out fast while holding on with all their might. The shark was going straight away and it appeared that he would keep right on going. The towels were the only thing keeping their hands from being cut to pieces by the line speeding through their grip. When all seemed lost and they were sure another twenty-five dollars was wasted on the sharks there was a sudden turn of events. The shark stopped abruptly when they had less than one hundred of feet of line left. They thought they had won the battle, but Mr. Shark regrouped, dived and started over again. Suddenly the line was tight and still. They stood there tense for what seemed like an eternity expecting the worst, then it occurred to them that the shark had wrapped the line around a piece of coral. What a revolting situation this was. They were not as much concerned about the money it was going to cost as they were about returning the line. Even with the money there was no easy way to get another line. In a less serious situation Don or Ken would have probably suggested the other one swim out and untangle the line.

Finally they decided that returning part of the line would be better than none, and in addition, they would give the fellow his twenty-five dollars. To salvage what they could, they were going to hook the Datsun to the line and try to pull it loose or break it. The ensuing conference suggested the possibility they might even pull the bumper off the car, but they decided to give it a try. While Don was backing the car up to hook the line to the bumper, a young girl about sixteen or seventeen, who was obviously pregnant, wandered over and asked what they were going to do. When Don said, "Get the line loose," she laughed at him.

Don said, "What is so funny?"

The young girl said, "That is not the way to get a line loose."

With sincerity, "How would you go about freeing the line?"

"For a package of cigarettes, I will get it loose for you."

Don looked this frail piece of humanity squarely in the eye and told her he would give her the cigarettes if she could get the line loose.

Without the slightest hesitation, she drew the line tight and plunked it like a bass fiddle player would plunk a string. The third time she plunked it the line came loose. Don gave her two packages of cigarettes and made another mental note concerning the native's ability to do things.

The group conceded the sharks this battle, but knew they had not won the war yet. However, it was getting late so they returned the line and drove to the Joe Ten store for the fifth time that day to get some Spam and a few other canned goods for dinner. They had dinner, held their evening board meeting, agreed the change in pace was just what they needed, but tomorrow they must get back to business.

The fifth day was anything but dramatic from the standpoint of coming any closer to their goal of finding the ravine. It was the same old routine of chopping their way through the undergrowth and sword grass. They would signal with their pistols periodically and get together to exchange any new findings. The monsoon rains added to the general misery. By nightfall the weary trio had a bite to eat and fell into bed. They did not have to be rocked to sleep.

They came to the end of the sixth day with only eleven more jungles to search. John's only comment to this unhappy bit of information was, "When you've seen one of these (another unusable descriptive adjective) jungles you have seen them all." Ken gave John a shot of adrenalin that would last him a full week when he turned to Don and said, "I think the old man has about had it. Did you notice how he was lagging further behind today?" Don just smiled at the good natured jab, knowing full well that John would be the last to give up and kidding about his age was all the inspiration he would need. Dinner, prepared with a can opener, was eaten with relish, but Don could not pass up the opportunity to mention what would happen if their wives tried to put something like this

Joe Ten shopping center built at the site of the invasion. It was a motor pool when Don was there in 1946.

Employees of the Saipan Hotel selling the group raffle tickets on a cow.

over on them and call it an evening meal.

"Yeah, we are really going to appreciate those dolls when we get home from this little excursion," said John with some emotion.

Ken admonished him to, "Please drop the sentiment bit before we all start crying."

Don encouraged them by saying, "Before leaving this rock we are going to fix one real good meal. I know John can cook because he had lots of experience up at that fishing camp of his in Canada."

John's eyes lighted up like a pinball machine at the very mention of his beloved fishing camp. The next hour was devoted to a blow by blow description of last summer's activities. Don and Ken shared John's nostalgic memoirs and when that subject was thoroughly exploited they had their regular evening recap of the day, and planned the next day.

They woke up early on the seventh day, feeling good. Could it be that our explorers were getting in a little better shape? They drove to the old enlisted mens' club which had been promoted to "Hotel Saipan". The waitress told them there were still no eggs, so they took a vote and decided this had gone far enough and, by golly, they were going to have eggs for breakfast. It was a bad morning to make that decision, but having made it they set out to find some eggs which they intended to bring back to the Hotel Saipan and have a decent breakfast. They struck out at the grocery store, but found out where there was a egg farm on the Island. It took a while to get there and the eggs cost one dollar and twenty cents per dozen, but they had found what they had gone after. They bought three dozen of these precious eggs and headed back for the Hotel Saipan unaware that at this very moment the entire staff of kitchen help had just walked off the job. They were soon to learn that Joe Ten had some real management problems.

When they could not get the eggs cooked, they summoned the manager. A guy named Pete was an apprentice with no teacher. He apologized for the inconvenience and found someone to cook the eggs. Pete sat with them and volunteered that he had been the manager for the past two weeks. He told them a very sad story about how hard it was to keep help because most of them just did not want to be told what to do. Ken said, "I am beginning to feel just like I am home. He has the same problems that I do in my business." Pete also told them he was twenty-eight years old and this was his first try at the hotel business.

Don asked, "What did you do before you started to work for Joe Ten?"

"I was a photographer. I learned this while working for the United States Navy. Most everyone here who has a trade has learned it while working for some branch of the service.

Don's next question was, "Do you have any pictures of pre-war Garapan." Garapan was a city on the southern end of the Island that had been completely leveled when we invaded Saipan during World War II, you will recall.

The eggs were served by Pete, and he sat down again and told Don he did have a very good picture of the late city. Don was trying to find a picture of the Hotel Kobayashi Royokan where witnesses had said Amelia Earhart had been held prisoner after her plane had crash-landed near Tanapag Harbor on Saipan. Pete said the picture would show the Hotel. It really belonged to the Mayor, but he had the negative and would make them some prints for delivery the next day. This was very good news and they were visibly satisfied with their eggs, even if they were not prepared exactly as they had wanted them, and the price was the same as posted on the menu—no deduction for them furnishing the eggs.

On the way out the door they met a carpenter working on a door. They never passed up an opportunity to visit with any available native so they paused to watch him work. His tools were very crude and they learned that he had learned his trade from the Sea Bees. Joe Ten had contracted with him to fix the place up. Joe Ten wanted the ceilings straightened up and Ken admitted, "It does make me a little dizzy to look at the ceiling."

The carpenter said, "It is just too late to do anything with that ceiling as the termites have already gotten too much of a head start."

Just trying to make conversation, John asked, "What is the best material to build with here?" He had no idea this would evoke a long, learned discussion regarding building and tropical building materials.

The carpenter began by stating, "The only good construction material for the tropic is bamboo which is tied together. Nails and metal roofing material rust out quite rapidly with the ever present heat and high humidity. Concrete also deteriorates in time."

To change the subject, Don asked him about his family. He told them about his son who was in school in the Phillipines, but he did not expect him to come back to Saipan because there just was no opportunity on the Island. They left, feeling a bit guilty about being from the United States, which was responsible for this sad state of affairs, since we are the trustee for Saipan. They could put themselves in his place and realize what kind of mixed emotions they would have about sending their children off to improve their future, knowing it meant not coming back home. There had to be something wrong with this kind of system. Their understanding and sympathy did not pass unnoticed. They had made another friend and perhaps given this man a thread of hope that if enough people realized just how it was, then there might be a change for the better some day.

Another day in the jungles still did not turn up any clues as to where the airplane might be found. There were moments when Don thought they were making progress as some of the terrain looked a little familiar, but he had to concede that during his two year stay here he had traveled a great deal and did expect his subconscious recollection to alert him when he came across areas that had not been changed by the salvage companies. These places were few and far between. It rained harder than usual all day, so they decided to knock off early and go to the Style Shop. With a glamorous name like that it would be impossible to guess this was a third rate beer joint, and was about the best the Island had to offer. They had been here before and noticed one fixture was always present in the form of a twenty-four inch high midget from the Phillipines. This thirty pound doll was about twenty-five years old and could drink beer with the best of them. They made friends with Lucy the Midget, while Ken and John had their fill of beer. Don stuck to his principal of not drinking anything alcoholic. This seemed like the right night to have that dinner they had been talking about the night before, so they borrowed a one burner hot plate from Vincente Camacho and bought steaks from Joe Diaz. They also picked up a frying pan with a paper label on the bottom. John forgot to take it off before putting it on the burner. One hour later the burner still was not hot enough to burn the label off. Don and Ken told John he would have to peel it off to allow the heat to get through the pan. Four hours later they had some very rare steaks to eat. No one complimented the cook or left a tip. John's E.S.P. prompted him to ask them both to leave this world. They all laughed, had their meeting and went to bed.

By the eighth day John was taking full advantage of his self-appointed lagging privileges. He could be depended upon to be be-hind Don and Ken at any given time. He maintained he was the senior member of the expedition and entitled to certain lagging privileges. Whether or not he was entitled and without any votes of confidence, he continued to bring up the rear in unhurried fashion. He tried to further justify his slower pace by telling them that he had been trained as a detective and would no doubt observe things that they would run past. Don was just picking himself up for the thousandth time in the heavy going, and said something closely re-lated to fecal material of the male bovine and added, "John, no one, absolutely no one runs by anything in this jungle. In fact, we will be damn lucky to crawl by what we are looking for. He stepped on a rotten log that looked solid enough and went crashing to the floor of the rain forest again.

On the ninth day John's lagging turned into a very fortunate situation that probably saved Don and Ken's life. About twelve o'clock Don heard some chopping in the underbrush close by.

"Hey, Ken, is that you?" They had been making their way up the mountainside, so he knew John would not be that close by. They were in a strange place and they had been told there were wild boars on the Island that were capable of tearing a man to ribbons with their three inch tusks and mean dispostion. Don felt sure the hack-ing was that of a machete, but when there was no answer he picked a place as clear of growth as possible and got ready to face whatever was coming through the jungle. As the sounds got louder his heart beat a little faster. Don decided against calling out again, knowing whoever or whatever it was could have heard him the first time so why reveal his position further. After several minutes of this agony, Don saw Ken pass within a few feet of him and continue on until Don asked him in jungle language, with a few adjectives, where he

67

was going and suggested a place, because Ken had not answered when he called. Then Don told Ken in no uncertain terms, not to scare the hell out of him again like that.

Ken just laughed and said, "I am too beat to talk above a whisper. I thought if I kept leaning into the brush and hacking I would make it to here and collapse at your feet, old buddy, then you could carry me home, fix me a nice hot shower, charcoal a steak, and..."

"And you can cut out that malarky, but maybe we had better rest awhile and let John catch up. We have pushed pretty hard so it will likely take him at least a half an hour to get here." They checked their watches and settled down on a stump to wait not having any idea they were being followed most of the morning by a native with a rifle. They were on his grandfather's farm and he thought they were stealing his betel nuts which were worth a penny each. He was intent on eliminating two betel nut poachers when he could get them together in rifle range.

Don suggested Ken go back and look for John when he did not show up as they had expected. Still not fully recuperated from the heavy going, Ken suggested Don go back and do the looking while he waited under the tree. Little did they know that at that very moment their hunter had found a spot where he could line them up in his sights. As he drew a bead on Don, both Ken and Don stood up, causing the rifleman to drop his gun to see if they had spotted him.

"O.K., Ken, you wait here and I will see if I can find John." With that Don started back down the mountain. The native was sure Don had seen him and was looking for a place to hide when Don decided to fire his pistol to locate John. You can imagine what the native thought. Whatever he thought was compounded when John fired back within a few feet of the poor fellow and said, "Hello, why are you following my friends?" John explained that he had been keeping him under close observation for the last two hours. This revelation understandably rattled the native, who told him his name was Mariano Fawlig.

By this time Don had reached the spot and was surprised to find John talking to Mariano. He told them that he thought they were there to steal his grandfather's betel nuts.

John explained they were visitors and would not think of stealing his or anyone else's betel nuts and showed him his nice white teeth to prove he did not chew betel nuts—yet. To be more logical and convincing John said, "We are looking for some large guns," remembering the ones Don had seen overlooking the ravine they had spent nine days looking for.

Mariano quickly realized he had made a mistake and apologized for his intention to shoot them. He explained that he had waited to get both of them together so the other would not hear the shots and get away. John told him that he was a policeman from Garfield Heights and could have dropped him at any moment he started shooting, which made Mariano glad they were friends.

By this time Ken had come up and was introduced to Mariano who had started telling them that he did know where there were some big guns. Now that they were friends, he could not do enough for them and offered to take them to the spot. Don could not help but think what a difference a little understanding among men makes; one minute a man wants to kill you; the next minute he would give you the shirt off his back. Understanding—that's the key to peace.

With their new guide leading the way, they started on up the mountain with vigor and determination. Once again lady luck had given them a hand at a very curcial moment and turned near tragedy into guidance that would eventually spell success.

Looking across Bird Island to Suicide Cliff where thousands of Japanese and natives lined up to wait their turn to jump rather than face capture.

One of several landing craft deserted near Tanapag Harbor.

John broke the silence by philosophying, "The darkest hour is always just before dawn, you know. We have been approaching this thing the wrong way. In police work we send two cruisers instead of one when we really need to get things done. Now, we should send two cruisers instead of one."

Ken looked at Don who also seemed a bit puzzled and they both wondered if the heat was getting to John. Ken said, "Don't talk in riddles, What do you mean; send two cruisers instead of one?"

By way of explanation John said, "Don't you see we have been trying to do this whole damn thing by ourselves when we could have had the help of all of the people who live here. They don't care anything about that airplane, but probably someone could give us a lot of information."

Don interrupted to say, "If he can find the guns, the ravine will be pretty easy to find."

Ken added, "Yeah, but the airplane might not still be there. John is right. We must start taking the natives into our confidence so we will know what happened."

Don told them not to worry about it until they checked this lead out, but he agreed that if they did not find the airplane here, it would be best to talk to them. After all, they only had five more days to spend before their visas ran out and they wanted to have a little fun before leaving (maybe even catch some sharks).

John's arm was still sore and he agreed that some shark must pay for the pain and damage.

This informal board meeting of the trio far out in the jungle laid the groundwork for activities that were to change our knowledge of history later on. Even these principals had no idea, at this stage of the adventure, what a momentous decision this was and the role they were going to play in the adventure of the century. Mariano was in excellent physical condition and knew how to go through the jungle, so they progressed at a good clip. John could see no reason for lagging behind and did not want to miss any of Mariano's conversation so he proved that 'the old man' had what it takes when necessary. Both Ken and Don knew this, but liked to kid him anyway.

The conversation drifted around to betel nuts again. They were curious as to whether they actually did give the added pep they were supposed to. Mariano suggested John chew one, as they were soon to come to a very steep cliff. John didn't figure he needed anything to get him up the cliff, but accepted the challenge and started chewing one of the little red nuts. It did not taste either real bad or real good so he kept on chewing until they reached the cliff.

John reached the top of the cliff well ahead of the others. He is not sure whether it was the betel nut or the power of suggestion, but he was there watching them strain every muscle to make it to the top. According to him there seems to be some kind of hypnotic effect attached to the betel nuts. He did not care to become an authority on the subject and did not like the red color it turned everyone's teeth who continues to seek their help so he never tried them again. Ken correctly told him it was the combination of betel nuts and lime that colored the teeth.

The foursome finally reached the gun implacements. Don inspected them and found they were the same type of guns from Singapore, but contained the inscription Sir Henry Armstrong. The ones near the airplane were inscribed Sir Henry Williams, Singapore 1913.

Mariano was very disappointed when told these were not the guns they were looking for. He seemed hurt that he had not been helpful, but they assured him this was not their first disappointment on this trip. When it became his turn to speak again, he told them about a man named John Doway who probably could help them. Mr. Doway had lived on the Island for a long time and knew about every place on Saipan.

Just meeting John Doway was worth the trip to Saipan if they never found the guns or the airplane. He was 75 years old and formerly from the Yap Islands. He had lived on Saipan for the last 50 years. Ken estimated that under ideal conditions Mr. Doway might weigh in at 125 pounds. He gave them bananas and rainwater to eat, then introduced them to his thirty-eight year old wife and youngest child—six years old.

John just had to tell Ken and Don that here was poetic justice for all of the smart remarks they had been making about age.

Their admiration and awe pleased Mr. Doway and he continued to show them just what a remarkable man he was. He had all of his teeth and proved his agility by literally running up a cocoanut tree with a copra ring as his only aid. He had a U.S. Carbine rifle that he was very proud to own. They made a reappraisal of his weight and decided he would have to be soaking wet without a haircut to make 125 pounds with all his clothes on, which were adequate but very little more. He attributed his great health to drinking banana whiskey and chewing betel nuts. John Gacek assured him the betel nuts were beneficial, and he would be glad to cool off with a little of Mr. Doway's homemade banana whiskey. To say the very least, Mr. Doway was a most impressive little man and knew every trail on Saipan. This was the best news they had heard since coming to Saipan.

John Doway told them about two Phillipine Companies that came in and salvaged everything they could in 1951 or 1952. Micrometals and Comar Metals brought in bulldozers and really tore up the Island. He knew where there had been four large guns that fit

A Japanese bunker showing direct hits.

What the invasion troops had to face.

Don's description. He said the guns had been removed by the salvagers, but the concrete mounts were still there along with the gun bases. He agreed to take them to the site the next day.

They ate at the Hotel Saipan, and were still excited about the prospects of finally finding the spot. Don was sure they were on the right track now. The food was beginning to taste pretty good and they enjoyed dinner. It had been a long and trying day, so they put on their favorite mosquito repellent which, John insists, "The mosquitoes regard as manna from heaven and the only reason we continue to use the stuff is from force of habit."

Ken reminded him of the first night they spent without this 'manna from heaven.'

Don told them "to shut up and go to sleep because we are going to be carrying that plane out tomorrow." All were very tried so they did not have to be told twice. Tired as they were, they all drifted into dreamland with smiles of satisfaction on their faces.

As could be expected, Don was the first one up the next morning and bounced his two sleepy-eyed companions out with some Navy words of encouragement to get them in the harness for a days work. Ken and John knew this was the day so they dressed in record time and accompanied Don to the Hotel Saipan restaurant that had a full complement of help. Pete was all smiles again and sat with them while they had some more of their one dollar and twenty cent per dozen eggs fixed a little more to their liking. Pete would neither confirm nor deny that the janitor was recruited to fix them the last time. They didn't really care because he had brought them the pre-war picture of Garapan and even was persuaded to turn the negative over to them.

They went to John Doway's farm and had another round of bananas and rainwater. With this fortification of soul food, they set out to find the gun emplacements. After a laborious trip through jungle that would stagger the imagination of most mortals, the group came to a searchlight and tower. This did not ring any bells with Don, but John Doway told them to keep walking. The wasps were out in maximum effort today and the rain seemed to follow them everywhere they went. They finally reached a point where they had to slide down a 20 foot embankment. Don watched the others make a clumsy descent and thought he would be original and run down standing up. He fell about half way down and tumbled the rest of the way completely out of control. Fortunately he was not seriously injured. Mostly his pride was hurt. Knowing they were getting close to the guns quickly healed his pride.

After finding the gun mounts, Don immediately started looking for the ravine where he thought he could find the airplane. He first went to the right several hundred yards then came back and went to the left. The terrain had definitely been changed since he had been here. John Doway finally took them to a small ravine that looked as if it could have been the one Don had seen many years before. They started searching and soon came upon some plane parts. Further investigation revealed six screw type airplane tie-downs. John Gacek was the knowledgeable one about aircraft and became really excited when he discovered that the six tie-downs were in a "T" formation. There was not any question that an airplane had been tied down on this spot. Don could not recall whether the plane had been tied down when he saw it or not. To be very certain this was the area, they went back to search for the cave that Don and Smitty had opened in 1946. While searching for the cave they came across a cave that would accommodate about fifty people. Then Ken found a cave that John Doway did not know about and he had been on the Island since 1913. This is an indication of just how difficult the terrain was. They had to use machete marks on the trees to keep from walking in circles.

Even with all precautions they did lose their directions at one point and wandered out into a restricted area loaded with live ammunition. Fortunately for them a detail came by that was trying to de-activate the area and, after giving them hell for being there, the Chief Petty Officer Aiken told them to leave the area. After he explained there were all kinds of live shells, grenades, and torpedoes in the area that could explode with the slightest impact, they were glad to leave.

Lunch was long overdue when they found some sugar cane and ripe bananas. It rained constantly, so all they had to do to get some water to wash this diet down with was to hold their canteens under a banana leaf for a few minutes. Naturally they were soaked in the almost constant downpour. In fact, they never really dried out while on Saipan. By Gum (a substituted word) the next trip would not be during the monsoon season.

They picked up some of the airplane parts with numbers stamped on them. Satisfied with their find, they started sloshing back through the jungle, and reached the car about dark. When they arrived at the car a man was waiting patiently by the car. His name turned out to be Terry Pau Selereo. They talked to him about the guns and the airplane. He mentioned that they should see John Doway. They told him they had just finished spending the day with John Doway. He said he knew a man who had removed the guns. After much small talk, he said he would take them to that man at 4:30 the next day. He could not leave his job as a heavy equipment repairman before that time.

They were a little late arriving at their banquet that evening at the Hotel Saipan. A few minutes after they pulled in and got

A model house offered to the natives. This house was completely destroyed by typhoon Jean.

A native built house that survived typhoon Jean.

seated they noticed a very quiet reserved man had followed them in and sat a few tables away.

Don turned to John and Ken and whispered, "You know, I have a feeling that guy over there has been following us ever since we have been here."

John agreed, "He has turned up at some strange places, and it seems accidental until you get to thinking about it. In fact, we have bumped into him two or three times a day ever since we arrived."

Ken added, "I have noticed him sitting over there every time we come in to eat and, now that I think about it, he has always come in just after we do regardless of the time of the day. Who do you suppose he is and what do you think he is following us for? We were supposed to check in with the high commissioner, but he was in Washington trying to get some more appropriations or something; anyway he wasn't around to check with."

They figured the way to discover this stranger's intentions, was to talk to him so they invited him over to their table, after agreeing among themselves, to tell him very little about their mission. He accepted the invitation and told them he was from Carlisle, Pennsylvania, and said he was on vacation from his duties on Guam. His job there was connected with the repair of war material such as tanks, trucks, helicopters, etc., damaged in Viet Nam. He tried to explain that in a declared war the government does not try to repair, but considers everything expendable. In an undeclared war like this one, for some foolish reason known only to the government, the equipment is repaired. Most likely the cost of repairs is greater than the cost of new equipment, but until Congress declares a war the costly repairs must go on. They listened to all of this and pretended to understand. However, they were too busy trying to figure out just how this man happened to be in their life here on Saipan, and kept hoping he might say something to reveal more than the story he had told them about being on Saipan for a vacation. From what they had seen of Saipan there were many more desirable places to enjoy one's self. If he was there for any other reason they were not going to find out from his conversation so they joined in and talked about everything from soup to nuts. They told him they were searching for some big guns up in the hills. He asked if he could go along with them, but sensed from their silence that he had not made a very popular request and withdrew it immediately. Could it be that he was just lonely and on vacation? They continued to wonder as they made their way back to their humble little block house that looked very inviting after the long day. Little did they realize this man was to soon turn up in their expedition again.

They had their evening board meeting to plan the next day and decided that Ken and Don would go with Terry to find the guns and John would stay in town to talk to some more of the natives. They were running out of time and wanted a lot more answers before they left. With the plans all made, they leaped into the arms of morpheus again and dreamed about home.

They did some sightseeing in the morning, then Ken and Don drove out to a quarry where Terry was working on some heavy equipment. He was terribly busy and working up a good lather so they told him they would be back a little later. Ken thought it would be a good idea to go to the Style Shop and pick up some beer so they could all sit down and relax after Terry got through with his job. Then they would go and take a look at the guns to see if they contained the inscription, "Sir Henry Williams". When they got back with the beer Terry told them he was going to be tied up until late and could not take them to find the guns, but would like for them to come back over after dinner that evening.

John had stayed in town and had made considerably more progress than Ken and Don. He first called on Vincente Camacho from whom they had leased the house. Vincente was an avid gardener and orchids were his long suit. John had grown orchids for a hobby at one time in his very versatile life and recognized several of Vincente's prize blossoms. This was the start of a mutual admiration that turned out to be very helpful on many occasions. John talked to Vincente for three hours telling him that they really were on the Island of Saipan to find Amelia Earhart's airplane. He told him that they had found some pieces, but would like to get any information they could from any witnesses who had seen the plane or the fliers.

Vincente told John that the villagers were still fearful of the Japanese and would be very reluctant to talk. "As you know, we have had three hundred years of domination without self determination since the Spanish controlled Saipan. They sold us to Germany and shortly after World War I started, the Japanese seized Saipan to start expanding her empire. After World War II saw the defeat of the Japanese we were placed under the United Nations Trust with the United States acting as administrator. These people are not sure that the Japanese will not reclaim Saipan some day and, as a matter of fact, many of them wish it was returned to Japanese rule. This would, of course, be the older people. They realize the Japanese were very strict." He told them a story that John had heard before; that if anyone even threw paper or trash on the ground and the Japanese saw them do it the penalty could be having their hand cut off or making the guilty person pick up the litter and beat themselves in the face with their fist until they bled freely. Just in case this took too long the Japanese were likely to volunteer to

Tons of salvage grenades, bombs, shells, etc. are recovered every week.

A Navy plane that was shot down is recovered.

help with the extraction of the blood.

This was hard for John to imagine and harder for him to imagine why the people would want this to return, so he asked Vincente, "How could anyone in his right mind want any part of that kind of brutality?"

Vincente explained, "Of course no one wants brutality, but the Japanese were not too hard to get along with as long as everyone did what was expected of them and minded their own business. The point is, the economy was good under the Japanese. There was plenty of work and plenty of money. While discipline was tough, my people did not have the hardship and lack of opportunity that exists today."

John was reminded of the carpenter working at the Hotel Saipan who had told him he did not expect to see his son back on Saipan to stay as there just was no opportunity to make a decent living on the Island. He felt there must be an answer to improve this situation and John really wished he could have told Vincente that he would get this changed. However, John knew there was very little he could do other than let it be known everywhere he went that this situation exists and our government is responsible. It is like our democracy—if we ever lose it, public apathy will be the reason.

Vincente went on to tell John that he would be glad to act as an interpreter to get whatever information the people would give concerning the two white fliers. He knew several who had seen them on Saipan. Vincente held an office in the municipality and was very much respected. John was certain this would help with the interrogation.

John was overjoyed with this offer and could hardly wait to tell Ken and Don. He continued the conversation with Vincente,

"It still bothers me that anyone could accept Japanese domination and their cruelty."

"Again, the older people remember it as a time of prosperity. Good living, plenty of food, choice of religion were the benefits. The Japanese were very strict and there was lots of killing and we were definitely second class citizens, but there were no money problems. There were even opportunities for the children to do things and make money to go to the movies. This is not the case today."

John said, "I know what you mean. We had a depression during the early thirties while you were having prosperity with the Japanese preparing for war. It was a terrible situation. No matter how badly you wanted to work, there just were no jobs. No one had any money to pay you if you did work. Many people begged for jobs just to get something to eat and many worked without pay just to have something to do and keep their minds occupied so they wouldn't "blow their minds". This is hard to realize now, but it happened, so I can appreciate your problems here. What was it like when the war started, Vincente?"

"First of all, I must explain that the war started for us on June 14, 1944 with the Americans invading Saipan, and not December 7, 1941 when the Japanese bombed Pearl Harbor and you went to war. Just before June 14th the Japanese told us to leave the villages. Unless you had relatives who had a farm, there just was not any place to go except to the caves up the mountain. My family took residence in a cave. We were very crowded in a small cave and our grandfather, who was past seventy, lived in the cave with us. He was in very poor health at the time, but we loved him very much and did all we could to make him as comfortable as possible under the trying circumstances. The Japanese ordered a seven o'clock curfew. No one was allowed to be seen after the curfew went into effect in the evening. Grandfather was suffocating in the cave and went to the mouth of the cave to get a breath of fresh air. A Japanese sentry saw him and shot his face off, killing him instantly. This will give you some idea how strict they were and how little regard they had for human life."

John added, "It is a damn poor commentary on our aid program if they know this harshness and would still prefer it and the prosperity that accompanied it to what they are getting today." With that parting remark he bade Vincente goodbye, telling him they would see him later and make some calls on the natives. They parted with a bond of understanding between them.

When Don and Ken arrived back at the house, John was sitting on the bed making notes on the events of the day.

Don spoke first, "Did you just get up. I suppose you have been sacked out all afternoon."

John could not restrain his enthusiasm as he spoke, "I made us a friend who is going to help us interview the natives. He will work evenings as an interpreter and, as a matter of fact, he is lining up some people for us to talk to this evening."

Don said, "Ken can go with you and I will go back out to see Terry again, but it looks like suddenly we are getting the run-around there. I guess it is not too important to find those guns anyway since we have the airplane parts, but I would like to be positive they are the same ones since we did not find the airplane, as I had seen it, all intact."

Ken reminded them, "It's time to eat. Let's go get it before the ants get it all." Both Don and John knew there were plenty of ants on Saipan to consume everything, so they made tracks to the one menu eating spot to see what surprise was in store for them tonight.

Their strange friend from Guam and Pennsylvania came in a

The Grotto, a hugh rock cavern with crystal clear ocean water entering through the tunnel in the background.

John ready to take a dip in the grotto. He came out in a hurry when he saw a man-o-war.

John, a pistol expert, shows the rest how to shoot.

John, Ken, Don and Jack relax while waiting for their equipment to come back from Saigon, Vietnam.

few minutes after they sat down, and instead of keeping at a distance acted real friendly. He sat down at their table and wanted to hear all about their exciting day.

Don told him that nothing much had happened since their guide was tied up with his work. Their supper came in good time and they held the ants at bay with different tactics, they had learned, while they ate. To date, Don held the record for thumping an ant the farthermost across the room with his middle finger. Ken claimed knife flipping honors, while John was content to brush them away or drop something to scare them if they came too close. They had to admire the ants for their sporting blood and determination. They kept coming back in the face of overwhelming odds. Don got so expert that he could flick them away in rapid succession with his left hand and never miss a bite with his fork in the other hand. Ken preferred to hold his table knife in his right hand and carefully bring the spring steel blade back while the ants came closer; then zing, he would let go and put every creature within range in orbit (and hopefully not in someone else's goulash). There even was a joke about the fellow who found an ant in his soup and called the waitress over to tell her about it. She said, "Don't talk so loud or everyone else will want one."

After they had their fill, they got up and let the ants have an undistrubed picnic. Don drove back out to Terry's place, not knowing what more he could learn, but thought he might make another date with Terry to take him to where the guns were supposed to be.

When he got to the house Terry met him in the yard, where he had one light bulb hanging down. He was very proud of that light. The Chamorro pay for electricity by the bulb and Terry could not afford one in the house, but this one in the yard was his pride and joy. He brought chairs from the house and asked Don to sit under the light. The numerous children sat at a respectable distance, awed at having a visitor. Terry sat back under that light and was really king here. They talked about many things and Terry said he would still take Don to the guns when he found time to be away from his job. The equipment was old and required constant attention to keep it going. (He never got time to take Don to the spot while they were there.)

In the meantime Ken and John had gone over to Vincente's house. He first took them to see a policeman, Jose B. Magofna, who was an uncle of Mariano Fawlig, who was going to shoot them for stealing his grandfather's betel nuts. He told them that after the Japanese had captured Guam, he was put on duty as and interpreter for the Japanese. Then when the Americans took Saipan, he joined the 6th Marines as an interpreter for the United States. After extensive questioning, he remembered the plane they found with John Doway. During the interview Vincente said his father-in-law saw a white lady come into the seaplane base at Tanapag Harbor that had top security. He thought it was about 1937. He did not know what happened to her after that. John told Jose that he too was a policeman. This did not seem to impress Jose much; he maintained his deadpan expression throughout the interview.

Vincente said, "I have something to show you." He had three pictures of the gravesite that was supposed to be Amelia Earhart's. He told them they should see the Padre, Father Sylvan. It soon became obvious this fellow was going to tell them very little, but John got the impression a lot more had happened that Jose knew. John said they would see the Padre.

At nine o'clock that evening they went to the church and met Brother Nolan from Yonkers, New York. He suggested they see Father Arnold, but he was away for the day holding Mass on one of the other Islands. John and Ken said they would come back the next day and see Father Sylvan.

The next day they met Father Sylvan and another priest. Father Sylvan was a big man, about two hundred fifty pounds and standing an erect six feet, four inches.

He asked, "What is your mission?"

John, "We came over to try and locate Amelia Earhart's airplane. Don is quite sure he saw it on Saipan when he was stationed here in 1946." Fr., "I will tell you what I know about the Amelia Earhart mystery." He had heard a great deal from the natives and had worked with Fred Goerner when he was on Saipan gathering data for his book, "Search For Amelia Earhart". He talked for three hours. There was no doubt in his mind that Amelia and Fred Noonan were on the Island in 1937. He said he would assist any way he could to help solve the mystery. He suggested they come to him for anything they could think of that he could help them with and said the gravesite would be a good place to start. Then he excused himself, saying, "If I am going out in the jungle with you, I had better get out of these vestments into some working clothes. Then we will go to Liyang cemetery and you can see the gravesites."

This had nothing to do with their airplane theory, but as long as they were here, why not try to piece the whole story together. It was another of those uncanny decisions that kept leading this group closer to being the ones who would solve the mystery.

Father Sylvan came back into the room attired in a baseball cap with CHIEF on the front. He was wearing walking shorts, combat boots, and had strapped to his waist a machete that hung nearly to the floor. With his height, that was a formidable looking piece of equipment. The three nearly gasped when they saw him.

He said, "Are you ready gents?"

Mealtime was when they found cocoanuts or bananas. They drank when it rained.

John demonstrates how to open a cocoanut with one stroke of his machete.

Types of salvage being recovered.

Still completely overwhelmed at the sight of this giant of a man, Don managed to recover enough to say, "Yeah, let's go and see that cemetery."

As they walked out the door and surveyed their tiny Datsun, all were hoping Father Sylvan could still pray in his working togs because it was going to take some kind of miracle to get them all into that car. Apparently, a change of clothes does not close the effective means of help from upstairs to a priest, if that is what was required, as they did all four squeeze into their mini-transportation unit. They were off in a cloud of coral dust.

Father Sylvan had them stop at the Japanese hospital that had been bombed; and then at the Japanese prison that became infamous after the Allies accidentally dropped a bomb on it prior to the invasion. There were two American pilots being held in the prison at that time; one was killed by the bomb. The Japanese were so enraged, they had to make someone pay for bombing their prison so they took the other prisoner out in the courtyard where there was a pit for solitary confinement. This was located between the men's and women's sections of the prison. In full view of all of the prisoners in both sections, the American prisoner was drenched with fuel oil and reduced to ashes. There are conflicting stories as to whether he was beheaded first with a samurai sword, as the Japanese liked to do, or whether he was placed in the small solitary confinement pit and burned alive. In either case it was unnerving to be standing on the spot where this atrosity took place. Father Sylvan told them how one of the fliers was later identified by a class ring that turned up, but the other has to go down in history as an unknown soldier unless someone finds the prison records. He continued to tell them how the Japanese were fastidious record keepers and unless these records were destroyed during the invasion it could still be possible to determine who the other flyer was.

John said, "That information could be in the tons of records that were shipped to Washington and have never been translated."

John felt a wave of resentment come over him as he said, "With all of the people working for the government and many of them without much to do, you would think our leaders would be grateful enough for the sacrifices of those who died to make an effort to find out what happened to them and relieve some mother's or father's mind. The truth might be horrible as it would be in this case, but nothing is worse than anxiety. At least when you know all hope is gone it is possible to adjust and carry on. To carry through life with hopeless hope never allows for any piece of mind. Maybe that is why we are here looking for Amelia Earhart's airplane. If the mystery could be cleared up as to just what did happen then many people could go on about their business with a much more peace of mind." Then he posed a question that made them all think, "Do you have any idea how many million man-hours has been spent wondering what happened to Amelia and Fred?"

"You know you are right about all of that John," Don said while thinking back. "But I worked with graves registration at times while I was here during the occupation and they really tried then to find out who everyone was. We would send home to the parents or wife, any little momento that could be associated with a soldier who had died in combat. They worked hard to identify everyone, but then that was the military; it had a greater respect for fallen comrades than ever-changing government officials who have pretty short memories about such matters."

They all agreed that if there were tons of records stuck away in the archives, these should be translated and made public. Father Sylvan was impressed with these rugged men's humility and consideration for their fellow men.

They recreated the miracle that got them into the Datsun and drove to Liyang Cemetery where there had been a previous excavation for the bodies of Amelia Earhart and Fred Noonan. At this stage, this was nothing more than a sightseeing tour and they could not know that this general area was soon to become a big part of their adventurous lives.

After spending some time at the cemetery, they drove back to the church and got comfortably seated for a long recap of all of the information Father Sylvan had been able to pick up from the local people and other investigators he had worked with on the Island. He realized they now had a contagious virulent form of the Amelia malady that could only be cured by exposure to some of the people who had seen Amelia Earhart and Fred Noonan on the Island of Saipan during 1937. His first prescription for this disease of intrigue was a suggestion that they call on a woman named Matilde San Nicolas.

This lady was married to a Japanese in 1937. His name was Shoda and he had passed away. Matilde remarried a man from the Yap Islands by the name of San Nicolas. She told them she was in Garapan living back of the Kobayashi Royokan Hotel in 1937 and was twenty-four years old at the time. She saw a white lady with a burn on her arm and face and who apparently had dysentry, as she made many trips a day to the outhouse in the courtyard back of the Hotel. It was a well known fact that the Kobayashi Royokan was used to house political prisoners and this woman, according to this witness, was under constant guard. When shown a picture of Amelia, Matilde was certain this was the woman she had seen many times.

John asked, "Did you ever talk to this woman?"

A Japanese mortar.

Another example of the live ammunition being gathered up by the salvage crews on the northern end of Saipan.

"No, but my mother talked to her many times."

"Who was your mother and where did she learn English?"

"My mother's name was Hosepa Diaz Fausto and she could speak good English because she originally came from Guam." She went on to tell them how this white lady had seemed to get progressively weaker. Then one day she gave Matilde's sister, Consolation Fausto Arielo a white gold ring with a white stone in the center. After that they did not see the white lady again.

John curiously asked, "What happened to the ring?"

"Before Consolation died she gave the ring to another sister, Delores. Before she died, she gave it to me. I gave it to a niece named Inointion Trinadad Tenaio who teaches school here. She is now age thirty-five and is in Chalan Kanoa village. The other man was here and wanted to see the ring, but it has been lost. We are still trying to find it."

Matilde's husband could speak excellent English but said very little until they were ready to leave. As was the custom there, they had gotten permission from him to come and talk to his wife. His parting remark was, "God bless you, I will pray for you. I like you and hope you find what you are looking for here on Saipan." They knew he was sincere and thanked him for letting them come into his house.

Their honest approach and talking with these people, instead of down to them, had made them another valuable contact. The word would get around that here were some regular guys who treat everyone the way they themselves would like to be treated. In most instances, getting accurate information depended upon how the individual being questioned felt about the person questioning them. These people have a remarkable way of not understanding or not remembering anything they do not care to divulge. These fellows were building bridges of friendship that would open a lot of doors for them in the future.

Vincente Camacho was a tremendous asset to them. He would start each interview with, "Don lived on the Island of Saipan for two years and likes it very much." This approach always brought smiles and nods of approval. They were off on the right foot from the beginning.

Then John would start by saying, "We are here to investigate the white woman flyer who was here along about 1937. Could you give us any information about her?" If the witness knew anything worthwhile the questioning would continue along this line. If it turned out that this person did not know anything or did not care to talk about pre-war Saipan, the conversation was diverted to something else, resulting in a pleasant visit. On more than one occasion this unhurried attitude and genuine interest in the natives turned out to be very helpful. In a more relaxed atmosphere memories often improved. Even if the person they were talking to could not give them direct information, they often could refer them to someone who could. Without this kind of assistance, anyone trying to make a complete investigation would become hopelessly lost or be led down blind alleys so time consuming that years could go by without finding the entire truth.

Vincente said they were not too far from Ben Gruerra and a talk with him might be helpful. Ben was a brother of Scuz Gruerra who was the Chief of Police under the Japanese. His tenure and actions directed by the unfeeling Japanese wasn't the least bit popular. Most all of the natives felt this man could have been less bent on making the Japanese happy for his own benefit and considered the welfare of his own people a little more. Vincente figured if it had not been Scuz doing the dirty work someone else would have been appointed to satisfy the Japanese. He was inclined to give everyone the benefit of the doubt, which accounted for his popular acceptance from his peers.

A short drive brought them to the home of a brother of the former Chief of Police. It was one of the finest homes on the Island. His working hours were spent at the Land Claims Office. With Garapan City completely destroyed to make the invasion of Saipan, most of the records of land ownership were also gone. It became necessary to set up the Land Claims Office to try to establish who had the right and title to Saipan property. He explained this took a great deal of time and Ben said it would be many years before it all got straightened out, if ever. He was a very gracious host and they spent six hours here. When the questioning got around to pre-war subjects, John could detect an attitude of a man trying to hide something. Ben's deadpan expression went even deader when there was a reference to his brother, Amelia Earhart, or anything relating to the 1937 era. He would discuss things that happened, but cautiously weighed every word.

John's years as a detective finally convinced him this was a poor place to try to get information and wound up the interview by asking Ben if there were any people of his acquaintance who might help with their investigation. Ben gave them the names of Pete Foifoi, a trusted native, and told them they should see Francisco Pangelinan, who was a truck driver for the Japanese. They later found out Francisco was not on the Island at the present time.

They were rapidly running out of time and after this bad experience of spending six hours and getting nowhere it seemed like a good time to go back to their trusted friend, Joe Diaz.

They told him they had just come from trying to locate Francisco Pangelinan. Joe looked at them a little disgusted and said,

A torpedo that missed. All kinds of material are being salvaged by an ex-Chief Petty Officer Aiken.

Natives line up for their pay. They average about $130 per month for this dangerous work.

"Don't you trust me? Why didn't you tell me before that you were here to investigate the white flyers?"

They all sheepishly listened to his berating and by way of apology told him they wanted to investigate as quietly as possible, but now needed someone they could trust to direct them to useful people. Their sincerity convinced him he should accept their apologies and try to be helpful.

Joe Diaz first told them that his father had been a truck driver and worked with Francisco in 1937. He had access to many places of top security including Tanapag Harbor. He further stated that his father, Antonio Diaz, could tell them a great deal about what had happened to the flyers initially, as he was called out early one morning to start building a road to bring the downed airplane from the jungle to Tanapag Harbor. Unfortunately Antonio Diaz was suffering from a heart condition and had been taken to Guam to the hospital. Joe said it might be well to talk to his mother and his sister who had a very frightening experience back in 1937.

They were so excited about this new development that they went directly out to see Joe's mother. Mrs. Antonio Diaz was very gracious. It was nine o'clock in the evening and they still had not eaten so she offered them some bat soup. Admittedly this does not sound like the delicacy it is regarded to be on Saipan. It is made from fruit bats that bring around five dollars apiece when they can be found. Don and Ken convinced her they thought it was good, but figured they could sleep better if they did not overeat which was a very polite way to refuse the second helping. According to his buddies, John never has any trouble sleeping and will eat anything cooked or raw, impressed his hostess by smacking his lips and asking for more. He thought it tasted like noodle soup and would likely have gotten the recipe except that fruit bats prefer Saipan to Garfield Heights, Ohio.

After the hospitality and much small talk, the group sat down and began seriously questioning about the airplane. Mrs. Diaz said she remembered one morning in 1937 (year was established by the age of one of the children) an airplane flew over and was sputtering as if in trouble. She said her husband, Antonio, was called out early that morning by the Japanese to report for work. He was one of the few people on the Island who could drive a truck. It had been some time since she had talked to him about it, but she was sure Antonio would be able to tell them a lot more when he returned from Guam.

She said that in 1957 the Central Intelligence Agency came to their home to find out what they knew about Amelia Earhart. The man was very abrupt and they told him they knew nothing. He warned them to keep on remembering nothing. Later the Navy came and questioned them. They still said nothing, afraid that this might be a check-up of the C.I.A. John was trying to establish why she and her husband had not told what they knew prior to this time. He was convinced that this was information that they had not given out prior to this moment and that it was all true. John knew he and the group must talk to Antonio Diaz when he got out of the hospital.

Mrs. Diaz told them they should talk to her daughter, Anna Diaz Magofna. She had seen a white man beheaded later that same year. She was only seven years old at the time and it was such a horrifying experience that she had nightmares for years after the incident took place. She told how she and Antonio would have to take her in bed with them at night to get her settled down again. They cautioned Anna that she must never breath a word of it or the entire family probably would be put to death by the Japanese. To a very young girl this was almost too much of a burden to carry.

John, Ken and Don thanked her very much, told her they would see Anna before they left Saipan, and very much wanted to meet her husband; hoping he would have a speedy return to good health.

It had been a long hard day. They did not realize how exhausted they were until they tumbled into bed. John dropped off to sleep immediatley while Don and Ken pondered about whether they might not have slept a little better with a second bowl of bat soup or a trip to the Saipan Hotel. Tomorrow was going to be a very busy day that would require maximum strength. Soon the roof was being tested by the syncopated snores of three tired men.

After breakfast the next morning they decided to have one more go at the guns, so they drove to the restricted area and talked to Chief Petty Officer Aiken and asked about the location of the large guns. He simply told them he was not familiar with the area, his only interest was to get the place deactivated. He explained to them that his men were continually confronted with the natives, especially kids, slipping into the area to steal shells and grenades. They would use the hand grenades to fish with. The plan was to get a boat and take the grenades out a ways from the shore, pull the pin and drop the grenades into the water. This would kill the fish or stun them so they would float to the surface to be picked up. It was a very workable plan except every once in a while a grenade would go off prematurely and kill someone or mangle the children. Naturally, since Chief Petty Officer Aiken was in charge of the restricted area, he got some of the blame every time one of these incidents occurred.

Convinced this was a losing proposition, they went back to Chalan Kanoa to see the school teacher about the ring Matilde told them she had given to her niece. The teacher could do little

A German gun taken out of the jungle is mute evidence of their world domination plans prior to World War I.

Entrance to San Antonio Village that was completely destroyed by typhoon Jean.

more than tell them it was white gold and had a pearl on top. She did not think it had been a very expensive ring, but would continue to look for it. John offered her one thousand dollars for it.

They next went to see Mariano Fawlig again. He took them to see Louie Igatol. They sat on the floor, as he had no furniture. He had been a truck driver's helper for the Japanese working at the Tanapag seaplane base. His truck driver was Joe Blass.

John asked him, "Could you remember the names of any of the other truck drivers at that time?"

He named: Antonio Diaz, Francisco Pangelinan, and Ramon Macynaga. They were more certain than before that they just had to talk to Antonio Diaz. He was an elected official to represent the Island, so must be dependable. If he was anything like his son, Joe, he would be cooperative, and Mrs. Diaz had already assured them that Antonio would be glad to see them when he was well enough. Getting over Ameliaitis was going to take longer than they figured and would require at least one more trip. With these thoughts in mind, they set out to find Joe's sister, Anna Magofna.

Protocol would have required they get permission from the husband to talk to Anna at her house so they went to her mother's place and Anna was brought over. Joe had gone along. When Anna came into the room Joe talked to her first in their native Chamorro language to tell her these three men were his friends and could be trusted. He would like for her to tell them what she knew about the white flyers.

Anna could understand English very well, but could not express herself well, so they talked mostly with Joe translating her explanation of how she was coming home from school one day, when suddently she saw two Japanese watching two white people digging outside the cemetery. She did not dare go any closer or let the Japanese know she was anywhere around so she hid and watched. When the grave was dug, the tall man with a big nose, as she described him, was blindfolded and made to kneel by the grave. His hands were tied behind him. One of the Japanese took a samurai sword and chopped his head off. The other one kicked him into the grave.

John asked her if she thought she could still find that grave.

She was sure she could because she had to go by it on the way to school every day until the invasion destroyed Garapan.

Don suggested, "We are going to have to leave here before we will get to check this out, but we will be back. Could you draw us a map?"

"Sure, I will draw a map so you can find it." She drew them a map, but for a lot of reasons to be explained later they would have never found the grave if she had not been able to go along and point it out to them. They would have missed it by about a mile. They had the map; their Amelia fever had gone up two more degrees. They were planning to leave the next day and the wheels were turning in their heads making plans to come back. Leaving was difficult right here, but they had no choice; their visas had expired.

Home sounded good now. There were many arrangements to be made at the last minute and the main thing was to get all of the bills paid. They started with the car rental, for which Ken thought he could use his American Express Card to settle up with Joe Ten Car Rental. Nothing doing. They wanted cash on the barrelhead, so cash it was.

Feeling a little short of cash now, Ken said, "I had better go to the bank and get some money." He was sure his American Express Card would be honored there. He was wrong again. They acted like they had never heard of such a thing, but said they would take his check. This was something he had never heard of before. Why would a banker, of all people, turn down a credit card and take a personal check. He decided not to look a gift horse in the mouth and said he would take one hundred fifty dollars.

The banker had different ideas, "Fifty dollars."

Ken, "That's not enough to get us all the way home. I need at least one hundred dollars."

"How about seventy-five?"

"I really don't think I can pay the rest of the bills here and make it home on seventy-five."

"O.K., then we will let you have the hundred."

Don, "Take it quick! If I walked into a strange bank I bet they would not let me write a check for fifty cents. They would run in the vault and lock the door."

With that transaction over, they went back to their hut to settle up and add more to the Joe Ten bank account. In fact, they were going to add a great deal more than they had figured on. When they took the place, they were told it would cost them five dollars per day. They misunderstood by thinking this was for the room. When they were handed the itemized bill, they found out this meant five dollars per person per day or a total of fifteen dollars a day instead of five. They did not make any headway negotiating this time. Between them, they scraped up enough to pay the bill. They thought there was nothing left to do now except pack their suitcases, say goodbye, and catch the morning airplane, with built-in thrills, back to Guam.

John had one more small chore to do. He had seen some rare tropical fish at one of the stores and thought he would thrill his son, who had a hobby aquarium of tropical fish. He bought the fish and some chemicals to condition the water appropriately for salt-water tropical fish. This was the beginning of a series of bad experiences that increased John's already adequate vocabulary of descriptive adjectives that cannot be used until the children have gone to bed.

While delivering the car back to the rental place, John was driving and Ken was sitting in the back seat with Don. It was about 90 degrees. Don looked at Ken a little concerned and said, "I think you had better take a bath before we leave. You are getting pretty ripe." Ken thought at first he was kidding, but Don said, "I am serious." Don was sitting on the windward side and getting the full benefit of the decaying seashells they had thrown in the back seat of the car and forgotten about. Just as Ken turned ready to slug Don for his reference to his B.O., he caught a nostril full of an odor that would gag a maggot on a gut-wagon. They had John stop the car and they sorted out the dead overripe ones, which were easy to recognize with the sniff test. They divided up the rest. If they did not smell bad they assumed they were O.K. That was an assumption that nearly cost Don his happy home when he got there.

The next morning they were anxious to leave, but were informed that the plane could not take off because typhoon Gilda was in the area. Joe Diaz's wife and some friends were at the airport with beautiful flower leis. This was the first of four trips they were to make with leis before the fellows finally got off Saipan. They were told to come back tomorrow after the storm had passed by. John was already starting to worry about his rare tropical fish. What another twenty-four hours of this heat would do to them, loomed in his mind. He could have saved himself a lot of future worry if he had taken them back to the store or mercifully given them the coup de grace at that moment. Never-say-die was a way of life with all of them and John really wanted to surprise his son, so he continued his education and on-the-job training for the care of tropical fish.

They considered getting the car again and going out to the gravesite while they waited. They decided this would not be the thing to do as someone might see them and ruin everything for their next trip. Besides that Ken reminded them that their money was running low and they were not off this Island yet. They did not have to wait too long to have plenty to do.

Typhoon Gilda hit with a fury that they could not adequately describe. There was nothing much they could do except wait it out. John and Ken poured themselves the last of the Long John Scotch while Don slept. He had seen typhoons before on Saipan many years before. He had told them before he went to sleep that they blow a while, everything gets calm, they come back the other way, then leave. This is exactly what typhoon Gilda did. Of course there was the little inconveniences of no electricity, no food, but plenty of rainwater as it came down in torrents. The average person might be inclined to wonder what you do in a situation like this and how you survive. The answer is, if you are there, you have no choice. You wait until it is over. If you don't get blown away it is unlikely that much else will happen except your nerves get a little shattered. Just knowing you are in the middle of a hundred mile an hour wind does not give one confidence, but the natives learn to accept this as a part of life. If they get wiped out, they start over with a little less than they had before. Life, health and peace of mind are the really important things in life. Anyone who just had to leave Saipan that day was in bad trouble because no one left. Nor did anyone leave the next day. The girls were there with the leis as soon as the storm passed, but Gilda was still in the area, and a threat, so all planes were grounded.

John, Ken and Don were beginning to reveal that they were normal human beings about this time. They became less polite

Antonio Diaz's home in San Antonio Village before it was destroyed by typhoon Jean.

with each other (which is the understatement of the year). They were restless and anxious to get home. John got quite a number of suggestions about what to do with his tropical fish. In fact, Don and Ken got quite hostile about all of his concern. They didn't mind him worrying about his precious little creatures, but they saw no reason for being included in the project. They were starting to have their own worries after forty-eight hours of delay.

CHAPTER V

HOME AGAIN AT LAST

On the third day after they were supposed to leave Saipan the sun came up in all of its splendor, the birds were singing and the airplanes were flying. The group got their things aboard the plane, said final goodbyes and accepted plastic leis from the girls who had given up on live flowers after the third try. Just the sheer joy of being on the way kept them from noticing the fallacies of the airplane this trip even though it was the same one they came over on.

The short trip to Guam started out to be completely uneventful, but that all changed when they pulled up at the unloading ramp. Who should be at the airport to meet them? None other than their acquaintance from Carlisle, Pa; the one that met them every evening at the Saipan Hotel for dinner.

He greeted them with a big, "Hello there, I am glad to see you made it. What are your plans," as if he did not know about their flying schedule.

Don said, "It is 10:00 now and we do not leave until 5:00 so I guess we will get a car and drive around a little."

Ken spoke up, "You live here; what is there interesting to see?"

The new self-appointed host said, "I have a car and must go to the depot to check in then I will take you around." He first took them to two huge quonset buildings that Don pictured as about the size of Cleveland Stadium. This is the place where tanks were being repaired. Their host got them security clearance and took them through the compound. He then gave them the key to his apartment telling them to get cleaned up and he would take them to lunch. No one argued with that suggestion. A hot shower and a good meal would hit the nail right on the head. On the way over they agreed not to talk about their find on Saipan at his apartment as it might be bugged. They also agreed it would be better to not say anything of significance to him. They just could not figure this fellow out. They figured sooner or later the truth would come out so they forgot about him while they enjoyed the luxury of the hot shower.

He picked them up about two hours later in a Navy personnel carrier and took them to an officers mess. A marine saluted him at the gate. A sign at the place indicated it was reserved for the rank of captains or up. It was a real "swanky" place and Ken just had to ask if the food was any better than the Saipan Hotel. They were to soon find out it was better than most any place they had ever been.

They were given white gloves and directed to a cooler with a selection of every imaginable kind of steak. When told to pick out what they would like, Don asked if he could take two. It had been a long time since they had seen meat that looked like this. After making their selection, they took it to the native cook who had a charcoal fire going and he fixed it just the way they ordered it. Don could not eat another steak, but they did all have apple pie and coffee. They told their host about typhoon Gilda and that all they had to eat was sardines, crackers, cocoanuts and bananas, and high winds blew in a new assortment of bugs that tried to deprive them of these meager rations.

A longer than expected drive about the Island had them rushing to catch their plane. This time it was a beautiful jet. The only unhappy person was John. His rare tropical fish were starting to look pretty sick and it still was a long trip home. There was a refueling stop at Wake where the last rites were administered to one of the fish. They would be coming to Hawaii next and would have a few hours layover. John got the salt brine chemicals out that he had bought with the fish. He was planning to change the water at the next stop and see if he could not perk the fish up a bit. The directions for the brine were in Japanese and there were no likely looking interpreters on the airplane so John would have to wait until he got to Hawaii.

When they landed, John headed straight for the police station. He first tried to find someone to read the directions on the chemicals. When that failed, John asked if he could borrow a cylinder of emergency oxygen. After several minutes of this emergency treatment the fish appeared more lively and John was much encouraged until another one started doing all kinds of peculiar maneuvers while they waited for the plane to Los Angeles. Then tragedy struck; two more fish collapsed and died. The three deceased rare specimens got a very unceremonious burial in the trash can as the final boarding call was being given. John still was determined to get the rest of those fish to his son.

John met a man on the trip to Los Angeles who seemed to know a lot about tropical fish. He offered a lot of advice, but most of it required a lot of equipment more commonly found in pet shops than airplanes. Anyway, John picked this man's brains enough to figure the only way he could save his remaining fish was to readjust the Ph of the water with the chemicals. This man could not read Japanese, but he did suggest about what he thought would be the right amount. John was extremely grateful and kept watching the little fellows, hoping they would stay alive until they reach Los Angeles.

While all that was going on, Ken and Don were discussing the next trip back to Saipan. They would take tape recorders and get a good photographer. They decided it would be a good idea to go

Antonio Diaz being interviewed at his home before showing the group where he helped build a road to Amelia's plane.

Mr. Diaz explains how he built a coral road into the jungle marsh to haul Amelia's plane out for the Japanese.

back and record the witnesses they had talked to on this trip and get pictures of them. This would provide them with proof of any claims which might be disputed. Ken knew he could rely on Jack Geschke to make this next trip.

When the plane landed, John wasted no time in going to the washroom to change the water and add the chemicals. The plunger was broken on the sink so Ken suggested they put some of the chemical in the toilet bowl and let the fish swim there until they got the water fixed up in the fishbowl. They watched them swim around in the toilet bowl for a while and the fish seemed to be improving so Don and Ken left. John went to the sink and started mixing up the water to take the fish on to Cleveland. A small boy walked into the restroom unnoticed by John and went into the first stall.

He saw the small fish swimming around in the toilet bowl and didn't think that should be. Just then John caught a glimpse of him and let out a bellow that would have waked the dead, but it was too late. The kid pulled the handle and John's investment in tropical fish went down the drain. He wanted to cry.

Don had called Florence to have her call the other wives so they could meet them at the airport in Cleveland. Don said his home looked like a $300,000 mansion after being on Saipan. Ken and John were happy to be home again, too. They wanted to get the airplane parts analyzed and prepare for the next trip. All in all there was much excitement. Organized effort gave way to everyone talking at once with more ideas and plans than the average individual could have coped with. There was no mistaking their intent now to prove or disprove this was the airplane they had traveled nearly half way around the world to find. They were equally determined to go back and locate the gravesite that Anna Diaz Magofna had described and given them a map of its location. In addition to the map and the airplane parts they brought back 75 rolls of 8mm movie film to help explain their trip. This was processed and, since they were all amateurs with the movie camera, they only wound up with about 600 feet of decent film. It was either badly underexposed if taken in the jungles where the sunlight just does not penetrate, or grossly overexposed if taken out in the sunlight, which is much brighter than anyone realized. This paltry dozen rolls of worthwhile film out of 75 convinced them more than ever that a professional photographer was an absolute must for the next trip.

Robert Stafford of the Cleveland Press wrote a story about them for his paper. Ken had met him before. The circumstances were much different.

Many people touch our lives on one or more occasions. Such was the case with Ken Matonis and Robert Stafford. It all goes back to the Korean War that was very real to Ken. Not only did he fight up to the bitter end, he had the traumatic experience of having to hold a brother in his arms on the battlefield and helplessly watch his life come to a premature end. Michael Matonis paid the supreme price. The circumstances of his death and many others have caused Ken to have a lot of thoughts about how important timing is to our lives.

Ken was attached to the 32nd Regiment of the 7th Division in Korea. His brother was in another regiment also in Korea. They would correspond when the action permitted. One day Ken received a letter from Michael stating that he could get transferred to the 32nd if Ken would get him a letter of acceptance. This sounded like a wonderful idea so Ken ask the CO to write him the letter. About a month later he came into the platoon area and they had a great reunion. There was talk of ending the war so they might be going home together. What a celebration that would be!

They were up on the front, but there seemed to be a little let-up in the action for the next six weeks while the political powers got ready to talk peace. Good men were dying on both sides every day while these politicians found time in their busy schedules of protocol and cocktail parties to discuss peace. Then tragedy hit Michael and Ken.

They were laying communication wire from an outpost to the MLR (main line of resistance) when the enemy tanks opened fire. Ken does not know by what miracle he was saved, but Michael did not make it. He died in Ken's arms that had to cause Ken to go into a state of shock. He wondered why it had been Michael and not him. He had to suddently realize how infinite death is and just how short life is. Carlyle said it, but as Ken held his brother and watched his life ebb away he had to realize there are remedies for all things but death. He had to wonder why he had ever requested that letter of acceptance that brought Michael to the spot where he would die. His more rational subconscientous mind should have prevailed and sent him a quote from Dryden when he said, "No king nor nation one moment can retard the appointed hour." He still had to wonder.

But Lincoln said, "Life is for the living" and indeed life did go on. At least the struggle to stay alive went on because the North Koreans decided it was time to put on a big push to strengthen their bargaining position at the peace table-like take as many lives as possible and sacrifice a lot of their noble sons for a few words, a period, or a comma on a piece of paper that would be violated at the first advantageous opportunity. That is all civilization has learned about living together in the last few thousand years. Most regretable. There was not time to be philosophical. The big push was on. The ranks of the 32nd were being thinned out to the point replacements from the 24th stationed in Japan had to be moved in.

Ken had survived and was sent to Japan for six weeks, delay in route, while Michael's body was processed. He then brought Michael to San Francisco on a ship and took a train from there to Chicago. They were transferred to another train for the last leg of the journey to Cleveland. About an hour out of Cleveland a reporter from the Cleveland Press boarded the train and rode on into Cleveland with Ken. The reporter was Robert Stafford. Ken told him, "A lot of other guys died, too, let me tell you what it is like and you print it like it is." Mr. Stafford told him the public is not ready for that. Michael and a lot of guys weren't ready to die either.

Jack and Don study the map Antonio Diaz drew to indicate where Amelia's plane landed.

CHAPTER VI

BACK HOME

November of 1967 slipped away rapidly with the group trying to reestablish normal daily living. Don went back to his ceramic tile business, John got back into action with the Garfield Heights Police, and Ken dived into a backlog of work with his commercial janitorial service business. It was most difficult for any one of them to get much done. All of the news media along with television and radio people scheduled them for various types of programs to relate the details of their adventure. With this kind of publicity, these new celebrities were stopped by all of their friends and total strangers to get the story of their trip directly from 'the horse's mouth'. All were congenial fellows and tried to convey the excitement and drama of their experiences. They would always end with a vow to return soon and bring back substantial evidence to prove what had actually happened to Amelia Earhart and Fred Noonan. This last proclamation never failed to stimulate more enthusiasm and conversation on the part of everyone present.

The few rolls of film that turned out were shown to guests at their homes with profuse apologies and appropriate matrimonial comments from their spouses that inspire one to do better next time. The contrasts of exhilerating beauty and deplorable existence of many of the people on Saipan were vivid pictures in the minds of Don, Ken and John. There were not adequate words for them to explain and describe these scenes to their satisfaction. Every time the subject came up, one of them would ask, "Who are we going to get who would be capable of capturing what we saw on film?" How could they know that the solution to that question would almost miraculously fall into their laps as the solution to so many of their problems did during their entire adventure?

December found everyone caught up in a flurry of activity centered around Christmas, and winding up the various businesses for the year, so little other than conversation was accomplished, to bring any kind of light into their adopted mystery. John was assigned the task of finding someone to analyze the airplane parts. He dived into this with his usual relentless energy. It was determined that Alcoa had made the aluminum for Lockheed during the thirties. Further effort found an analytical chemist who was a great help in establishing the vintage of the metal.

What appeared to be a simple problem of analysis was not so simple. First the metal was analyzed by Crobaugh Laboratories to establish just what percentage of various metals went into the final alloy. They were especially interested in copper content, as this had changed in the late 30's to a point that their metal could be tied to the middle thirties by its copper content. Also, information had to be obtained from German and Japanese sources to rule out the possibility that they might have been using this same copper content in their aluminum alloys.

Alcoa was most helpful in getting them the alloy analysis for the entire period of 1930 to 1940, as well as information on the German and Japanese airplane materials. Neither used copper in their aluminum alloys as tin was satisfactory and more available.

Finally they had something tangible that was checking out on all accounts. They had established that the metal in the airplane parts they had brought from Saipan were made prior to 1937 by Alcoa.

Even John's investigating ability was taxed to the limit when he tried to tie the numbers on the airplane parts to Amelia Earhart's Lockheed 10 E. It was understandable that this company had doubtless been plagued with many requests which had been blind alleys in the search for that famous airplane. However, it seemed to take an undue amount of effort to find anyone in the organization even willing to part with or supply a numbered parts list for the 10 E series, which certainly had to be available. John's persistance finally paid off with that list and an explanation that it would be almost impossible to establish whether or not this was Amelia's airplane just from the parts list. This was true because there had been many parts replaced prior to and during the final flight, with no records kept of specific serial numbered parts. Most part numbers would simply reflect a catalogue number for ordering replacements. This was discouraging, but efforts went on. They could not give up without exhausting every possibility.

Florence Kothera was becoming a full time secretary with telephone calls and letters to every conceivable person who might possibly have any information regarding that airplane. Nearly all of her efforts provided no clues. She and Don read every book obtainable on any of Amelia's activities to partially satiate their avid interest with ever present hope of coming across some tiny shred of information which could be helpful in carrying the investigation still further. They reasoned that as long as their search could be kept alive there was always a possibility the entire mystery could be solved.

There were many times when they talked about "How was it possible to get so involved, and were they being foolish for pursuing something that had been given up as a lost cause by many many people before them?" In spite of any such doubts as to the logic or their sanity, the same determination continued to grip this circle with growing passion. Even though Don was not absolutely sure about the plane, to stop now or even slow down was completely unthinkable.

The slowdown of business activities after the first of the year gave the entire group more opportunities to get together and start planning their trip back to excavate the gravesite using the map that had been given to them by Anna. Jack Geschke had his International Inn and other business ventures under control at this point and was making

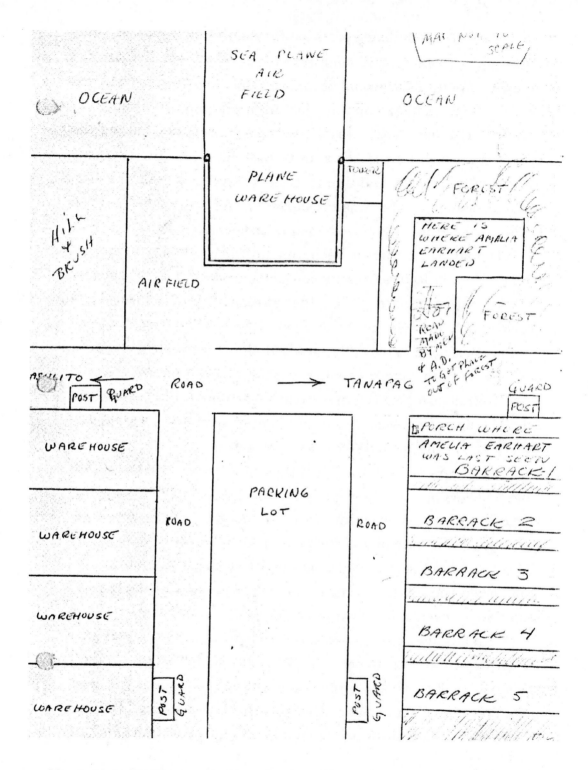

Mr. Antonio Diaz's map showing where Amelia's plane came down. He helped build the road to take it out of the forest.

plans to go with them on this trip. Their consistent, bubbling accounts of the last trip would no longer allow him to remain a silent partner in this great adventure. There were going to be several moments in his immediate future to make him wonder why he had become so inspired. Two hundred mile-an-hour typhoons are something less than inspiring when you are in the middle of one, as Jack was soon going to be, which would put him in the same category as General Custer's men who wondered, "what am I doing here?" In fact, Jack had many opportunities to ask them to tell him again how wonderful it was on Saipan after a day of being drenched by the ever present rains, stung by wasps, and attached every night by limitless hordes of mosquitoes that John swears can stand flatfooted and harpoon a tall man square on his behind. (Author's note: This is supposed to be a factual report, but in all fairness, I have to concede that description has been modified a bit to keep this a family type book).

Jack has an interesting habit of looking at his wristwatch every few minutes when a meeting takes longer than he feels it should or he had rather be some other place. This little characteristic became quite hilarious to the rest of the group when they were out in the jungle with no place to go and during the typhoon Jean when nobody was going anyplace. This is getting ahead of our story, however, so let's skip back to Cleveland for a couple of months of preparation for the second trip to Saipan. They thought with Anna's map they would have no problem finding the gravesite. They were just as convinced that they could expect to find Fred Noonan's body there.

Being fairly certain they were about to make history now, they set out to find a photographer who could record the events as they took place. They decided it should be on 16 mm film and someone who could get better than twelve rolls out of seventy-five should be in charge of that detail.

They first approached a well known television personality specializing in travel and adventure series. He first planned to go, then found he had other obligations. This put them right back where they started until one day John decided he should get his weekly haircut.

For John to decide he needs a haircut is an optimistic assumption based very little on the facts. Most of his hair turned to skin long ago, but it gives him confidence to sit in the barber chair and visit with old friends while the barber pretends to earn his money. Anyway John's decision to go to Danny's clip joint was another action directed by Fate.

Danny said, "Heard you had a trip to Saipan. Tell me about it."

While John was talking, Marty Fiorillo walked in the door. John had met Marty about a year before and listened to him tell about going to Africa, Alaska, digging up Indian graves in Arizona and many other interesting trips. After Danny and John greeted Marty they asked if he had moved back to Cleveland or was just on a buying trip.

Marty, who is never at a loss for words, gave them a rundown on his Frontier Arms Inc. gunshop in Cheyenne, Wyoming and told them that he was only here to replenish his supply of special guns for big game. He was outfitting another safari that required special equipment. His partner, Earl was holding the fort in Cheyenne.

At the first break in the conversation, Danny broke in with, "Marty, John was just about to tell me about his trip to Saipan to try and find Amelia Earhart's airplane. I know this is something you will be interested in hearing."

Marty said he had read something about that trip and was very much interested in hearing all about it.

John needed no more encouragement. His steeltrap mind had already sprung. He planned to put on one of his best performances and by the time he got out of that barber chair he would have a recruit for the photographer's job or he was no judge of human nature. It was an inspiring description of all that had happened and John ended by say-ing, "We are going back the first of April to tape the witnesses, make a movie, and excavate for Fred Noonan's body." It probably was the word 'excavate' that really turned Marty on. His real first love is ar-chaeology and here was an opportunity to do some real exciting work.

Marty spoke right up, "I am a pretty good photographer. I have over $5,000 worth of equipment and I would like to go with you fellows."

John said, "I am just one of the group. I will have to get their ap-proval, but I know we could use someone with your talents and equip-ment. We are on a pretty limited budget and so far this whole deal has cost us a lot of money. With some good film, perhaps we could make enough to recoup part of our expense."

"Talk it up for me, John. I really would like to make this trip."

John could hardly wait to get the group together to start talking up for Marty. Later they found out Marty had just gotten a haircut three days before and had just accidentally dropped in to pass the time of day. Anyway the group had another coffee and cookie session at the Kothera's house and Marty was elected to the high post of Chief Pho-tographer. This turned out to be one of the best decisions the group ever made. Not only did Marty get them excellent pictures and mov-ies, but he turned out to be the only one who knew anything about dig-ging remains. Without his help they no doubt would have thrown out all of the evidence they went 9,000 miles to uncover. He, also, proved to be invaluable on several occasions in interviewing people after the second trip was over. In addition, he got them all revolvers, as they had given the ones they used on the first trip to people on Saipan who had helped them.

Marty got his safari taken care of then waited six weeks while ev-eryone got shots, visas, etc. They found out he was a perfectionist and a most lovable fellow. They were to find out that he could be painfully exact when it came to taking pictures and was inclined to quit regularly when they could not see the need of having the light just right for every picture. They were to learn this is the difference between acceptable and real first class pictures.

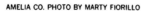
AMELIA CO. PHOTO BY MARTY FIORILLO

Joe Diaz explaining his father's map showing where the plane went down.

CHAPTER VII

HISTORY IN THE MAKING

They were all finally ready for the historic second trip to Saipan. John double checked to see that he had Anna's map of the gravesite. This was wasted effort. Without Anna's going out in the jungle with them and pointing out the exact spot, they never would have found it. They would have been using the wrong crematorium as a guide.

Marty had carefully checked and packed his equipment. This was later attested to when the equipment went to Saigon, Viet Nam first and still got back to Saipan in good condition.

Ken tied up all of the loose ends he could as far as his business was concerned and added to the equipment that was worthwhile taking on a second trip. The Cuyahoga Cleaning Contractors Company would just have to get along without him for a month.

Don worked extra hours, postponed some jobs, and farmed out the rest so he could leave with a reasonably clean conscience.

They all met with their wives and friends at Jack Gesche's International Airport Inn for last goodbyes. Florence gave Don some last minute instructions about bringing home any more shells to annoint the carpet with. John was kidded some about bringing home some rare tropical fish. Finally zero hour arrived. They drove the few blocks to Hopkins Airport. Ken was the last to check his baggage. The other eleven bags, including Marty's photography equipment had been checked on the way to the International Inn.

They had a rather uneventful trip as far as Guam. Naturally, John went right to sleep. Ken and Don remembered that it would be a twenty-four hour journey, with stops, so they got in some 'shut-eye' at every opportunity. When they landed at Guam, Ken was the only one with any baggage. Don called Florence and asked her to check with

Pan American, once they were on Saipan there was no telephone service.

Florence found out that the eleven bags had gone to Saigon instead of Saipan. Pan American said they would put a tracer on it and get it back as soon as possible. They flew on to Saipan via the Trust Territory Airline. This was still a nerve shattering experience for the professionals who had made it before. Marty and Jack survived only because they had been told what they could expect and that the trip did not take very long.

They rented a car and drove to the Royal Toga, with intentions of staying there. They were informed that the rate would be $12.00 per person per day. Jack was helping finance this expedition. He looked at his watch and said there must be something more reasonable since they were going to be here a month. The rest agreed that sixty dollars a day would put them in the tourist class.

When that was brought up, it caused Ken to remark, "Here you bums are trying to go first class and you don't even have any baggage. How do you expect to get checked into a nice hotel without even having a suitcase?"

In unison, "Go ahead and rub it in, wise guy, we will all be wearing your clothes before the week is over." They had no idea just how prophetic that crack was going to be. They had assumed their own things would be coming on the plane the next day.

John, Ken, and Don had learned to stop at Joe Ten's and get Joe Diaz when they had a problem. Besides it was time to introduce Marty and Jack to this wonderful friend. They told him about going to the Royal Toga and that the management wanted them to buy the place just to stay there for thirty days. Joe got the picture. He took them to his uncle's place—he said could be had for $5.00 per person per day. This sounded real great until they got there. It was not much more than a shack in Chalan Kanoa. Joe was busy telling his uncle where to send each one of several raga-muffin children. They would all be farmed out to different relatives to make room for the paying guests. Joe told them his uncle was sick and would have to stay with them. After looking the place over, they could understand why he was sick. They would have explained to him that it was unhealthy to keep pigs, chickens, and goats in the house, but knew the Chamorro would likely have told them that he had not lost any in years. The odor was enough to convince Jack to check his watch again and head for their Datsun. It didn't take a board meeting for the rest to determine this was a bit too rough for them. He offered all he had.

Joe suggested they try at the Saipan Hotel. In fact, this was another Joe Ten enterprise and he took them over to negotiate a price. They were familiar with the Saipan Hotel and expected to see their friend, Peter, again. They found Peter had been replaced as manager by a woman. After much conversation, she finally agreed to furnish them two rooms in the converted barracks for $4.00 per head per day. Jack looked at the quarters and looked at his watch again, but knew it was this or nothing. At least it was an improvement over the last place they had looked at.

They did not have much equipment to get since most of it had gone to Saigon, Viet Nam. Ken did go to the airport and pick up his clothes and the few items the rest had carried during the trip. They spent the rest of the day just resting up from the long trip and getting oriented to the time change that bedevils all airline travelers.

The next morning they got up early and went to the restaurant for bacon and eggs. Nothing had changed since they were here before. The rice dish tasted about the same. Jack looked at his watch several times during his initiation to this type of breakfast. Marty ate it like a real trouper, but John, Ken and Don were silently amused by his facial

Joe Diaz pointing out the location near Tanapag Seaplane base where the plane went down. The very ill Mr. Diaz felt it his duty to show them the exact location.

Japanese, Saipanese and Americans help recover the Japanese war dead for return to Japan.

expressions that denoted certain reservations about this kind of bill of fare. They knew at this particular moment, Marty would rather have been back in Wyoming at his gun shop where the deer and the antelope play and breakfast is an inspiring experience.

After breakfast, they all agreed there was a lot of work to be done, but nothing to do it with. They would 'get going' with the taping and filming of interviews just as soon as the equipment arrived. They were to spend the next five days trying to 'get going'. While they were waiting for the equipment to arrive, they drove around Saipan visiting people they had talked to before, introducing them to Marty and Jack, and setting up interviews to be held when the equipment arrived. The Island was beautifully appointed with all kinds of tropical flowers and flowering trees, and Marty could hardly wait to get his camera equipment to make a permanent record of this aspect of Saipan.

Every morning after breakfast for five days they would drive to the airport to find they still had no equipment. They were beginning to worry that it was lost forever when on the sixth day a couple of pieces came on the Micronesian Airline. This gave them hope that the rest would be along and the trip would not be a lost cause. They also were tired of wearing Ken's clothes and he was tired of sharing his limited supply.

Their intentions were to take all of the pictures and tape the witnesses before they did any digging. This was pre-determined so that if they did find anything, they could leave immediately with the evidence. While reviewing this plan on one occasion, it occurred to them that if Amelia had been sent on a spying mission for the United States government she would have chosen to fly from East to West instead of from West to East as they set out to do before wrecking the airplane in Hawaii. Her reasons would have been the same. That is; after taking pictures of Saipan and flying on to Howland Island, the next stop would have been Hawaii, or she could have turned the information and pictures over to the Coast Guard ship *Itasca* which had been sent to Howland Island to help guide them there. If she had gone from West to East she would have had to carry the film through customs in several foreign countries and taken the chance of having her mission discovered—something that might have provoked the Japanese to attack when we were less prepared for war than we were December 7, 1941 when they attacked Pearl Harbor, starting the Pacific phase of World War II.

Saipan is not a very big island and a day's driving would bring them by the Joe Ten store at least a dozen times a day while they were waiting for the equipment. They always stopped and bought pop, smokies (Smoked fish), and a few items to combat the heat, mosquitoes, or other discomforts of Saipan life.

On the seventh day Marty got his camera equipment so they could really 'get going'. They decided to do as much filming as possible before taping; a very fortunate decision. Within three weeks nearly everything was going to leave the Island in the furious 200 M.P.H. winds of typhoon Jean.

Don describes Marty's picture taking as something unreal. "We would be driving along with five of us crowded in the Datsun. Marty would suddenly see a flower or some object that he thought would make a good picture so we would stop the car and all pile out. Then we would wait for an hour or two for the sun to be just right for Marty to get the light he wanted. This kind of action evoked a lot of uncomplimentary comments from the rest of the group and had Marty resigning regularly."

Marty would alternate between, "If you know more about it, you do it, I quit," and "you guys brought me 9,000 miles to get some good pictures, now leave me alone while I get that job done."

Most of the time they left him alone except for a lot of good natured heckling. They admit now that he got unbelievable pictures, capturing Saipan as they saw it.

After seven days of filming everything from flowers to fortifications, this project was done. Jack looked at his watch and wondered what was happening at the good ole International Inn. He had not been given much to do up to now and had seen the Island several times so was beginning to wonder what he was doing there. That was soon to change. They all assured Jack that when they started digging in the jungle he would have plenty to do and they could use all of the help they could get. That suggestion of him swinging a pick out in the rotten jungle reminded Jack of the time he was on Saipan while in service and caused him to look at his watch again.

It was now time to start with the taping. John was put in charge of this. They felt his ability to extract information, from his many years as a police officer, was a definite advantage. The rest would go along to keep the conversation moving, but John would have the recorder and ask most of the questions.

The first interview was with Antonio Diaz, Joe's father, and a very substantial citizen on the Island. He was 59 years old and had been in the hospital at the time of their first trip so this was their first opportunity to meet this man. He still was a very sick man and certainly had no reason to tell them anything except the absolute truth. This interview took place on Palm Sunday, April 4, 1968.

After proper introductions, they got right down to business. Mr. Diaz had been called inside the Japanese seaplane base, Tanapag Harbor to build a coral road into the jungle to bring out Amelia's plane. The plane had gone down in some pinelike trees and was damaged very little. There were no airstrips on Saipan at that time, but they figured it was logical for her to try to land as close to other airplanes as pos-

Japanese in charge of collecting the war dead with Mayor Sablan's wife enjoying a look at pre-war Garapan.

Several Japanese were found in this cave.

sible since she was out of fuel, according to the last report to the *Itasca*.

Mr. Diaz drew them a map of the area as he remembered it showing where the plane was located. He pointed out where the Japanese had him help build the coral road to bring the airplane out.

The interview started inside, but Marty had to have more light to get good pictures so they asked if they could move the furniture outside if they would bring it back in afterwards.

Antonio said, "The airplane no got gas."

John, "It ran out of gas?"

"Yes, run out of gas."

"How many were there?"

"One man and one woman wearing a jacket and pants."

They showed him a picture and asked if it was something like this.

"Yes, that looks like them"

"Do you recognize them?"

"Yes."

"How did you know they were Americans?"

I saw them on the veranda being guarded by two Japanese."

"M.P.'s?"

"Did you know they were American?"

"The Japanese foreman said they were."

"You were driving a truck at the time?"

"Yes, there were six of us."

"If we take you to Tanapag, could you show us where the plane went down?"

"Yes, I could do that."

"Did the airplane have one or two engines?" At this point they had some dificulty making him understand so they showed him a picture of Amelia's airplane.

He said it was like that one and the Japanese later had some like that too.

"Was there any damage to this airplane?"

"No damage. No, no damage."

"She landed on the beach right here?" pointing to the map.

"Yes, and just a little bit inside the trees."

"But it didn't hurt the airplane?"

"No, it was no broke—good."

"Was the airplane painted a metal color, or what color was it?"

"Shiney." Then looking again at the picture he pointed out the two engines and two tails and said, "it looked like that."

"Are you sure?"

He said he recognized the plane, but could not be too sure it was the same plane. This will give you some idea how honorable and how hard this fine old gentleman was trying to tell the truth.

They then got into the Datsun and drove out to Tanapag Harbor. On the way out, he reiterated that the plane had come down on Saipan and was not damaged. He also explained that anyone who came into the area without authority would be shot on the spot.

John asked, "A few years ago when Goerner was here to talk to you, according to his book you said something different. Would you explain this?" His granddaughter read the passage from the "Search for Amelia Earhart" to him, then translated it. This was done so there would be no question about his understanding the question. They had some conflicting testimony that had to be straightened out before they could get to the bottom of what had actually happened to Amelia's airplane. In the book Diaz was supposed to have said the airplane was brought in by ship.

Mr. Diaz said he did not talk to Mr. Goerner. He said they came to his home and his foreman talked to them. He said at that time he could not talk English as well. They said they would get a friend who could translate, but they never came back. They went to Guam and he never saw them again. He denied saying anything in the book.

At Tanapag Harbor he explained that after building the road to bring the airplane out, it was loaded on a ship and probably sent to Japan; he was told it went to Japan. Misinterpreting one or two words can change the entire picture in situations like this.

"How long did it take to get the plane out?"

"Two weeks."

"What time of the day was it when they came down?"

"About three o'clock in the morning."

"Were they cut up or hurt?"

"No, they were lucky."

"Did she smoke?"

"I don't know."

"Do you think they killed them on this island?"

"I don't know. I didn't see that if it happened."

"How long were you a Congressman for Saipan?"

"Fourteen years. I quit because we have too much problems with the budget."

"How old are you?"

"Fifty-nine."

"What year were you born?"

"1909."

John turned to the rest and said, "Everything checks. You can't cross him up on anything."

It now was Mr. Diaz's turn to ask some questions. "Were the woman and man spies?"

John answered, "They may have been spies."

"Maybe the Japanese kill them, I do not know." No one talked about anything like that because the Japanese would kill anyone they

John and Jack study bones in one of the hundreds of caves to determine if they are American or Japanese.

The Japanese had good maps and regrouped regularly in the search for their war dead.

thought knew too much."

"What do you think they came to Saipan for?"

Don said, "I think they wanted to get some pictures of the way the Japanese were preparing the Island for war. They were not supposed to be doing that, but we could not be sure or could not stop them without some pictures to show to the rest of the world. I don't think she intended to land here but we can't be too sure of that either. This may have been part of the overall plan. This would have been a good opportunity for us to come to the Island and see what was going on. Apparently the Japanese had this all figured out too and had no intentions of letting anyone know they had landed here. Amelia had confided in friends that this would be her last 'stunt flight'. She may have known the calculated risks. She said if she got back she would devote the rest of her flying days to scientific advancement. She also left some things with her personal secretary to be destroyed in the event that she did not return."

Mr. Diaz did not reveal the thoughts going through his mind. He was a very sick man and asked to be taken back home, if there was nothing further he could help them with.

They drove him back and took some pictures of his nice home with all kinds of flowers growing all around. Little did he or they know it would soon all be blown away by typhoon Jean. They had made another friend on Saipan with their warmth and understanding.

It had been a very interesting and productive day. They had talked to the man who helped bring Amelia's airplane to Tanapag Harbor and he had shown them the very spot where she landed on the beach and plowed into the jungle with practically no damage to herself, Fred, or the airplane. Mr. Diaz had gone to the trouble to make them a map for future reference. This was all very exciting, but they learned of much greater excitement that was taking place on the

Island.

A group of Japanese were given permission to come to Saipan and recover their war dead to return them to Japan. It is customary to have the remains of any good Japanese returned to the homeland when they died. For centuries they have worshiped their dead and want them close at hand.

At their meeting that evening, they decided such an event only happens once and maybe they could learn something by volunteering to help bring the bones out of the caves and various other places around the Island. They got up and had breakfast so fast the next morning that Jack didn't even have time to look at his watch.

John thought it would be best to get permission from the local police since they were in charge of the yellow helmeted Japanese detail gathering up the bones. They drove to the north end of the Island and found Captain Antonio Benevente with Chief Petty Officer Aiken. John had no trouble getting on common ground with him by showing Tony that he was a police officer from the States. Captain Benevente said he would ask the Japanese if it would be all right for the Americans to help. Permission was granted and they picked up their burlap bags and started for the hills. That is all except John. He decided this would be a good time to interview Captain Benevente to find out what he might know about Amelia Earhart.

John switched on the tape recorder and began the questioning. Tony, as the captain preferred to be called, was very cooperative. He said he himself did not see Amelia, but was very certain that she was on Saipan in 1937. He had talked to the former Chief of Police, Vincente Sablan and Ben Gruerra. Both had denied any knowledge about Amelia until two years after the United States took over Saipan. When they decided it might not be too risky to tell the truth, both admitted she had been there. The rest of the group kept screaming for John to hurry it up a little, knowing it was his habit to lag behind. Don finally came back to see what was going on and got in on the end of the interview where Tony was telling about two intelligence officers from the United States, New York he thought, who came to Saipan in 1961 and again in 1963 to question a lot of people and do some excavating.

These are the same ones that talked to Antonio Diaz and his wife. When they told them they did not know anything about Amelia, the officers told them to be very certain they never told anyone anything in the future. Captain Benevente went on to tell how Josephine Akiyama had seen Amelia when she skipped school back in 1937 and took lunch to her brother-in-law who was working for the Japanese military. It all tied into what everyone else had been telling them.

John wound up the interview prematurely and went with the rest of the group to help gather up Japanese war dead. They worked two days at this task and saw many strange sights. All told it was estimated that 15,000 bodies were gathered up, and there was no doubt that this was about the hardest work any of them had ever done. The Japanese had excellent maps.

The bones were placed in huge piles. After a blessing ceremony by the Japanese, that included throwing on incense, flower petals and planting a flag, they were reduced to ashes in one of the most weird bonfires anyone will ever see. Marty got fantastic movies of the cremation. The ashes were carefully gathered up after they cooled and placed in boxes for shipment back to Japan to a war memorial.

On the second day of looking for bodies, they were working on the northern end of the Island. Don showed them suicide cliff where thousands of Japanese lined up and waited their turn to jump to their death in 1944 rather than be taken prisoners of war by the United States. Their minds had been so poisoned by political propoganda,

John and Jack carrying their lunch to work in the jungle.

The remains of a Japanese soldier in a cave.

that anything was better than capture. There may have been one blessing in disguise to this propaganda for the benefit of our adventurers. Anna Diaz Magofna was only seven years old when she saw Fred Noonan beheaded, but it impressed her all the more because he was a nice looking man and not a beast the Japanese had taught everyone to believe. She might not have remembered the exact spot so vividly if this had not made such an impression on her young mind. The beheading was bad, but after the Japanese soldiers came to Saipan brutality was very common and she saw much of it.

That same afternoon, Don took them to see the Grotto. This was a cave with a small opening at the top that developed into a huge cavern about fifty feet down. The unique feature about it was that it had been formed by the ocean tides flowing in and out. In the center of the huge room was a beautiful pool of ocean water fed by a tunnel out to the ocean. Don explained that he and Smitty used to swim here, but you had to be very careful to know when the tide was going out or you could be sucked through the tunnel and drown.

It had been a long and hot day so John decided to take a swim. Don cautioned him against it since they did not know about the tides and he had seen that water leave with such force nobody could have possibly stood up against it and survived. John could not be persuaded to listen to reason. He stripped down to his birthday suit and surveyed the sheer rock sides of the pool that were from ten to twenty feet high and asked Don, "How do you climb out of the pool?"

Don answered, "The best you can without getting cut up" and watched John make a rather pathetic attempt at doing a swan dive. He came up like a Polaris missile and climbed up one of the rock sides with agility that would have put a mountain goat to shame.

They all realized this took a double dose of adrenalin to perform that fete and asked John what happened. When he got his breath he explained that he had seen a man-o-war about the size of a battle-ship coming straight at him. That ended the swimming except for telling Vincente Camacho about the hair raising experience. He advised them not to swim in the grotto, as sharks and all kinds of treacherous ocean creatures had been seen in that pool. John assured Vincente that this was good advice but was no longer needed.

Jack looked at his watch and said it was time to get cleaned up so they went back to the Saipan Hotel. No hot water, as usual, but this was offset by the lights working. They never seemed to have both at the same time. In fact, they never had hot water and the lights worked only part of the time. Don figured the ground was jinxed because this is where he stayed in a quonset when he was in service. He added, "I just threw that in for you boys." They looked at him as if they were going to throw him out, so it was a normal day.

Jack had been pretty quiet for the last two days so they asked him what he thought of the whole operation. He had been in the service in World Warr II and figured, " . . . . . helping honor those Japanese war dead was like honoring the plague." With that, he looked at his watch and got up and washed his hands again.

The next day they had decided to take it easy and go fishing. They caught lots of fish including bonita and tuna. While they were busy relaxing John got into a conversation with the Captain of the last wooden hulled, diesel powered ship named the *Four Winds*. Captain Jurisprudence was a Phillipino and invited them to have dinner on his ship. They readily accepted, feeling certain any menu would be superior to that of the Saipan Hotel. They couldn't know they would be the last guests Captain Jurisprudence would ever entertain on that ship. Twenty-four hours later it would be on the bottom of the Pacific Ocean.

The Captain was an excellent host and they all had a good time.

Jack did not look at his watch once and Marty had no filming to do so he relaxed completely for the first time in days. Don and Ken were interested in watching the crew fish, while John talked to the Captain. One of the rugged little seamen caught a fish and proceeded to eat it whole and alive. A seaman on the other side was disgusted at this display of uncouthness. He caught a fish about the same size and pointing to his fellow sailor said, "He is a savage, you do not eat a fish like that in company." Don and Ken agreed, but were a little surprised when he showed them how to be a gentleman. He bit the head off first and spat it out, then proceeded to eat the fish raw, "You kill them first." Don said, "Now we know." Ken started humming, "To Each His Own." They both walked away to find the rest of the group. They thanked the Captain profusely and someone said, "We will be seeing you." They were to learn that would be very soon and under some very unpleasant circumstances.

They went to bed early that evening with great intentions of putting in a full day interviewing the next day. They woke up early and went down to the restaurant for some more soul food (or sole food, as it was). The waitress said there was a typhoon named Jean headed for Saipan and would get there about noon, so they had a few hours to prepare for this emergency. They first went to see Joe Diaz to find out what they should do. They were thinking of going to the Japanese bunkers where much of the population went when there was a storm on the way. They remembered going out there after typhoon Gilda on the last trip and the sanitation was pretty bad (another understatement of the century). Jack is pretty "antiseptic" and when he got the full impact of just how it would be in those overcrowded bunkers he looked at his watch twice and said he would stay where they were. Anyway, Joe told them the Saipan Hotel was built by the government and had footers twenty-five feet in the ground. By this time the wind

143

Saipan Police Chief Benevente emerges from a cave during the search for war dead.

Burlap bags were used to bring the bones to designated spots for cremation.

was up to 50 mph and it was only eleven o'clock. They asked Joe what he was going to do. When they realized he had not made any special preparations, they asked him to come with his family to stay with them since it was a safe place. He looked out the window and saw the trees bent over so did not wait for a second invitation. He started gathering up his goat, his pig, and a champion fighting cock. According to Don, it had never won anything, but had never lost either, so it was a champion. Joe said he had to bring a friend. Actually it was a relative of Joe's wife, a seventeen year old boy from the Yap Island. Joe had taken him to raise along with his three children. John said they could take everything except the pig. Joe protested that it was a very fine pig. John stood firm, "You can bring the goat to have milk for the children, but the pig will just have to take his chances here." Joe put him back in the pen and never saw him again.

They all got back to the Saipan Hotel and settled down to listen to honky-tonk records being played by the local radio station while Jean gathered momentum. The roof started to lift about 7:30. They got Marty ready with the camera to record the action, but the prayers of the others must have been answered as it never blew off. There was no glass in the windows of the bathroom and the wind was coming through the bathroom doorway and making so much noise a person had to shout to be heard. John, Ken, and Don decided to close the door. These three husky men could not get it closed against the force of Jean. Joe came in from the other room and said it would be better to leave it open as it was liable to blow open anyway and kill somebody. They left it open.

John said, "Boy we are lucky we are in a concrete building. We would have been screwed now if we had stayed in Chalan Kanoa with Joe's uncle."

Jack said, "I wonder if this is going to hold up," as he looked nervously at his watch and glanced at the pulsating ceiling. He remembered the conversation with the carpenter who had said the termites already had too much of a head start on the roof. They were watching buildings go all around them. Suddenly, about 8:00 that evening, it all stopped. They knew they were in the eye of the typhoon now and the worst was yet to come.

The honky-tonk station was playing "Blue Water" during the lull when a loud knock on the door made them all jump up to see what was happening. There stood Captain Jurisprudence from the *"Four Winds"* with his first mate and crew of eighteen. The first sailor in line had absolutely nothing on. One had no shoes. One had only a life jacket to cover his brown body. Their clothes had been blown off them. A few only had shorts while others' clothes were torn to shreds.

John asked them to come in and tell what had happened to the *Four Winds*. The Captain said it sunk and they were lucky to get to shore. They had hung on to tangan tangen tree roots near the water and had their clothes blown off during the storm. Don noticed in the dim candlelight that Captain Jurisprudence had one eye closed and asked what had happened to his eye. The Captain said something blew into his eye early in the storm and that it was very painful. He said he had to get to a doctor or he might lose that eye. John said they had a first aid kit and would fix him up. They tried to see what was in his eye, but the candles just did not give enough light. John was still fumbling around in the dark in his room trying to find the first aid kit. He finally found it and selected a small tube that he figured was eye ointment. About the time he was ready to put it in, Don's sharp eyes noticed it was tooth paste. With this the Captain begged them to take him to the local hospital while there was still time. He said they would have about one hour before the storm struck from the other direction.

146

Just then an announcement came over the honky-tonk radio station, "All unnecessary road traffic shall be kept to a minimum with only emergency and official vehicles permitted." This was repeated in Chamorro. He continued, "As the intensity of the storm increases it will be necessary to turn off the power. This will be around twelve noon." This was a rather facetious announcement, as most of the power was already out, with lines blown down.

John, Ken, and Don decided they could get the Captain to the hospital so they set out. It was a mess. Lines were down, cows were all over the road, power poles and trees blocked the streets. John was reminded of the time during the last trip that he took to this same hospital when he lost the encounter with the sharks. They drove past the Japanese prison and where Joe Diaz's house was supposed to be. It was completely gone. There just was nothing left. They decided not to tell Joe when they got back. There would be plenty of time for him to worry about that after the storm was over.

At last they reached the hospital. It was Ken who was watching his watch now. They had less than one half an hour to get the Captain patched up and get back to relative safety. There was over a foot of water in the hospital, no lights, one doctor, one pharmacist, and three nurses. Everyone else had left to be with their families. They were operating by candle light. While they waited one boy came in with his head cut open by a piece of flying debris from a quonset. John recognized Lt. Cruz from the Saipan police force who brought him in. John went over and asked who the boy was. Lt. Cruz said it was his boy. He asked them to come by after the typhoon and he would tell them 85% of what they wanted to know.

Everyone was doing all they could so there was no way to ask anyone to hurry, but Ken was watching the wind start to pick up again and started walking in tight circles in the water. The doctor

Japanese remains being cremated.

A Japanese woman completing a shrine in memory of the war dead.

patched up the Captain's eye and thanked them for being patient and admonished them to make haste in getting back to the Saipan Hotel.

They realized that last remark was pretty unnecessary when they opened the door to go. The door blew off and sailed away. They thought their little pink Datsun was going to be airborne on several occasions. Ken asked John if he had ever flown a Datsun. The Captain was feeling better now and thought that was a pretty funny joke.

When they got back to the Saipan Hotel, they found all of the sailors in John's room. The Captain and his first mate insisted on staying in the other room with all the rest. He said you cannot fraternize with the men and maintain discipline. Even under these trying circumstances he wanted to adhere to protocol.

The sailors were piled one on top of the other completely beat; all sound asleep. Eighteen sailors crowded into one room with one double bed is quite a sight.

John, Ken, Don, Marty, Jack, six members of the Diaz family, Captain Jurisprudence, his first mate, one goat and one champion rooster occupied the other room of the same size. They had one well ventilated bathroom. This kind of crisis changes modesty a little.

Typhoon Jean created havoc all of that night, the next day and most of the next night. The radio station stayed on the air with emergency power and this group continued to listen to the honky-tonk records and announcements about the typhoon. They got very little sleep as winds gusted to over two hundred miles an hour.

On the third day, all was quiet. They opened the door to see a beautiful Pacific dawn. The rain had stopped. As they looked out it took a while to realize that the only green they were seeing was the grass. There was not a leaf on any tree except the palms.

They expected to see all kinds of destruction. Actually they saw very little of anything. Everything had just blown away. It was truly unbelievable that the wind could come and go and take everything, that was not steel reinforced, with it.

Ken asked Don if he had any cigarettes. He had two wet ones. This was an emergency. They went to the bar which was in operation before the storm. Everything was blown apart. The cash register was open with some change in it. Don found some cigarettes and took a carton back to the hotel. Then they decided to take a trip around to survey the damage. The further they went, the worse it looked. The entire Island had been reduced to a junk pile. About the only thing still standing were the government built buildings and the Royal Toga hotel built by Casey Jones, the enterprising Seabee from North Carolina who parlayed 15 used Jeeps into a huge fortune. He married a Guamanian woman, which gave him the right to do business in Micronesia. This fabulous organizer now owns about everything on Guam, has leased the entire Island of Tinian for a cattle ranch. You will remember this is where the airstrips were built in World War II that provided the take-off for the planes which dropped the two atomic bombs on Japanese cities—ending the war. The point was very clear, that the United States government and at least one man, who has made a fortune from surplus war materials, knows how to build buildings that will stand up through typhoons. It made this group sick to know this, know that our government is responsible by choice, know that these typhoons come regularly (they had been here twice and seen two of them), and while they were realizing all of this, they were seeing the remains of the entire population of Saipan completely wiped out— their entire wordly possessions gone with the wind. Don was the first to remark in somber tones, "We could do something about this, if anyone cared. What the hell are we doing over here, if we are not willing to provide these people with some kind of house they could at least ride out these typhoons in? Why should they keep on being blown away while our government squanders millions? There has got to be a way to handle this situation differently."

John spoke up, "I can see why some of them had rather see the Japanese take over again. Almost anything would be better than this hopeless situation."

Jack was too shocked to even look at his watch. He agreed it was a sorry situation and just should not be tolerated.

Marty had been all over the world and seen a little of everything unpleasant. He hardly ever was at a loss for words, but this had him on the ropes. There just had to be an answer. He finally spoke up, "You know, there will be a few lines in the newspapers about this along with the other gory things that go on in the world and it will be forgotten by everyone except the people who are trapped and have to live without means of protecting themselves."

Ken added, "It is abundantly clear why the young people who get away from here have no desire to return. It is sad ... sad ... SAD with a capital S."

They saw an old man trying to gather up some scraps of lumber and sheet metal. They stopped to get his impressions and were surprised that he could greet them with a smile and friendly, "Good morning," which they agreed it certainly was. He said, "This is worse than the invasion when American battleships completely leveled Garapan City. There is still nothing on the site. Jean had taken about 98% of everything and left nothing but a macabre collection of bugs and gooney birds that seem to go with typhoons.

They were getting hungry and thirsty. The radio had informed them to go to the airport to get emergency food and water so they headed for the airport. When they got there they found a line nearly a quarter of a mile long—people waiting to get some food and water. They estimated about a third of the line-up was military personnel,

Don and Jack try to learn the significance of the shrine.

Don and Ken watching some of the 15,000 Japanese war dead being cremated.

and wondered how they got to Saipan so fast. Don just had to say, "Look what the typhoon blew in."

Further inquiry determined they were flown in by Navy PBY's along with the food and water. The Navy had the job of delivering supplies to all of the islands which Jean had hit.

By 10:00 ships were coming in unloading Jeeps, tents, rations, and a multitude of material necessary to get the Island back to normal operation. Marty said, "At least the military is on the ball. When they get the o.k., they get things done."

John said, "Do we stay here and starve in line or go and find ourselves some food?"

Another look at the long non-moving line convinced them to vote unanimously to fend for themselves. Don said, "cocoanuts and bananas are going to be hard to find so I suggest we go and see Father Sylvan."

His place was a shambles. They knocked on what was left of the door and noted that the church was still standing without too much damage. Father Arnold came to the door in a state of shock. They first asked if they could take some pictures. They had forgotten about food at the sight of the destruction. Father Arnold said he had worked 18 years building two classrooms each year; now he had nothing. They took some pictures to take back home and he had recovered enough to ask if they were hungry. He gave them Spam and warm pop. It tasted mighty good. They thanked him and said they would see what they could do to help him when they got back home.

They spent the rest of the day going around to the various villages and were amazed to find, by afternoon, most of them were trying to put a shack together out of scraps to have a roof over their heads. They were pleasant and not dejected, as could be expected after a tragedy like this. Seeing everyone working, suddenly reminded them that they were not tourists.

They had come here to do a job and had not done much of it. Marty was glad, now, that he had taken the pictures of the Island before Jean. There was not much beautiful about it now. They still had several witnesses to tape and the gravesite to excavate. They were ashamed to think about how they could ask for these people's cooperation at a time like this, but they must try.

First, they went to see Anna's mother and father. Mrs. Diaz was sweeping the water out of what was left of their house and told them that all the clothes she had left was what she had on. Antonio, as sick as he was, had a hammer and nails and was picking up tin to nail back on the house. Life went on and they could not cease to be amazed at how little distraught the people were.

The next day they got up at 7:00 and went to see Joe Diaz to see if he had anything left in the store to sell. He didn't, but he went to the warehouse and found some canned food and cigarettes. He picked what had to be the biggest native on Saipan—named Sam and put him in charge of the store. Joe said, "Give everyone all they want free." They took what they needed immediately and left the rest for their neighbors.

The group needed gasoline for the Datsun. One station was completely out of business. The other one could be pumped by hand. One complete turn of the crank was one penny's worth of gasoline. With gasoline forty cents a gallon it gave the pumper a good workout making forty turns. They needed ten gallons to fill up. That was four hundred turns. They were all completely beat, just watching this sturdy fellow fill up their tank and there was a lineup as far as they could see waiting. Ken said, "Boy, I bet he won't have to be rocked to sleep tonight."

With a full tank of gas, they took off for Joe Diaz's house or more factually, what used to be his house. He was busy building a 10'x10' building for his family of six. They decided their project would just have to wait until these people at least had a roof over their heads. The airport was headquarters for all emergency operations so they decided to go get a first-hand look at the Red Cross and the military in action. While at the airport, they learned that the airplanes were coming in loaded with supplies and taking anyone who wished to leave the Island back to Guam. John thought it would be a good idea to fly to Guam and call the wives as they would not worry so much if they knew they were safe. When he found out the airplanes were bringing absolutely nobody back to Saipan, he decided to let the wives worry a few more days. He said, "Most wives have to worry about something anyway so this gives them something worthwhile to worry about." He was told by the rest that he should be ashamed of himself. To which he replied, "I am, but what are we going to do? We still have some digging to do and you guys might need an old man for that job."

On the third day, the military had brought in huge electric generators and their lights were back to working off and on at the Saipan Hotel. Power had been restored to most of the Island and the army had a field kitchen set up to feed anyone who could not get good food elsewhere. This group preferred elsewhere. They got to be real experts at taking the top off cocoanuts with a machete in one stroke. Marty advises you to count your fingers each time you do that, but it is the way the natives do it. On the afternoon of the third day, they decided to drive over to Anna's to see how things were coming along. They met Pete, her husband, in the yard and they were amazed to see that he had a house built. It was even more incredible when they found out he was a lineman and had put in extremely long hours of overtime getting the power back to normal. John said, "I would like to see some-one work like this back home."

A Japanese helmet possibly belonging to a soldier in this collection of remains.

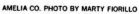

Last phase of cremation.

They apologized for asking her at a time like this, but they were running out of time and had to get at the excavation now or never, could she go with them so they would be certain they were in the right spot. She smiled and said, "O.K., I will take Francisco along so she can help, if I cannot understand you." Seven people in a Datsun is a carfull especially with Anna over 8 month's pregnant, but they made it to Liyang cemetery, as Anna directed. Don was already disappointed and puzzled. According to the map she had given them on the last trip, the spot was supposed to be near the crematorium. That was over by the Japanese prison. He told Ken, "I think we are getting the business."

John was trying to keep the conversation light, still feeling a little guilty asking her with all the problems of typhoon Jean and her delicate condition to come out here in the jungle. He asked, "How many children do you have Anna?"

Without the slightest hesitation she said, "Ten. I will soon have a dozen and laughed."

John said, "That is a nice family!"

"Yes, but it takes a lot of money. It is easy to make babies, but it costs a lot to feed them."

John could only say, "Well, what are you going to do?"

John said, "You tell Don where to go. He is a very bad driver and is liable to wind up out in the ocean."

She said, "Find the old road." Don still thought she was wrong.

They went by the former city of Garapan. John asked if she remembered it. She did.

They went too far and she had them turn around and go back.

John said, "How old were you when you saw the white man with the long nose executed?"

"Seven or eight. I was in the first grade in the Japanese school."

She explained that she was walking home from school and saw two Japanese with the white woman and white man with a long nose. The Japanese were having them dig a hole. They blindfolded the man, made him kneel, cut his head off with a samurai sword and kicked him into the grave.

Suddenly Anna said, "Stop here" and got out of the car. "Now we must find the old road and the cemetery. Then we must find the place where the Japanese burn them."

"You mean the crematorium?"

"Yes."

Don said, "That is over by the jail, Anna."

"No, there was one here." They suddenly realized that they would never have found the spot because they would have used the other crematorium as a reference point and nothing else would have checked out.

John, "O.K., we will go look with you."

She picked up a stick and started poking into the ground trying to locate the old coral road. She found the road and started looking for the crematorium while she explained how she hid so the Japanese would not see her. She said she did not know the man and woman, but knew they were white and they did not look ugly like the Japanese had said they were. She was afraid the Japanese soldiers would kill her too if they knew she had seen them.

John asked, "What were the Japanese soldiers doing while the man and woman were digging?"

"Bolero."

"What does bolero mean?"

Ken could speak Japanese and knew the answer to that. He said, "In common terms, it means B.S.."

John, "Oh, they were talking too much to notice you?"

"Yes, they were B.S.ing."

She was still trying to get her bearings in the thick jungle. The only thing helpful was that Jean had stripped the leaves from all the trees and jungle growth. It looked like one contorted mass of all sizes of ropes. It was tough going.

Anna was following as they hacked their way towards the cemetery. She stopped again and said, "I think it is near here."

John, "Do you want me to walk in here?"

"Yes, walk towards the cemetery."

John hacked and puffed until he had progressed a few paces. "Do you think this is too far?"

"That's not so far" and she started in towards him.

John was afraid she would trip and he would have to become a midwife out there so he cautioned, "Wait, Anna, I will cut a better path." She kept coming and was getting around better than he was. Of course he was hampered some by the tape recorder. He was trying to be Tarzan and Cecil B. DeMille at the same time. He got some pretty weird sounds on tape along with most of the conversation.

His only collected comment was, "Boy, this jungle is rough, huh?" Then he came upon some pieces of concrete. The others were looking in other directions so he called them over. John asked Don, "Does that look like concrete to you?"

Excitedly he answered, "Hey, you are right; that looks like it may have been part of a building!"

Anna was still making her way towards them and asked, "You find?"

John hurried towards her and told her to wait while he cut a better path so she could get a good look. "We have to take our time and be sure, Anna."

She was anxious to see what they had found. While taking her

A serious interview.

Joe Diaz and Don lining up witnesses to see the next day.

Some of the 15,000 bodies being cremated. Ashes were returned to Japan to be placed in a war memorial.

through the dense growth John asked, "Was the crematorium here made of concrete?"

"Yes."

"Then we have found it." He pointed out the piece and continued, "This is concrete. It is not coral, but this (censored) damn jungle is so thick you can't see — — — —." He used a four letter word starting with S that is better left unsaid for this family book.

Next, they found the cemetery and got their bearings. Anna's map started to make sense to Don now.

John located a ridge and told Don to get up on it so they could keep him in view and use him for a reference point to locate the cemetery.

Marty was better trained at determining the difference in materials and he confirmed that the large piece was concrete, and found several smaller pieces.

John turned to Anna, "Then this would be it?"

"Yes, I think. I never go too near. I just went down the road by the cemetery."

"Well, how far would it be from here, Anna?" He was referring to the gravesite.

"I remember some cocoanut trees before I got to the cemetery."

They had very little trouble locating these. John had to caution Anna not to lose her shoes, which indicates how impenetrable the jungle was and how hazardous it was for a pregnant woman to be walking thru it.

Don came in loud and clear, "Are you finding anything?" John told him to keep his shirt on. He said, "You know I took that off an hour ago." At least he was satisfied they had not gone away and left him standing on that ridge.

Then John told him Anna was pretty sure this is the spot because there was concrete there where the crematorium had been blown up prior to the invasion when our Navy guns leveled that end of the Island. They marked the spot with a machete. Anna continued to look around to be positive. She located a large breadfruit in the area and said it was about ten steps from that tree. It was an old tree and very large for that area. The tree was practically dead. In a few more years this reliable landmark would have been gone and it would have been virtually impossible to locate the exact spot again.

Ken was working his way to the spot and said something sarcastic or vulgar about the jungle which prompted John to ask him if he knew how to use a machete. Anna spoke up and said her little daughter Francisco was pretty good with the machete.

Ken got the point and said, "Never mind sending Francisco, I will make it sooner or later."

It took some time to cut a path so they could pace off the ten steps in the proper direction. They marked the spot. This gave them a fairly small area to dig. They were convinced they would soon be recovering Fred Noonan's body.

Anna began to tell them again about the beheading of the tall good-looking man with the long nose. She said she could not get a real good look at him because the Japanese put a mask over his eyes, made him kneel by the hole and cut his head off with the samurai sword. "This is what I see."

John, "You are sure that he was a white man?"

"Yes, Then I tell Mother, Mother I cannot sleep, why?" She repeated this until they understood she was having nightmares about this experience. Mrs. Diaz had told them previously that she would have to take Anna in bed with her for several years after that because she would wake up hysterical and it would take a long time to get her calmed down. The experience was almost too much for a seven year old girl.

John asked, "How deep was the grave?"

"That was not so deep. Not as deep as the Chamorro grave."

"About how deep would you say, Anna?"

"I cannot tell you, because I did not see in it . . . the Japanese might kill me if they know I am there."

"I see, but the Japanese did not see you?"

"No, I was hiding, then I saw."

"Then you told your Mother and Father?"

"Yes, I tell them. You talk to my Mother and Father, no?"

"Yes, we talked to them. We know you are telling us the truth about what happened."

Don threw in a question at this point, "You were seven years old then, Anna, what year were you born in?"

Without the slightest hesitation, "1930."

Back to John, "What did your Mother say?"

"You keep quiet, if the Japanese know you see, maybe they kill you."

"Umhumh."

"I never forget that I saw that. The breadfruit tree was standing there."

"The breadfruit there, it must be fifty or sixty years old, don't you think?"

"I don't know how many years that tree. It seems to be already dying."

"Yeh, but it is still here. Were there any other kids with you, Anna?"

"Yes, I think about five of the neighbors, but I don't remember them so much now, but I still remember the American man and how they cut his head off."

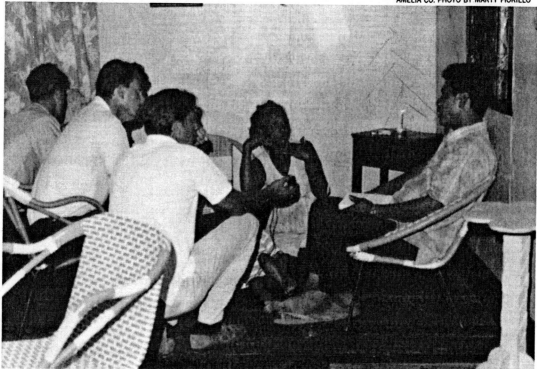

Mrs. Cabrera being interviewed again by candlelight with Joe Diaz interpreting to be sure she was telling the truth.

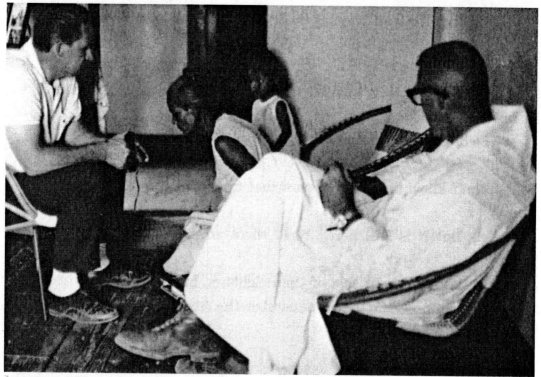

Father Sylvan in his robes and combat boots interviewing Joaquina Cabrera who saw an American man and woman in 1937 riding in a motorcycle side-car with their hands tied behind their back.

John, "Yeh, you see something like that you never forget it." He was a little bit wrong about that, maybe. They were going to meet a man who had obviously been involved in digging this very same spot who claimed he didn't remember anything about it.

Don asked, "What color of clothes did the man have, Anna? Do you remember that?"

"I didn't notice so much what kind of clothes. It was too dark maybe . . . green or blue. But I think green. Blue maybe."

Marty had been taking movies of all of this while John was doing the taping. He said it was getting too dark to take any more good pictures.

John said, "Just do the best you can, Marty."

Marty snapped back, "I will not take inferior pictures. There is not enough light now and I am quitting for the day."

Anna asked, "Do you think you can find this place now?"

"Yes, we have it well marked."

Anna almost fell while they were trying to get back to the car. She said, "This is not the right time for an accident."

They all agreed and cautioned her to take it easy. They told her they were going to try to find the bones.

Anna did not think they would find much after such a long time, but John said they would try and maybe they would only find the teeth. They asked her not to say anything about it in the village so they would not have a lot of curious people out there bothering them when they started the excavation the next day.

Don asked if she would like to go by the other crematorium. She said she would look at it, but this was the right one. She was sure by the cocoanut trees and the big breadfruit tree. Don stopped the car near the other crematorium. Anna said, "That's not the one."

John said, "There is no cemetery around here, no cocoanut trees, and no breadfruit trees."

Don asked if the other crematorium by the cemetery was as large as this one. She said it was larger. Then she described it in some detail. Don was completely convinced now that she knew what she was talking about. She said that it was used only for Japanese. Chamorro natives could not be cremated there.

They arrived back at Anna's home. Marty had the light he wanted again so he had Anna reinact the beheading while he took some movies of the action. It had been a busy day. They decided not to start digging until the next day so they could get most of it done without anyone being the wiser. The rest of the day was spent with more interviews.

They found Louis Igatol in a big warehouse filled with supplies and hundreds of children. He had sustained a leg injury during the typhoon, but consented to talk to them. John showed him a picture of Amelia Earhart and asked him if it meant anything to him.

Louis said when he reported to work one morning, the Admiral's car pulled up in front of some buildings inside the Tanapag Harbor Seaplane Base. He bowed down, as was the custom or demands of the Japanese military. He looked up from his bowing position and saw Amelia get out of the car with a Japanese admiral.

"Here is a picture of the American flyer that others have said was on Saipan, Louis, could it have been this woman that you saw?"

"That is the one. She was skinny and had short hair."

John said, "It is important that you be very sure. Don't just tell us what you think we would like to hear. It means nothing to us except we are trying to get the facts. Otherwise it just does not make one particle of difference to us."

"I am positive. She had on different clothes."

John, "She may have been dressed differently. This picture was taken in the United States."

Louis, "I would know her and she was dressed like that, but some different." He continued to be unshakable.

Don asked, "Did she look sad or worried?"

"She looked very tired and was hurt a little bit."

John asked, "When you saw her you were with that other man; what was his name?"

"Blass, Joe Blass."

John, "How old do you think Joe Blass is?"

"Younger than me."

"How old are you, about forty-five?"

"Forty-six."

John, "You were a truck driver, Louie?"

"No, I was a laborer at the compound."

Don, "Did you have to get a pass to enter the compound?"

"Yes, not too many people could get inside." He never did give any more accurate figures, but it was very restricted.

Don, "Did you ever see her again after that morning?"

"No."

John, "Louie, do you want to point out the difference in the clothes?"

"They were different, but that is the woman," he said as he pointed to the picture again.

John, "The face, the hair, that is the woman you saw when she got out of the car?"

"Yes, that is the woman."

John, "You, by any chance, don't know the admiral's name, do you?"

"No."

John, "I see, but the jacket was different?"

Matilde San Nicholas telling Lt. Gacek she lived one house behind the hotel where Amelia was held prisoner.

Matilde San Nicholas's house was one of the few that was not destroyed by typhoon Jean.

"Yes."

John, "You have been a big help. Did you see a man?"

"No."

"Do you remember what year that was?"

"No."

"How old were you at the time?"

"Maybe twenty."

Don, "The last time we were here your wife said it was in 1937."

"I will ask her when I see her."

John, "Hope you get to feeling better, God bless you. I would like to ask you just a few more questions."

"I will try to tell you what I know."

They left and picked up Mario Fawlig to help with the questioning. Louie could speak good English, but this was too important to take a chance on even one word being misunderstood or misinterpreted by either side. Here was another of many eye-witnesses who had seen Amelia shortly after she had landed on Saipan and was taken prisoner by the Japanese. While the others were gone after Mariano, John and Marty got Louie, with his bad leg, moved outside so they could take movies of the rest of the interview. About the time Marty was ready to start rolling the film, a cloud came over. It was a minor crisis. Amidst dogs barking and children playing noisily in the background, the interview went on. A squealing pig made Jack do a double take on his watch; but this was Saipan.

John continued, "Did you ever see a white woman on the Island?"

"No, That was the only one."

"When was that?"

"During Japanese times."

"Before the war?"

"The war was getting close. The Japanese military was here."

"Where did you see her?"

"I saw her get out of the car with a Japanese Admiral."

"What did they do with her?"

"They took her into the office."

"Did your driver, Joe Blass, see her too?"

"Yes, he saw her."

"What did he think?"

"Joe said, If I had a chance I would take her away."

"Is Joe Blass still living?"

"No. He was killed by an electrical shock before the war."

"How was the white woman dressed?"

"She had a light blue jacket, blue pants and she was carrying a purse."

"What kind of purse?"

"A sling purse, carried over the shoulder."

"Did she have long hair or short hair?"

"Short hair."

Mariano talked to Louie in Chamorro for a few minutes. He told the group that Louie knew the face in the picture was the same, but the clothes were different.

"Was it in the morning or the evening?"

"After lunch."

"Could everyone get into the compound or did it take a special pass?"

"Only authorized people got in."

"Do you know of any others who could get in?"

"I and two others is all I know, but there were more."

"How close were you to her?"

By pointing to the end of the tent they estimated about sixty feet.

"How do you know she was a white woman?"

"The driver told me. He was from Guam and he knew about American people."

"Did you hear about any American flyers or spies being caught on Saipan?"

"No, I never heard about any spies."

"Are you sure?"

"After the war, I hear they were spies."

"Do you think the woman you saw was the same woman they said was a spy?"

"Yes."

"Did you ever see the admiral before?"

"No. That was the first time I saw him."

Don said, "He could have been brought in from Japan or some other island."

"Maybe, I never see him before."

"Did you see the woman again after that?"

"No."

"Did you see any white man with her?"

"No."

Don asked, "Did she look nervous or scared?"

"She looked natural. Maybe a little sadness."

"Did both she and the admiral come out the same door of the car?"

"Yes, the woman came out the door first followed by the admiral."

"Did someone open the car door?"

"The driver opened the door."

"Then they were both in the back seat?"

"Yes, they both got out of the back of the car."

"How did you know the Japanese was an admiral?"

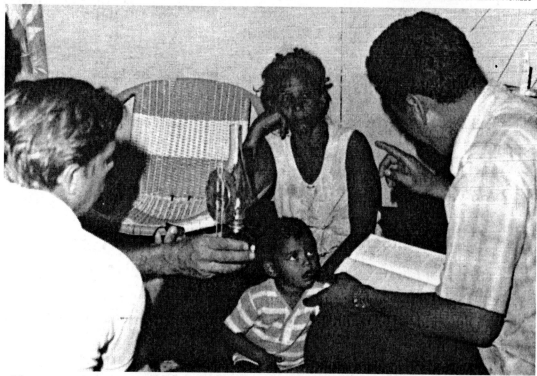

The second interview with Mrs. Cabrera. Joe Diaz is holding a copy of Fred Goerner's book "The Search for Amelia Earhart."

Father Sylvan's parish house.

"By the car. When that car is going around the Japanese has to bow, also the Saipanese. Only an admiral could ride in that car and everyone has to give respect."

"Did you see her come out of the building?"

"No."

"How long did you work for the Japanese?"

"When the Japanese first come in until the war. First I work for private Japanese; when the soldiers come, I work for the military."

"How was it working for the Japanese?"

"The military pushed us very hard; never let us sit down."

"What if you refused to do a job? What happened?"

"They clubbed you over the head."

"What happened if unauthorized people came into the compound?"

"They would kill them."

"How?"

"With a gun or a bayonet."

"Thank you very much, you have been a big help. Seems like everything went wrong in trying to get you on tape. One day the sun wouldn't come out, next you were sick, then came the typhoon, Jean, you were injured, but finally we made it. We will send some pictures of you back for the family. Hope you get along well with that leg. Take care of yourself."

The group was satisfied Louie Igatol was telling the truth. There was little doubt he had seen Amelia Earhart with the Japanese. Eager to get as many tapes done as possible, they next went to see Matilde San Nicholas. She had lived next to the Kobiyashi Royakan Hotel where Amelia was held political prisoner. You will recall that she had been interviewed on their previous trip and this was just to get her on tape for the record. It was somewhat of a difficult task with carpenters trying to put a house together around them and the fact that Matilde does not speak English very well. They had taken Father Sylvan along to translate for them. They finished this interview without coming up with any new information or any variation of her last story, which convinced them it was the truth.

Marty was reminded of the former Sam Rayburn, the Texas politician who served about as long as anyone in Congress. One of his friends asked him one day how he could see hundreds of people every day with all kinds of requests to which he always answered, "Yes, no, or maybe so". How can you do that without being caught giving a different answer when they ask you the same thing again later? Sam smiled and said, "If you tell the truth the first time, you don't have to remember what you said before to give the same answer the next time." The rest of the group agreed that it would be almost impossible to fabricate a story and remember the details six months later. This was to be the last tape of witnesses. Tomorrow they would start with the digging to see if they could find the remains of Fred Noonan.

When they got back to the Saipan Hotel there was a note for them to get in touch with Captain Jurisprudence at the Royal Toga Hotel and another telling them to contact Mr. Dirk Anthony Ballendorf, Associate Director, United States Peace Corps on Saipan. This caused Don to comment, "Boy did we get popular all of the sudden. I think we have better go see the Captain first; he might want to take us to dinner."

They had a good meal at the Royal Toga and went up to the Captain's room afterward for a good old fashioned bull session (most of which will have to be deleted). Ken started out by telling about a time he got rolled when he was in service. He was drinking in something less than a first class bar when a girl came over to have her picture taken with him. They slipped something in his drink to knock him out. He woke up, or at least the M.P.'s picked him up in an alley with just his shorts on. They marched him over to the guardhouse and stood him against the wall. He said, "What am I standing against this wall for with just my shorts on?" They told him they were going to search him.

John related a pretty wild story about a non-commissioned officer who had recently been rolled on Guam. Then he got into his experiences around San Antonio, Texas. He said you just did not go out alone at night. The rest got in their bit before the conversation got around to the *Four Winds*.

Captain Jurisprudence said he was going to Guam on Friday to call the home office. John told him he would not be able to come back. The Captain said he thought they would let him come back because they wanted that ship out of the way.

Marty got into the conversation with, "If you just leave it there, do you abandon it, scuttle it, or what do you do?"

Captain Jurisprudence answered, "I think we will salvage the engines, at least. It is not in too deep water so divers could work easily. We will have to have a company come from Manila to do that."

John said, "You were lucky that typhoon hit while you were in port."

The Captain said, "We started out, but the waves got up to eighteen feet and we came back. Lucky that we did or none os us would be here. We were lucky, too, that we were in the eye of the typhoon so we could get over to your place. That is the first time I have ever been in the eye of a typhoon."

John said, "Wasn't that something? It was nice; you remember when we were in the center of that eye, how quiet it was; there wasn't a breath of air. You could hear a hundred miles, you know."

Jack Gesche added to this bit of exaggerated phraseology by say-

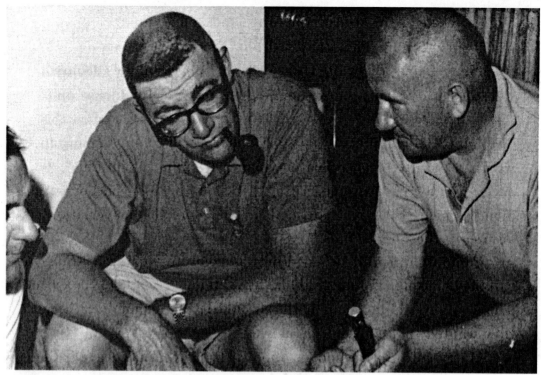

Father Sylvan's information being taped by John Gacek.

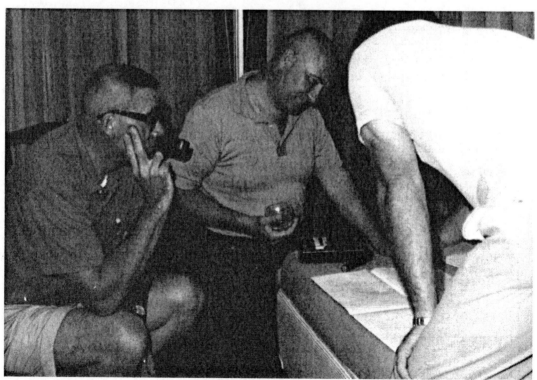

Father Sylvan being shown Antonio Diaz's map.

ing, "Now, John, I have told you a million times not to exaggerate."

John's quick recognition glance and good natured smile caused Jack to revise this down so, "Would you believe fifty times on this trip?"

That seemed more acceptable so the conversation went on.

John continued, "After it was so quiet, then the wind started to pick up. How big is the eye of a typhoon, anyway?"

The Captain took that one, "Sometimes they can be as big as a hundred mile radius."

"Doesn't it come back with more force then?"

"Oh, yes, from the other direction; it usually is a lot stronger."

"When we were at the hospital getting your eye treated, it started picking up pretty well. We could hear the metal being torn off the roof. I thought to myself, "I don't know whether we will ever make it back or not; but we decided to give it a try."

Don said, "I am glad that building held together, there are a lot of cracks in that building now that were not there before. You could hear the ceiling vibrate like ..." He made a fast harmonic noise that likely was close to what was going on at the time.

John said, "I have never seen anything like this. We went through typhoon Gilda last year, but it was nothing like this. You couldn't see your hand in front of your face ... and you guys were down there hanging onto the dock, what an experience!"

Ken said, "This S.O.B. just never let up. It just kept going without a break until the eye reached us."

Captain Jurisprudence said, "You should have seen us on the ship. We couldn't see anything either." Then the first mate told how he was trying to help keep the pumps going from the bridge and keep the ship headed into the twenty foot waves. The Chief Mate came up and said, "Every wave is tearing us to pieces." The Captain noticed they were being pushed into shore. He gave the order to abandon ship. They jumped and were all washed ashore.

They kidded the Captain about abandoning his ship. They didn't think good captains left their ship—they just went down with it.

"That's a lot of B.S. . . . We were within the three mile limit—not out in international waters. It is still our ship."

Don asked, "Will those motors still be good?"

"Yes, but the machinery will all have to be torn down and cleaned up."

The Captain then told about how he tied a briefcase with all of his money and his ship papers to the roots of a tangan tangan tree when they made it to shore. The next morning when he went down to get it, the rope was there, but the briefcase was gone. He hired some divers to try to find it, but so far nothing.

Captain Jurisprudence then told them about being in the Phillipine armed service that had to go underground when the Japanese took over the Phillipines. He said one day they were having lunch—consisting of some sweet potatoes—when a detachment of Japanese came their way. He had just been circumsized. He was told to run down and get some help from some of their buddies. Just as he started, the Japanese opened fire with machine guns. He said, "I could hardly walk before, but I set a new speed record and you know, I didn't feel any pain. Boy, was I scared—just a kid, you know. Another time, an airplane came by strafing. An empty cartridge hit me on the back. I really thought I was done for." Then it got real gory when he started telling about how the Japanese treated the populace when they were being beaten and had to retreat. All of the men would be lined up in the church or biggest building they could find and be shot down. Children would be tossed up in the air and caught on bayonets for a game. Everyone the Japanese could catch would be massacred.

Collaborators were either burned at the stake in public places or, in some cases, the men would be castrated and forced to consume their own testicles. These are gruesome bits of war that everyone likes to forget, but it happened. The Captain had some very narrow escapes. Then he added, "But the war is over now. We don't hold any animosity and I don't think the Japanese do."

The Captain had spent considerable time in Viet Nam. He could not understand our actions there. He outlined the terrorist activities and wound up by saying, "..... the United States has so many soldiers over there, most of them never see a Viet Cong, in fact, they see more V.D. than they do V.C. He thinks we should either win the war or get out. The rest agreed that Hanoi should be given about two weeks to pull their troops out. If they didn't; start with Hanoi and level everything north of the DMZ. John added, "That sounds pretty harsh, but its no Sunday School picnic over there now. Why let it go on and on?"

Don reminded them that they had to get up early and had a big job to do. With this, they told the Captain goodbye and drove back to the Saipan Hotel for a restless nights sleep.

Ken and Marty bounced out of bed early the next morning and got the rest of the crew into high gear. The day had finally arrived to start digging to see if they could find evidence that Fred Noonan had been executed where and like Anna said he had.

Marty said, "Where are the digging tools?"

They had planned to purchase these at the Joe Ten store, but that typhoon, Jean had everything messed up. Don hunted around the hotel while waiting for breakfast to be served and came up with a coal shovel. They figured this would do for a starter. As soon as the stores opened, they would see what Joe Diaz could come up with in the line of picks and shovels.

Louis Igatol being interviewed in his temporary quarters after typhoon Jean. He sustained a foot injury during the storm.

Louis Igatol positively identified Amelia as the person he saw with a Japanese admiral on the restricted Tanapag base.

It didn't take them long to find out this was no job for a coal shovel. Ken had been on the business end of that shovel and he thought they would have a hard job with a steam shovel. It was going to be a hard job, but first they had to get some picks and shovels. Don suggested they go see Father Sylvan. He was an early riser, and since the priests had built the church and school they must have tools around.

This was a good decision. The padre fixed them up with picks and shovels. They dug for a couple of hours. The dirt was not too hard with so much rain all of the time, but getting through the network of roots was something else. They unearthed a firebrick that brought them all to life. Don was the first to comment, "Anna was right."

Marty suddenly realized it was time to start checking more carefully or they might miss something. While the rest of the group expected to come upon a human skeleton that would be impossible not to recognize, Marty had excavated before and knew better. He said, "We must stop right now and get a screen to sift the dirt." He explained that teeth might be all that would be left after so many years. The others reluctantly agreed and ceased digging to decide where they could find some one quarter inch mesh screen, Marty told them would be best suited for the job.

John said, "You fellows keep digging and piling the dirt in the middle. I will go and find a screen somewhere."

It was not until he was down the road, in a fog of coral dust, that it occurred to Don, "Do you suppose that old rascal plans to take the morning off and will come dragging back here this afternoon telling us he could not find any screen?"

Ken said, "That thought occurred to me, also, and he has the car, the lunch, the water, and a lot of nerve if that is his idea of how to get out of some work. I wouldn't put it past him, but I guess we will just have to wait and see."

John found a piece of expanded metal on the back of a refrigerator (at the Saipan Hotel) which he removed uncerimoniously since he had no tools. He found a carpenter to nail this on the bottom of a dresser drawer—and he still refuses to tell where he got it. The carpenter bored two holes about six inches apart as per John's instructions. On the way back to the gravesite, John misappropriated some clothes line to loop through the holes for handles. In less than an hour he had come up with a real professional screen that even merited Marty's approval.

Don had to tell John, by way of apology, that they figured he had skipped out on them, now that there was work to do. John returned the compliment and told them to give him some dirt to sift. They all complied with that request at once, causing John to drop the load on his foot. After that, they became serious. It was hard work. Digging and sifting went on in monotonous fashion until they were about a foot deep. Then they started coming up with bits of bones. They were all excited, and Marty practically uncontrollable. The rest had hoped to find large bones, Marty knew they were finding good evidence. Marty insisted they put every particle in bags and envelopes. They found some ammunition that should not have been there. Marty said, "This grave has been excavated before." By evening, they were completely exhausted, but very happy with the results. They would be back early the next day.

John led the parade into deep sleep and was the first up the next morning. He had no trouble getting the others into action. On the way out to the gravesite, they decided to ask Father Sylvan to go out with them. After all, someone should be giving them permission to do this digging. Father Sylvan told them it was outside the consecrated cemetery and if they had any trouble to tell them he had given them permission.

They were digging and Ken was sifting. Suddenly he dropped the sifting box and plucked what appeared, at first sight, to be a gold nugget about two inches long. They all crowded around while he carefully scraped the dirt away. It was gold all right and turned out to be a three tooth bridge. Father Sylvan was impressed more than ever and said, "I think you are really onto something now." This inspired them to keep looking. They could not be too sure the small pieces of bones they were finding were human, but there was no question about that gold bridge. They started wondering out loud how they would find Noonan's dental records. That could wait; back to the digging.

By the middle of the afternoon, the sun was unbearable. They had not missed Jack Geschke until he came walking up with some cold pop. How he got it cold was a secret he would not reveal, but they all agreed it was about the best thing they had ever tasted. It tasted so good that Don spent the rest of the day climbing cocoanut trees gathering cocoanuts to keep them working. He explained why the milk in the cocoanuts from the trees is cool while that from those on the ground is always warm. John said, "The cocoanut milk was probably great for baby cocoanuts, but I sure would like to have a tall Scotch and water right now." Then he went into a long lecture on thirst being a problem of mind over matter. He had learned in the service that six ounces of water a day will provide enough moisture for survival. The more he talked, the drier he got. It was not long before he had Don bringing him freshly cut cocoanuts.

They were dirty and tired when they got in that evening and hoped the water would be on when they made it back to the Saipan Hotel. It wasn't. They borrowed some soap and went to the ocean. The water was cold and the soap would not lather. They knew there must be something better so they went to Joe Ten's later to get some

Catholic Church at San Roque Village. Completely destroyed by typhoon Jean.

A goony bird. Hundreds of these follow typhoons and become stranded.

canned food; he solved their soap problem. He introduced them to Cold Power—a soap powder that would lather in salt water.

That night they went looking for a tavern. The Style Shop was all blown down. They reminisced about happier times there when John had taught the native girls to do the polka and Don introduced the jitterbug. About all they knew before was the twist and old fashioned two-step. They had been under a lot of strain with the typhoon, and living so close, and it was beginning to tell. They were getting less jestful with their barbs and criticism. When one person made a suggestion the rest vetoed it or had a different approach. Marty resigned for the forty-something time that afternoon telling them, ... It was an impossible situation without more organization. They conceded he was right. They must get better organized and lay out a definite program to follow. Everyone would be bound by it and NO BACKTALK FROM ANYONE. The program included a trip to Guam to notify their wives that they had made it through the typhoon and would soon be coming back to civilization. John was selected for this job since he would be the one most apt to talk his way back. There were still restrictions against anyone coming to the Island. Not even reporters were allowed. The official reason was that extra people put increased demands on the food and water supplies.

Don said, "The real reason they do not want anyone over here is that they don't want the outside world to know how sorry a situation it really is. I am ashamed of it, too, but let's at least face the truth. These people are suffering almost beyond human endurance and we are responsible. Something needs to be done."

Jack spoke up, "I am going to help this situation. You fellows can make it without me now and I am over-due back home. I will leave so they can feed at least one reporter. The whole mess makes me sick, SICK."

The rest of the group agreed Jack, Ken and John should go to Guam the next morning. John would make arrangements and reservations for their trip home and come back. Jack would proceed on home. John and Ken were supposed to be back that day, but they didn't show up.

Don and Marty finished digging the gravesite down to what Marty said was the bottom. They had handled a lot of dirt in that 6'x6' grave and came up with a lot of bones and teeth as well as an assortment of other items, including the firebrick, 30 calibre and 45 calibre shells, cocoanut cloth, some charcoal, the gold bridge, and some amalgam fillings, which Dr. Baby later told them was positive proof that a white person had been buried there.

On the way back, they stopped by to see how Louis Igatol was getting along with his bad leg and show they were more interested in him than just for what he could tell them (it was this kind of consideration and genuine interest in the natives that enabled them to make the discoveries they did). Louie was feeling much better, but still unable to go to work. Marty noticed he had one real big cauliflower ear and asked him if he used to be a wrestler. Louie was turned on in a hurry at the mention of his ear, "The blankety, blank Carolinians are no (censored) good. My son and I stopped at the Smiling Bar to have one beer after a hard day before going home to dinner. Twelve 'slopped-up' Carolinians jumped my boy. Naturally I piled into them."

Don is a pretty healthy specimen, but he said, "I had rather be on your side Louie", while watching this big muscular man turn livid as he told the story. "One of those dirty birds picked up a piece of coral which you fellows know is jagged and razor sharp. He hit me on the side of the head with that so hard I went to my knees. That made me mad. My son and I worked those twelve over pretty good. They were all on the floor when we left. This ear has never been the same since."

Don said, "Where did the tent come from?" He was commenting on Louie's new quarters.

Louie said, "They threw me out of the warehouse and gave me this tent to live in until I can get around well enough to build myself another house."

As they drove, it was unbelievable how many little shacks had been pieced together in four days. Life, such as it was, looked to be almost back to normal—waiting for the next typhoon to blow it all away again. They could not understand why the government did not provide these people, who were more than willing to work, with some decent materials to work with. About that time they came to a huge stockpile of government plywood with armed guards standing on top to see that none of it was used for a roof over the heads of the natives. Their emotions and disdain for our great political expediency left them speechless, but each knew what the other was thinking.

They drove to Mrs. Joaquina Cabrera's to tape an interview. She had told them before that she had seen the white woman in the side-car of a motorcycle and that she knew who the driver was. The man who drove the motorcycle was dead. He was killed by an American bomb, but his wife was still alive. She suggested they go see her. They were not too sure about this woman's testimony so they went to see if Joe Diaz knew her. It was his aunt. He suggested they go back and talk to her again. Joe talked to her in Chamorro for a while explaining these were his friends. Then he turned to them and said, "She is telling the truth. I did not think so when you first came to me, because she had never told me that story, but it is true."

They went from there to see the motorcycles driver's wife. She had remarried and was living in a one room house 6'x6'x7' built since the typhoon. Joe told the husband, "These are my friends and they

An enlisted men's club gutted by the typhoon.

Typhoon damage at the harbor.

would like to talk to your wife about something that happened a long time ago. It is nothing bad or anything to cause any trouble, they are just trying to find out what happened to a white woman flyer who was here in 1937. Do you remember the white flyers?"

"Could you come back tomorrow?"

They left before they had another opportunity to go back.

The next day, there still was no sign of John, which caused Don to have bad thoughts again about good old John. "Those pot-lickers are over on Guam living it up, while we get everything done here. They were to find out later that it was quite different. John and Ken were going without sleep and food, trying to get back. John was tearing his hair out trying to find a way (and John does not have much hair to spare).

While driving about the Island, Marty saw something at Isley Field that he wanted to photograph. Don was supposed to shade the camera. He was standing there baking in the sun for what seemed like hours while Marty waited for the right beam of light to appear. At the perfect moment, Don decided he had better go relieve himself if he is going to stand there all day. As he walked towards the bushes, the communication gap was interpreted by Marty as downright insubordination and he quit again. Don never did say whether they got him calmed down enough to get that picture or even what they were supposed to be taking a picture of in the first place. I think it was a traumatic experience for everyone and they mutually agreed to forget it.

They went back to the priests house to thank them for everything and say last goodbyes. While they were visiting, there was a light knock on the door. There stood a carpenter with the tools of his trade. He said he was from Tinian and was sent by the Father there to help any way he could. He was not to be paid by them, but they would have to provide him with food and shelter for as long as they could use him. Guam sent a priest in his early 20's. Father Andre. He had worked two years on Saipan drawing up plans for the present church. This church was not damaged, but the entire school was wiped out. There would be plenty to do.

Don asked Father Andre if he was a friend of the nuns in the Convent that had been a naval hospital, as Marty was back on the staff and wanted to get some pictures of the damage there. Father Andre said he did know them and he approved of the picture taking so they drove to the Convent.

It turned out to be a very joyous occasion. In spite of the destruction, the nuns jumped up and down like they were on springs at the sight of this man. They all loved him dearly and were very emotional in their greetings. They welcomed Don and Marty and said they had a delicacy for them. They were served baby cocoanuts for the first time. These were peeled and sliced and tasted like marshmallows. The nuns felt sorry for Marty. He had forgotten his hat and the sun was focused on his bald head that already had the appearance of a red snapper. One of the nuns told him to put his handkerchief over his head. She took a square of cardboard from a box, the corrugated shipping kind, and carefully marked the center and drew a circle around this about the size she thought Marty's head would be. She then cut from the center point the way you cut a pie. The points were turned up and it made a very acceptable hat when placed over the handkerchief on Marty's head. They had learned something else.

Don asked the Mother Superior, "How will you ever snap back after this storm?"

She answered, "God only takes away to provide something better."

Don decided that was a pretty useful piece of philosophy. Here they were with almost total destruction. They were not crying in their beer or Holy Water. They were happy and would soon have things ship-shape again. Marty and Don could not help but be very impressed with their attitude.

He remembered one other statement Mother Superior made, "If America would only stop drinking and smoking for one minute, this whole Island could be rebuilt to withstand the next typhoons that surely will come." She went on to say they had 500 chickens before the typhoon and only lost 28. This had to be a miracle.

In the meantime back on Guam, John had found an attorney who would take him and Ken back to Saipan. He had a twin-engine plane he occasionally used for charter trips. He charged them two hundred dollars, which is about ten times the commercial rate. At those prices, John insisted on being the pilot so he could log some twin-engine time. Ken can tell some stories about the landing. Anyway, when Marty and Don got back to the Saipan Hotel the bad boys were there.

Don spoke first, "O.K., now tell us what you found so enticing on Guam that it took days to get back. We didn't even know if you were coming back. Figured you may have gone on home."

Ken hesitatingly said, "I know you are not going to believe it but we were a lot worse off over there than you were here."

"That's right, Ken, we are not going to believe it, but go ahead, anyway and tell your story. You have had time to make up a pretty good one."

"As I was saying, before I was so rudely interrupted, we first called the wives. Everything is all right on the home front. We couldn't get back that day so we tried to get a room. All of the rooms were taken by reporters who thought they were coming over to Saipan. The government did not want any reporters or political people on Saipan. We are not supposed to put our 20 years of progress on parade

36 room school destroyed by typhoon Jean. Father Arnold had built 2 classrooms per year for 18 years.

An automobile repair garage damaged by Jean.

yet, or not wash our dirty linen in the public's eye, or something like that. Anyway, John and I spent the night in the terminal. We couldn't get out the next day so we found a room. It was a real dump with cockroaches, bedbugs, the works! That put real determination in us. The next day we looked up Captain Findley, who was in charge of the Guam Airport. We told him our clothes and other things were on Saipan and we had to get back."

Ken went on, "Captain Findley could not help us get back, but gave us a bottle of whiskey that I guess was supposed to ease the pain. It did a little. Then we found this attorney who normally brings people over here for $50. Seeing we were in a panic, he charged us $200. John wanted to fly. He brought us in hot and bouncy. The owner bailed him out of the embarassment by saying he had to get that landing gear fixed—and he probably did after that landing."

John said, "It wasn't that bad, not a good landing, but not too bad."

Ken smiled and said, "You have your opinion and I will have mine." He turned to Don and Marty, "Believe me, I am glad to be here."

After thinking about it for several minutes, Don and Marty accepted this highly improbably story because it sounded so simple to be anything but the truth. They declared it some kind of a holiday and decided it was time to have another round with the sharks. Marty owns a custom gun shop in Cheyenne, Wyoming known as Frontier Arms. He meets customers everywhere he goes so he had brought an elephant gun along as an example of his craftsmanship. Now was the time to see what kind of shark gun it was.

They went to Joe Ten's and got big chunks of Australian beef and headed for the dump. Lo and behold, no sharks. The porpoise were around that day and sharks will not come near these fish.

They planned to leave the next day and went to say goodbye to Joe Diaz. He told them there were 70 to 80 people waiting to leave Saipan, but he used his influence and arranged it so they could leave. As it turned out, John was the only one to leave. He said he would check again on their reservations back and wait for them at the Guam airport, as they were supposed to get the next plane.

John had a long wait, meeting every plane that arrived from Saipan for the next twenty-four hours. Lady Luck was to intervene again. Don went to see the dispatcher and found out that his daughter had married Don's cousin. There was a Navy PBY warming up on the ramp that they had been told could not carry another ounce and get off the ground. James Bell got them on it. They did not have time to pay for the car so they gave Brother Gregario $120 to give to the car owner and if it was more to bill them. They later got a bill for the extra amount which they paid without a question. Doubtless the car rental agency got the money.

Ken, Don and Marty were seated near the pilot of the PBY. He asked them if they would like to get a good picture of a Russian fishing trawler. Marty got a camera out quickly and the pilot dived down, scattering bearded Russians all over the deck. The pilot explained that the trawler had been 'fishing' just outside the three mile limit near Saipan for several years, but they must have caught all of the fish because they moved out forty miles after the Pueblo incident.

The Navy got them a personnel carrier to transfer their luggage. They saw John at the airport. He was tickled pink to see they had made it. There is no telephone service to Saipan so all he could do was wait.

Then came the real bad news. John told them when they did not show up the day before, he had to cancel their reservations and could not make any more until they were there on Guam. The agent said they were booked for five or six days. Captain Findley was pressed into service again. This time, after some real persuasive effort he got them booked on the 5:30 plane.

They had some time to kill so they grabbed a taxi and went to an open air market and bought a whole stalk of bananas. In retrospect, they now think it may have looked a little strange for four grown men to be riding around Guam picking bananas off a stalk and eating them by the dozens.

John wanted to see the Chief of Police to tell him their story about Amelia. John and Captain Quintanilla had a good gabfest with the Captain telling him the most pressing problem on the Island of Guam was juvenile delinquency. John said, "Just like home. I guess the world is about the same where youth is concerned."

Captain Quintanilla said after Pearl Harbor he was on Saipan. The Japanese put him to work helping to build airfields. He said one of the first airplanes to land there was the Japanese Betty which is almost the exact replica of Amelia's Lockheed 10E. He said the people on Saipan knew about Amelia, but many would not talk.

His Chief, before he retired in 1936, told him the American government had hired him to go to Saipan to see what was going on in the way of fortifications. He was met at the dock by Suz or 'Quemoy' and not allowed to leave the ship. He said, "I have talked to many natives and there is no doubt that Amelia went down on Saipan."

Captain Quintanilla asked them to let him know when they knew for certain whether they had actually recovered the remains of Fred Noonan. They assured him they would.

They had a little time left so they went to the beach and got their customs clearance shells. They had found out from the last trip that decomposing snails got you through the customs without any delays. As soon as an official opened a suitcase and got a whiff of that odor, it

Father Andre, Don and Marty are given cocoanut milk by the nuns that can still smile after being wiped out by the typhoon.

U.S. Naval Hospital that was converted to a convent. Destroyed by typhoon Jean. Nuns plan to rebuild.

was slammed shut and passed.

They had decided to play a little joke on John so on the way from Saipan they fixed up a cigar box with some small rocks in it and told him it was the bones. He guarded it with his life all the way home before they told him Marty had the remains in a camera case.

There was one more call to make before leaving the Island. They would go by and see what Mr. Ballendorf and the Peace Corps had to say. After the usual introductions all around they went to his upstairs office. There was considerable sparing before they were told why he wanted to see them. Then Mr. Ballendorf said Fred Goerner had asked him to look them up to offer any assistance he could, especially with Lockheed. They were told Mr. Goerner had a complete list of serial numbers for Amelia's Electra 10E.

Mr. Ballendorf said he had been on Saipan for two years and was looking into the Col. Ellis mystery. You will recall he had been in the area in the early twenties and predicted Japan and the United States were on a collision course that would lead to war sooner or later. He seemed to disappear very mysteriously after that without anyone having been able to find many clues since then.

John explained that he had written Lockheed for the numbers and then called them up. They told him they had not gotten his letters which just points up how difficult it can be to try to trace a lead out. They could see no logical reason why the numbers should be so difficult to obtain unless it had to be cleared with some government agency. They reasoned that the airplane companies do a great deal of war contract work for the government and would not want to do anything to jeopardize that.

Mr. Ballendorf was curious as to how they had gotten started in this search. Don cautiously told him his story and explained how he had tried twice to interest Goerner in the information he had, but they never got together. Then there was more discussion about the Ellis affair. He said he was getting absolutely no help from the government towards helping solve this either. Apparently Col. Ellis liked to drink a little when that was not too popular so was considered to be a little strange. They wished him well on the project.

The trip home was uneventful otherwise. They made the stop for refueling at Wake Island; a couple of smells from the customs at Hawaii cleared them and his sinuses, no doubt.

San Francisco was beautiful and Hopkins Airport in Cleveland even looked better. They were met there by their wives, who had to be the most welcomed sight on earth. The only thing they could not understand was why the fellows did not stay on Hawaii for a visit. Florence said she would never get that close and not spend a few days. Don hazarded a guess that perhaps it was because the sad memories of John's last experience there with the rare tropical fish.

They were all anxious to get to their own homes, so the party broke up with plans to get together after they all got rested up. There would be much to do and many things to check out in the next few months to conclude this adventure.

CHAPTER VIII

THE SEARCH GOES ON

In the weeks following their return, there were numerous occasions to relate their exciting stories about Saipan and more specifically what they had found. They were in the newspapers, on radio and made several television appearances. Many, many people contacted them with bits of information.

One of these interested parties was a former Marine, Richard Kulesza. He was with the 2nd Marine Division, 8th. Regiment on Saipan. He told about how he had taken a detail of 16 men up to the cave area to bring out the natives and the Japanese. They spent 27 days on this project and heard rumors about the two white flyers that had been there prior to the war. Survival was the most important thing at that time so little attention was paid to any such stories, but he is sure in his own mind now that the stories were true. He said the Saipanese were not the kind of people to fabricate stories or tell lies. They spent several hours looking at pictures Richard had taken relating to Saipan and his service days.

They spent considerable time discussing Amelia's flight with Col. Paul Briand who wrote the book, "Daughters of The Sky". He suggested they talk to Lt. Col. Gervais. He was contacted later at his home in Las Vegas. Don first explained about the airplane he had seen on Saipan while there with the occupational forces. Don was trying to find out from this flyer, if he thought there was any possible way the plane could have landed there. They decided it had to be carried up to the area the same as the big coastal guns. Col. Gervais said he had spent ten years on his studies of the Amelia Earhart flight. One thing he was very positive of was that he has no doubts that she was on Saipan. He has plenty of evidence to support that with the people

These nuns come from all of the surrounding islands. They sing for Don and Marty in spite of their convent being destroyed.

A curious nun checking Marty's camera used to take 10,000 feet of movie film to record their adventure.

he has interviewed, etc. It was his contention that a lot of work has been done on this mystery, but little has been turned up as tangible evidence of what really happened.

There was one other point they could agree on even though their information came from different sources; they felt the United States government knew or knows a lot more than it is willing to reveal, even at this late date. Some top level civilian and military personnel made repeated visits to see Amelia while she was waiting for the airplane to be repaired after the Hawaii mishap. You will recall a decision was made to reverse the direction of the flight and go from East to West which certainly was better suited to a trip they would have chosen if any espionage was to be included in the Pacific.

They agreed on one other point. It was important that everyone doing research should proceed on separate paths and check their respective information at intervals to see how much of it double checked. Eventually some tangible evidence would turn up. At this point Don had no idea he would be the one to prove what had happened to Amelia and Fred. Naturally he hoped this would be the case, but there had been a lot of disappointments up to now.

A meeting of the group was held to see what more could be done to find out what had happened to Fred Noonan's body. They were quite certain they had one piece of the head that would match. The problem would be to find the remains that had been dug up in 1944 by Billy Burks and Everett Henson under the direction of a Marine Captain, Tracey Griswold.

Captain Griswold was supposed to live in Erie, Pennsylvania. That was the nearest so they would start with him. They placed a call to his home and were told that he would not be home until later in the evening. John asked to have Griswold call back when he returned. They figured they would still be in session and it would be nice to have the entire group know what they found out from the Captain. The meeting went on for a few hours while they made decisions to send a delegation to talk to Billy Burks and Everett Henson if they did not get the information they needed from Captain Griswold which reminded them that he had not called back and should be home by now. At that crucial moment, John had to leave on some police business so Marty placed the call.

This time Mr. Griswold answered the phone. Marty began the conversation with, "Hello, Mr. Griswold?"

"Yes."

"You don't know me. My name is Marty Fiorillo. Earlier this evening Lt. Gacek placed a call. Did you get the call?"

"I got it when I got home."

That's alright, I wondered if perhaps you didn't get the message and John had to leave. We thought we would give you another try just before we left." Marty then explained their trips to Saipan and the fact that Mr. Goerner had mentioned him several times in his book. Then Marty said the group would like to come to Erie to meet with Mr. Griswold or pay for his transportation to Cleveland to talk over anything he might know concerning Amelia.

Mr. Griswold's response was, "As I told Mr. Goerner when he was in here, the pathetic part about it is that I can't tell anybody anything because I wasn't mixed up in it."

"I understand that, but the thing we would like to talk to you about . . . not about the bones because if you did not have anything to do with that we can understand that you could not tell us anything about those."

"Right."

" . . . but we would like to talk to you as a matter of record on our part so we can close the door on this phase. Maybe you can shed some light on some things that happened on Saipan while you were there. It may help us out. We will never feel finished on the part of Goerner, Henson, and Griswold unless we talk to you. Because this way we have talked to all parties then we can sum it up by figuring it was just another one of those deals."

"You are at liberty to come to Erie. I am here most of the time. Give me a call and tell me when you are coming and I will certainly be here."

"Well, would this weekend be too soon?"

Mr. Griswold said that would be too soon as he would be out of town on business. He asked if they were in Cleveland temporarily or lived there.

Marty explained, "To be exact we live in Garfield Heights, a suburb of Cleveland. There are five men doing this work and if you did not have anything to do with this, I might add, it is just as important for us to talk to you as if you did. We will explain that when we see you."

"Right."

"We are not trying to prove one way or another whether the government used her for a spy. We are just trying to find Amelia Earhart and Fred Noonan or trying to exclude all material that is not factual."

"Well, I would be interested in talking to you. I just wonder if we could make it some time next week?"

"When would suit you?"

"How about the middle of the week?"

"Good, I will talk to the fellows. Most likely two of us will come next Wednesday. We will call for a definite appointment before we leave."

With this settled there was not much left to do except decide who would make the trip. They could have saved that time as it actually

203

A private home destroyed by typhoon Jean.

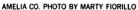

Nuns cleaning up the convent in Chalan Kanoa Village after the typhoon.

worked out the following week. They were not able to get together in Erie, but Mr. Griswold had to make a trip to Chicago so they had an hour to talk to him at the Cleveland Hopkins Airport.

This was a very pleasant meeting with the gist of the conversation being: Mr. Griswold said he had been on Saipan during and after the invasion. He had been in intelligence work on previous invasions, of other islands, but was not in that capacity when on Saipan. He said he would go along with the theory that someone from Washington had ordered a detail to dig up what might possibly be the remains of Fred Noonan and or Amelia Earhart. He then said, It wasn't me, but the person apparently did use my idenity—my height, my weight, my image and everything about me, but it wasn't me.

They liked Mr. Griswold and wanted to believe him, but there was a seed of doubt in their minds that during one of the worst phases of the Pacific Campaign even the CID would have gone to the bother of trying to disguise the personnel selected for a grave excavation where two privates were selected at random to do the digging. Still, Mr. Griswold had said this was the case. It was possible, they conceded, but they had to try to find why this was so mysterious, if possible.

At their next meeting, they decided to obtain a picture of Mr. Griswold when he was about thirty years old and visit Billy Burks and Everett Henson. The plan was to show them nine pictures of men including the picture of Mr. Griswold. Their thinking was that if he was the man they were looking for, he likely had some very good reasons for not wanting to admit he was that person. If he was not the person they were looking for, it would be better to know that rather than carry doubts. If it turned out that he was the Captain in charge of the detail and they could produce enough evidence to that effect, it might change the situation to where he could or would tell them what he knew about the previous excavation on Saipan. The least they could hope for would be a request that they drop any investigation relating to his part in the Amelia mystery because he was not at liberty to divulge any part he might have played. These decisions were to cost them a lot of time and money without the expected results. It would all end with, "I don't remember" ringing in their ears thus destroying their last possible known lead to where the body, they are certain is that of Fred Noonan, is located.

John and Marty were the most available to find Billy Burks and Everett Henson. Billy was last known to have been in Dallas and that was the closest so they would start with him.

John was able to get the photograph of Mr. Griswold and the other eight pictures of an assortment of men about the same age. His next move was to locate Billy Burks in Dallas if he was still there. It took a little effort, but John's training in police work paid off again. John and Marty flew to Dallas to interview this witness. On the flight down, they laid out their strategy. The first thing to do would be to tell the witness what they had done on Saipan and then ask him if he would tell them about his experiences there.

They checked in at the Hotel Adolphus which John and Marty rated a little above the Saipan Hotel. John said, "Ken told us we must try to be conservative and save money."

Marty surveyed the surroundings and said, "We are saving money."

With Billy Burks brought over from the Merchantile Bank, John began, "Marty, I am going to begin here by giving Billy a little shot of what we have been doing, why we have been doing this and how it was started because Don saw the airplane on Saipan. That way Billy will realize we are here on an adventure and not interested in causing any problems for anyone. We are just trying to prove to the world that we can come to a conclusion on the Amelia mystery." He looked to Marty for approval and smiled when Billy showed his understanding by relaxing in anticipation of hearing their story first.

Marty started his cameras while John explained how Mrs. Morrissey and everyone had been very cooperative. He went on to tell how the natives on Saipan were very reluctant to speak to anybody because they still have the feeling the Japanese are going to come back. John added, "I think they may be right because we are starting to give away some of those islands and if we don't do a better job of taking care of our responsibilities, we had better get rid of all of them."

Billy asked how many people were living on Saipan. Marty stopped his camera long enough to tell him there were various estimates ranging from four to eight thousand without anyone knowing for sure.

John continued to tell how the children were going to school and learning English. This has caused the natives to learn the same language so they are loosening up some. "Anyway," he said, "they decided to talk to us." Then he explained how Anna was coming home from school and saw the tall white man beheaded in 1937.

"She was in the first grade in the Japanese school. We asked her when she was born. She told us in 1930 so that checked out O.K.."

John told Billy how Anna had found the old coral road by poking around with a stick, how they had located the breadfruit tree that was 114 inches around, about the three cocoanut trees she used for landmarks. After she became oriented she pointed out a spot out in that patch of jungle outside the cemetery and told them to dig in that six by six foot location. She said they would find the bodies of two Americans in the same hole.

John continued to tell how they dug down about three to three and one half feet and started coming up with pieces of bones without any idea of what they had or if they could ever be identified.

The last official visit anyone made to the "Four Winds."

Captain explaining his impending return to his home in the Phillipines with the "Four Winds."

At this point, John started showing Billy some pictures they had taken of the old jail and other Saipan scenes. Billy recognized many of them and they brought back old memories.

Billy then told them a little about the invasion. As soon as it was secured they moved on to Tinian. After that was taken the 1st Battalion of the 6th Marines came back to Saipan and waited to be rotated home.

Marty showed him the picture that included the large breadfruit tree and asked him if anything in it looked familiar. He said the large forked tree looked like one near the spot where he and 'Snake' Henson had dug on orders from an officer named Griswold.

John and Marty asked how far the tree would have been from where their detail had dug. Billy thought about it for a few moments and said about as far as it would be across the room.

John, "About thirty feet?"

"Yes, I would say about that much."

Marty, "That is what Anna had us step off. It would have to be the same spot."

Billy quickly added, "You must remember I wasn't very much concerned about how far it was. I certainly wasn't thinking ahead of a day when I would be asked that question."

John asked, "How in the heck did you get in a situation like this; did you volunteer?"

Billy promptly told him he never volunteered for anything. He said maybe, " 'Snake' and I had gone to get a drink of water or something. This captain came up and told us to come with him. He didn't say please, or would you mind, or anything except "let's go"."

John asked, "Was this right after you landed?"

"No, see we landed in June. Seems like it took us about three weeks or nearly a month to secure the Island. Then they put us back

209

aboard ship and we went on over to Tinian. After that was secured they brought us back to a place I always called the back harbor. We waited until September or maybe November for transportation back home. Anyone that had been there since 1942 were being sent back home."

John asked, "What was the officer's name?"

Billy, "I just said it the other day and now I can't seem to think of it. I believe it was Griswold."

"That's right."

"I'm going to tell you the truth. I have forgotten so damn much of that stuff. On anything like this, I always try to be real, real careful. I don't want to start talking and tell you something that I might not conscientiously realize I was telling you a lie, but I might be trying to tell you what you wanted to hear. That would be just as bad as telling a bald-faced lie, if it winds up with you being misdirected in any way, shape, or fashion. I told Goerner this and I feel the same way now."

John and Marty assured him that they only wanted the truth.

Billy said this whole affair did not seem to be as important to him as it did to everyone else so he did not remember all of the various details about where they stopped on the way to excavate, etc.. "I am sure I can't tell you too much because I did not know what was going on. Griswold did not tell us anything except what we were to do. Then he told us to forget it. I have tried to do that. However, the way he ordered us to forget about it certainly suggested that it was important."

While thinking more about it, Billy continued to say, "The main thing I remember about this was: how important it seemed to be to Griswold. I do remember some headstones and an old broken down fence of some kind. It looked as if it had been abandoned."

John asked, "Do you remember how he (Griswold) knew where he was going?"

"No, it seems like to me, he stopped and asked directions one time. He had his quarters down near this stockade where the natives were confined. We came by that. He stopped to talk to someone or get some notes or something. After that he seemed to know exactly where we were going. He took us there. He did all of the driving."

John, "When you were digging, do you remember how deep you you dug?"

"It wasn't very deep."

"Would you say about waist deep?"

"No, I don't think it was that deep."

Marty asked how far they dug altogether.

"About two feet. It seemed like we were just digging up a shallow grave where someone had been hurriedly dumped in. We were doing everything we could to get the hell out of there. I am due to go back to the States . . . something I couldn't even dream or visualize and they got me out there grave robbing . . . I'm going to get excited and re-member something—forget it! There's no way!"

John, "Somewhere along the line, I got the impression someone asked who are we digging for or something like that."

"Snake asked him. He would question a damn fence-post some-times. I mean, you know, he was one of those kind of guys and he was the one that was doing all of the talking."

John said, "Then he told you it was Amelia Earhart."

"No, he said did you ever hear of Amelia Earhart. Naturally everyone has . . . that was about the limit of the conversation. We dug for a while, more or less like a routine detail as if this guy had this in-formation. He wanted to show on some report somewhere that he had acted on it."

The "Four Winds" after typhoon Jean that put this last diesel-driven wooden-hulled ship out of service.

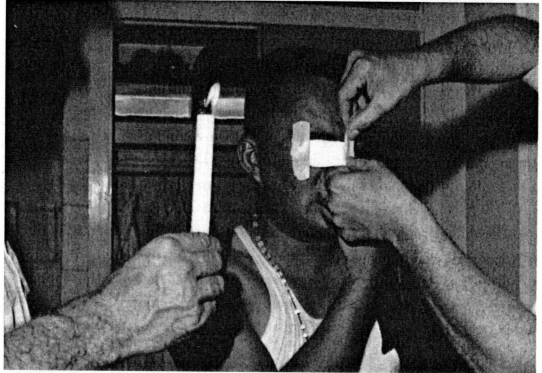

Captain Jurisprudence getting emergency eye treatment by candlelight during typhoon Jean.

John, "In other words he knew what he was doing. He had specific orders and he was carrying them out?"

"Yeh, he knew what he was doing and where he was headed."

" . . . but you didn't see any paper or any map?"

"No, I don't think so. It is possible, but I don't remember if I did."

Marty, "When you picked up the bones, did you screen the area?"

"No, just picked up what was handy. There was no thorough search. It was like we were trying to satisfy some order. It seemed like we were making a superficial search . . . and maybe if it was so secret they were going to go over it with a fine toothed comb later. We had no way to know that. It just looked like we were trying to satisfy the captain and get out of there."

Marty, "Could you tell whether you found a whole skeleton or more than one?"

"No, I wasn't even interested in that."

"Do you remember seeing any skulls?"

"No, just a lot of bones."

"In other words you just picked up whatever was handy without knowing or caring what it was?"

"That is exactly right."

"Did the bones look as if they had been there for quite a while?"

"Oh yes, you must remember we were there in 1944. That would have been seven years . . . and seven years in the tropics can do a lot. That soil has a lot of acid in it. Then the rains wash everything on down . . . there was no casket or anything . . . in fact it looked as if they were trying to hide something as the grave was not in the cemetery and wasn't marked."

This last remark perked John up. "It wasn't in the cemetery, then; it was on the outside; out in the jungle?"

"Well, no it was in a clearing at the base of the breadfruit tree. It wasn't jungle then."

John, "You can see how it looks now. And that was after the typhoon. If that typhoon had not stripped all of the leaves off the trees you couldn't see that site."

"That sure surprised me to see the jungle had taken over like that, but I was in enough jungles to know they take over everything."

John, "That's right and it was damn miserable digging when we were there—roots going every direction and all tough as rawhide."

Billy then said, "There is one thing too that you have to remember that at the time she was buried this cemetery had been maintained. My later association with the Japanese convinced me that they were very industrious people that did not waste anything. I would say that, as far as the physical looks of that Island, it would look a little bit better after twenty-five years of Japanese rule than it would after twenty-five years of American rule."

John agreed, "That's true."

Marty then asked, "How far out from the cemetery fence would you say this grave was?"

"It seems to me like it was about twelve to eighteen feet."

"Everything you say jibes with our location," was John's laughing comment. "Now I am going to tell you more about what we did. It amazes me, though that you can be so accurate after all of these years."

Billy, "I have done some survey work and can remember terrain very well. I have been an instructor in maps while in the service which makes a person a better judge of distance."

Billy, "I was more concerned about what I was going to be doing next week than I was about what I was doing then."

"You left that quick, did you?"

"Yes, we left the next week. When we left we didn't have our service records with us nor our seabags. Didn't even have our pay records with us. When we got back to the States they gave us fifty dollars and gave us a thirty day leave."

John laughed and said, "that was a big deal wasn't it? You couldn't get out of town with only fifty dollars."

John then said, "I want to show you a picture of the cemetery." Billy remembered the angle in the cemetery and told them how she was facing. Then Marty gave him the nine pictures that included Tracy Griswold.

Billy said, "The thing I remember about him was that he was a tall spare man similar to this one," holding up Griswold's picture. It had taken him less than two minutes to pick it out.

John asked, "Do you think that is him?"

"Yes, that looks like him to me."

John said, "That's Tracy Griswold." Then John explained, "He doesn't say he wasn't the man very convincingly. He just says, in effect, I think you are on the right track and leaves you dangling. He said he was in the Pioneer Battalion." This struck a familiar chord with Billy.

John said, "I know you are anxious to get away. Can you remember what you did with the bones? Did you put them in something?"

"Seems like it was a box ... might have even been an old ration box."

"Then those were given to whom?"

"I don't know. We put them in the Jeep and left, but I assume Griswold took them."

Marty asked, "Have you ever seen him since then?"

"Not to my knowledge."

Then they showed him a picture of Josephine Akiyama that Don had taken when he was on the Island in 1946. She was an exceptional-

John visits with part of the crew from the "Four Winds" during 200 m.p.h. winds.

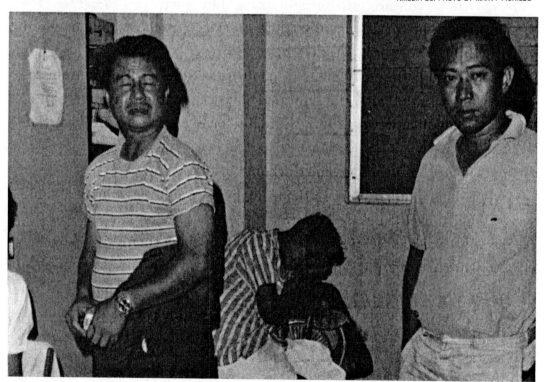

Some of the sailors trying to fit into the oversized clothing loaned to them by Ken, Don, John, Jack and Marty.

ly pretty girl on Saipan and they asked him if he had ever seen her before. Billy said he had seen Griswold talking to many people in the compound and remembered particularly seeing him talk to a pretty girl several times . . . that could possibly be the one. She could have been Griswold's informer.

John said, "Do you think he could have had some hanky-panky with her?"

"No, I wouldn't say that because I liked Griswold and he was a very fine man. It might have been a temptation, but I don't think he would fool around there even if he was that kind which I don't think he was."

Next they showed him a picture of Anna and discussed the possibility that she might have been the one that helped Griswold get the information to know where to dig.

Billy told about how some of the girls would tease the fellows by being topless bathing beauties. John told him that this was still a bit of custom on the Island. That is, some of the older women go out into the ocean with topless suits to take a bath.

Billy then said, "It is quite obvious Griswold got the right information from someone. I know damn good and well he wasn't on the Island when it happened so he had to be told by someone."

John, "Right, you've got something there."

"He didn't all of the sudden get a hot flash from Washington saying hey go look at this deal out here. He wasn't about to go around digging up that whole Island either. To the best of my knowledge, he went to one place, one time and that was it."

John said, "This is just a shot in the dark, but do you think Griswold may have taken one of these women out in the jungle and they pointed the grave out to him. Then he went back at a later date with you fellows to do the digging."

I doubt that he would have taken anyone out in that jungle alone."

John, "Then he was a pretty decent man."

"Well, he was a smart man; he was a capable man; just because a man is a little smarter or in a better position than I am in is no reason to be charitable—it's just the damn facts. If a man'a a good man, he's just a good man. If he had worked hard to get somewhere, I am not going to knock him."

John, "It takes a good man to have that kind of position in the first place."

"That's right and I can't fault the man in any way, shape, or form."

John, "He is a very intelligent man. You talk to him and you can see he knows what is going on. I just cannot understand why he does not either tell us he is not in a position to tell us and to please leave him out or tell us what happened. At this late date, I can see no reason why there is anything to hide, if there ever was. Of course if he is sworn to secrecy, I can't blame the man, but what is there to hide other than the government not notifying the nearest of kin if they knew what happened?"

Billy, "You kinda' have to have a feel for what you are doing. You kinda' have to go along with the authorities who put you in that position, otherwise you are not the right man for the job."

Marty and John agreed with this and asked if he would like to go back. Billy said he had no desire to return to Saipan. He had seen enought of it during World War II.

John told Billy that they had seen the gravesite that Goerner had excavated. It was very close and he explained if they had not had Anna to direct them, they never would have found the right place either.

They said goodbye and went back to the airport to catch a plane for the West Coast to see 'Snake' Henson. They were already wondering if he would be able to pick Mr. Griswold out of the picture lineup as easily as Billy Burks. If he could, there would be no doubts in their minds that they had talked to the right Tracy Griswold.

When they arrived in California it was too late to see anyone but they were able to make appointments to see Mrs. Akiyama's attorney, William Penaluna and Mr. Henson the following day. They had hoped they could convince Attorney Penaluna that they were on the right track and see if he could not arrange an interview with Josephine Akiyama. It was purely academic at this stage of the investigation, but since she had knowledge about Amelia, they would have liked to talk to her. They did spend a couple of hours of pleasant conversation with these nice people and learned the lawyer's primary objective was to get some property restored to the Akiyama's that they had lost during the war.

Their appointment with Everett Henson was for late afternoon at the Henson's very lovely home. The first part of the session, that lasted eight hours, was spent with Marty and John bringing the Hensons up to date on the adventure while a beautiful meal was prepared that put California hospitality second to none.

'Snake' Henson had turned out to be everything they had hoped for and more. He showed them some momentos from Saipan including a picture of a Japanese admiral and a small Shinto shrine.

After everyone had struck a monstrous blow at Twiggy by eating extra portions of all of the goodies, they settled down to some serious discussion. These adventurers could not help but think of the extreme contrast between this meeting and some they had attended on Saipan for the same purpose—to interview another witness directly involved in the Amelia Earhart case.

First they determined that Mr. Henson was forty-eight years old

Captain Jurisprudence showing Don where he tied his briefcase containing his papers and $300. The typhoon blew it away.

Front view of the Royal Toga Hotel that withstood typhoon Jean.

and a native of Kansas, Amelia's birthplace.

Then Everett lived up to his previous billing by asking the next question. "What prompted your beginning your search for Amelia?"

John and Marty took turns explaining how it all began on up through their last trip to Saipan being very careful not to disclose anything that would lead or mislead Everett in the information they hoped to get from him regarding his part in the digging in 1944. When they finished telling him how it started and what they had done, he asked, "Do you have any connection with Mr. Goerner, Tom Devine, Col. Gervais, Col. Briand, or any of those other people that were working on the mystery?"

They assured him that they did not have any working agreement with any of these people or anyone else. They had read Mr. Goerner's book and had talked to the rest of these people, but had no other connections with them. Everett had talked to most of these people on one or more occasions and was curious to know how they fitted into their work or investigations. Some very interesting points came up that partially accounted for the discussion that lasted nearly all night. However, they had to conclude that while a lot of investigation had taken place there had been very little tangible evidence produced to support the numerous theories.

John said, "We have a lot of tangible evidence to prove our efforts were fruitful, but first we want to hear your story and then we will show you what we have and where we found it."

Marty got his cameras set up ready to make a permanent record of Everett Henson's testimony. They could hardly wait to see if Everett could identify Griswold and see if his description would fit the one given them the day before by Billy Burks.

Everett had another question, "Have you been approached by any government officials?"

"No, other than Griswold." I asked Griswold, "Do you believe the government would do a thing like take the bones away and destroy them or file them away without notifying the next of kin?" He said, "Are you kidding; I did a lot worse things than that (presumably for security reasons during the war)." Then he said, "In fact with all five of you guys, if they wanted to shut you up, you would disappear just like that (with a single snap of the fingers)!" "

Marty said, "He looked right at us and we thought he was warning us, maybe."

John added, "We had a few interesting things happen on Saipan that we do not talk about, but we were extremely lucky all the way through. This adventure could have wound up a lot different on many occasions."

It was Mrs. Henson's turn to ask a question, "I have read so much that I don't always remember exactly what happened, but did Goerner talk to the eye-witness to the beheading?"

John, "No, and I'll tell you why. He came to the house of Antonio Diaz. He talked to the man, but there was a language barrier. They said they would go find an interpreter and come back. He was in a hurry to leave and never came back. Mr. Diaz told us that if he had come back he would have told him the same thing he told us and he would have broke this thing a long time ago. That is how close he was to getting the evidence he needed! Mr. Diaz gave us maps, he showed us where he helped take the airplane out of the jungle, and we asked him, "why are you telling me this when Goerner mentioned your name in his book? Why didn't you tell him?" That is when he explained that he would have told him, but he never came back."

Marty and John then explained that where Goerner actually did dig was very close and they could see how the mistake was made. They said they would never have found the right place by simply relying on a map. The eye-witness to Noonan's beheading that actually went with them out in the jungle and pointed out the spot was the reason they were successful. Without the eye-witness they could have dug for an awfully long time and likely not found the remains.

It looked as if the discussion took a turn towards others work so Marty cleared the air by stating, "We are not here to discuss nor do we have any intentions of trying to pass judgement on anyone trying to solve the mystery. We are not in competition with anyone."

John added, "The site we excavated is no secret. Father Sylvan and many of the natives will be glad to point it out to anyone that cares to go and take a look. There are no secrets concerning our adventure. We are only interested in facts and double checking all of those. That is the reason we have come to you."

Everett said, "Good, I am not on anybody's side either. I am a little ole bitty thing in this whole situation and I don't know anything except what happened to me. That's all."

With this settled, John said, "I would like to hear your story; how you were selected etc.."

Everett began by saying, "There wasn't much to it." He told the same story as Billy Burks about how they were selected by Griswold to go on a little tour.

John asked, "You didn't know who he was at the time?"

Everett, "Well, he had been with us for some of the time. In the beginning of this whole thing, I thought that he was attached to our outfit, but I had forgotten. My memory actually failed me there so I do have an old roster in my seabag of the old battalion. I got the roster and could not find his name on it so he was not attached to it, according to my roster."

"What was the name of your outfit?"

"Dog Company, 2nd Battalion, 18th Marines."

Rear view of the Royal Toga showing typhoon damage to the palm trees.

Army plane landing to bring in fresh water, food and medicine after the typhoon.

"Did you say dog company?"

"Yes, D Company or Dog Company ..."

"That was 18th Marines?"

"Yes, the 18th Regiment, 2nd Marine Division."

"What was Griswold's rank?"

"He was a captain and to go on with the events as they happened, we got a Jeep and drove up on top of a hill to the Japanese Admiral's house. We went through there. This picture is of another Japanese Admiral. I think he fought in the Russo-Japaneses war or something. Below the house was a carriage house. Inside there was a beautiful carriage. One like you would see in the movies."

John, "A horse-drawn carriage?"

"Yes, it looked like a carriage for royalty, very colorful, black and gold, you know the kind. I often wondered what happened to that darn thing. I thought at the time, brother, I sure would like to have that at home, but anyway up on the wall was a propeller with a leading edge of brass. It had some Japanese characters on it. I called Griswold's attention to that. He said, "Bring it." We took that. Then we went on down the hill to where the hospital used to be. We leveled it off. Our Navy leveled the dang thing off because when we leveled Garapan for the invasion the hospital had a big red cross on it and it was left until it was determined that the Japs had some artillery on top and were shooting back; they said level it; we leveled it. We went on past that 'annie-googling' off towards Garapan. We came to a large cemetery. It had the old German-type wroughtiron railing around the perimeter of the graveyard. Somewhere as we walked around we saw a statue of some kine of an angel."

"Right, I know what you mean", showed John was paying close attention.

Everett said that stood out, of course, and you will recall Goerner had a picture of it in his book.

John told him it was still there and that he would show them some pictures of it when they got to that point.

Everett went on, "Griswold went around on the inside of the island side and I went around the other way. He told us to look for some graves that might be anywhere on the outside of the perimeter of the graveyard. Well, I went around the bottom and he went around the top. Then I came across these two graves over there. I yelled at Burks and Griswold. They came on down."

John asked, "How did you know they were graves?"

"Well, they were the size of graves. They were outlined with white stones, rock, or coral, I suppose. We got down to the spot and Griswold said, "we will dig them up." We started digging. We ran into these bones and he put them in canisters and we left. We went on back to the area."

"How deep did you dig?"

"Oh, we were around waist deep. You had to put your hands on the ground to hoist yourself out."

"I see."

"...so we started back to the area so I asked Griswold."

"Before we get to that, how much of the bones do you think you actually got. I know that would be hard to remember, but what do you imagine it was?"

"I don't have any idea because I don't know how many bones make up a skeleton."

"In other words, you didn't get a whole bushel of bones?"

"We got quite a few bones out of there, yes, just how many, I don't know; we didn't count them or anything like that . . . I mean, when you are digging up somebody's grave you know how you would feel."

John agreed that would be an unpleasant task.

226

"You are right. I am standing there in hostile territory digging up somebody and wondering who."

"Did you wonder who at the time?"

"Yes I did . . . that is what I was going to say. As soon as we got through and started back I said, "What in the hell are we doing—who are we looking for?"

Griswold said, "Did you ever hear of Amelia Earhart?"

I said, "Yes."

He said, "Well, then that's enough said." Then he admonished Burks and I both to say no more about it. We didn't. I didn't say any more about it until I contacted Mr. Goerner.

John, "I know it is hard to remember details, but do you remember any other landmarks that you have not told me about?"

"There was a big tree about ten paces away."

"Would you know what kind of tree it was?"

"No, I don't have any idea what kind of tree it was."

"But you would say that it was a large tree for that jungle area?"

"It was one of the larger trees, right."

John continued, "Was there anything peculiar about the shape that you might remember?"

"I remember it as a great big forked tree. It had a big trunk that came up a ways and branched out into a big fork. Other than that, I can't tell you anything strange about anything I saw."

John showed him a picture of the tree. Everett said, "That could be it, but I could not swear to it."

They could understand this because the tree was practically dead now with a lot of the upper branches gone. It had been several years and trees change. They were satisfied, however, because that is the only large forked tree in the entire area.

John asked, "How far outside of the cemetery did you dig?"

The planes come in every 30 minutes for 3 days to keep Saipan going.

A witness studying the pictures used in the investigation.

"Fifteen to twenty-five feet outside the perimeter of the cemetery, as I recall."

"O.K. that is all we want to know." Then John turned to Marty with a big smile, "What do you want me to do, kiss him while you get some pictures? That is almost exactly what Billy Burks told us."

Next, John brought out the nine pictures that included Griswold. He asked Everett to look through them and see if he could pick out Mr. Griswold.

He looked through them until he came to the picture of Tracy Griswold and went no further.

John, "That's the man?"

"Hell yes, that's Griswold."

Mrs. Henson said, "Everett does have a terrific memory. My brother and he went all through school together. They recently went to a reunion. My brother sat there and ask him who everyone in the class was. He knew every one."

John, "I have what you might call cycles. Sometimes I can remember things when I was a kid three years old . . . you know, really vivid. Then I go into a slump and just can't place things."

Mrs. Henson, "He remembers things that I just can't believe. It's rather disgusting to me because I just can't remember like that."

Everett was still looking at the picture. He said, "There is no question about that being ole Gris."

John then showed him some recent pictures of Mr. Griswold to which Everett commented, "His eyes, nose and general profile is just about the same. I know that first one I picked out is Tracy Griswold."

John showed them the picture of the firebrick and explained it was to prove there was a crematorium nearby. Anna had told them this, but they would not know Amelia had been cremated until they got Dr. Baby's report. They had interviewed several witnesses that

knew she had dysentery so it all fitted together. The Japanese cremated anyone with any kind of disease and maybe in this case to destroy
identity. If the later was any part of their reason for cremating her
they were misguided because Dr. Baby told the group that cremation
was a form of preservation. It did, however, likely prevent Captain
Griswold, Pfc. Billy Burks, and Pfc. Everett Henson from recovering
Amelia's body when they dug in the same spot as our adventurers.
Even then the truth could have been known if a quarter-inch mesh
screen had been used to pick up the cremated particles.

Then a horrible thought occurred to John. He wondered if her
remains had been found, would the world have been told or was that
the reason Captain Griswold had orders to find the grave and recover
the remains. These could have been destroyed or filed away so there
could never be anything but rumors about what really happened to
Amelia and Fred. Having spent his life as a policeman, reminded him:
without a body, it is nearly impossible to prove a murder . . . but why?
Why would anyone, especially the government, want to conceal their
identity? Was it possible for our government to spend millions and
millions of dollars, when this nation was in the depths of a depression,
just to keep the public from knowing what was going on. He couldn't
believe it. Maybe his whole thinking process had gone bye-bye. All of
these thoughts went through John's mind when the full impact of
what Billy Burks and Everett Henson's testimony began to make
abundantly clear to his detective mind that he had talked to the right
Tracy Griswold. Also, that the digging mission had seemed very important to Griswold which meant it likely was very important to someone else . . . but who was that someone else? There had to be some
answers somewhere. John and Marty decided then and there that
Tracy Griswold had to be contacted again, now that he had been positively identified by two witnesses—the very two that dug up the re-

mains that had to be Fred Noonan and turned these remains over to him.

Mrs. Henson brought in some fresh coffee that jolted the adventurers back to the completion of their interview. John asked Everett if there was anything else about Griswold that would help prove this was the right Tracy Griswold. This prompted Everett to relate a conversation that removed all possibility of this not being the right Griswold.

Henson began with, "We were laying there one night . . . I think it was just he and I talking. Just shootin' the breeze, you know."

He said, " 'Snake', what are you going to do after the war?" We were having general conversation like that . . . we got to talking . . . where are you from . . . all that kind of jazz. He told me in that conversation that he was from Pennsylvania and that his family was in the stove manufacturing business named Griswold. I said, "My Grandma had one of those stoves; I remember the stoves . . . the Griswold stoves." I had forgotten all about it until Fred (Goerner) came on the scene. In the conversation with him this all came back to me. I told him Griswold was with us. I had forgotten his first name, but I did remember that he had told me his family was in the stove manufacturing business. I was glad I remembered that because it proved I was not an idiot or trying to cook up a lie or something like that."

John said, "Well everything matches. I can't see how he can deny that he was the guy, now."

Mrs. Henson said, "Now that you have this, what are you going to do with it?"

John told her, "We have 10,000 feet of movies shot on this investigation on 16mm film. These are still in the cans. They all came out beautiful, thanks to Marty, but they have never been narrated, never been cut, spliced or put in any sequence. We just filmed the events as

231

they happened. Now what we will eventually do is make a movie out of it and if possible write a book. None of us are very well grounded in these fields so we will have to go along and see what works out. We want to present our story as authentically as possible and in any way we can. We had exceptional luck all the way through, maybe we will have some here when we are all through with the investigation."

They had visited until the wee hours of the morning. It had been another long day, but a very productive one. The parting words of Mrs. Henson had to sum up all of their feelings when she said, "I think it was a very bad thing to let Amelia's mother die without knowing what had happened when it is quite apparent now that they knew."

Everett Henson then said, "There is no doubt in my mind that Amelia and Fred were the first casualties of World War II."

John says, "I have to go along with that, but that has not been our primary aim. We would like for them to have the credit due them. Anyone that lays their life on the line and loses their life should have a little recognition."

They all agreed on that and said, "Goodnight."

AMELIA CO. PHOTO BY MARTY FIORILLO

The road in towards the gravesite.

CHAPTER IX

THE HUMAN REMAINS FROM SAIPAN

It would seem that when someone has made a spectacular discovery, about all that is necessary is to reveal it to the press and all problems would automatically be solved. Such was not the case with these adventurers. It was going to take a great deal more than just finding an authority to identify the human remains and become instant heroes. They were not at all sure they had anything of value. Only proper evaluation by an expert would put them in position to tell their whole story. As Don put it, "there had already been too much speculation and not enough tangible evidence connected with the whole Amelia Earhart affair."

These fellows had learned to be cautious with every move. They wanted, most of all, to be certain they were right before making big headlines. In fact, making headlines was the farthest thought from any of their minds. They had set out to find Amelia Earhart's airplane. There was considerable evidence to prove they had found parts of it and many witnesses who verified its presence on Saipan.

Now that they had what should be the remains of Fred Noonan and possibly Amelia Earhart, even more care must be used to be absolutely positive.

John was selected by the group and put in charge of the bones. It would become his obligation to find someone who could make proper identification. He soon discovered this was a formidable assignment. Where do you start looking for someone to identify a body that had been relegated to history?

History—that would do for openers. John decided he would call the Natural Science Museum in Cleveland. They would surely be involved in this type of work. When a woman answered, John began

Liyang Cemetery showing the Angel that Billy Burks and Everett Henson remembered seeing while they were excavating the grave in 1944.

Liyang Cemetery showing how the jungle takes over. This is cleaned up once a year.

explaining that he and a group of fellows had recently made an expedition to the Pacific to locate a missing person. He further explained that they were successful in locating some human remains and were most anxious to contact an anthropologist of some stature that could possibly help with the identification. This is one time when John's winning ways took a recess. She listened for a while, then issued this challenge, "What right or by whose authority did you bring back the bones?" Before John could answer that question, she asked another, "Did you check with the Public Health Department?"

Quickly deciding this was a sure loser and could cause all kinds of grief, John said perhaps he should check with them first and hung up. He sat motionless for a few minutes wondering what to do next. His mild state of shock began to subside by letting his worry mechanism take over.

John had a deep seated philosophy that put the brakes on his worries immediately. He firmly believed that if you can do something about a problem, do it. If you can't do anything about it, don't waste time worrying about it. This is doubtless the reason he can go to sleep anywhere at any time of the day or night. So what could he do at this point? He could explain that Father Sylvan had given him permission to remove the remains, but what about the Health Department? Would they really be interested in someone who had been buried thirty years? That did not seem very logical to him. Anyway he decided at that moment it was time to find out. There was use in taking chances. He called Dr. Addelson who does autopsies in Cuyahoga County. John knew he could rely on this man's advice. Dr. Sam Gerber was also consulted.

Dr. Addelson relieved John's mind about any legal aspects and told him not to worry about the Health Department. The remains he had would not come under their jurisdiction at this point. One piece of red tape had been set aside. There still was the problem of finding someone to make the identification.

John let a few days go by while putting his brain through mental gymnastics trying to come up with the right person solid enough for the task at hand. He called on an old friend, Dr. Carl Brudzinski, and learned that he had gone to school with a Dr. Raymond S. Baby. Dr. Brudzinski explained that Dr. Baby is tops in the field of anthropology, is a genuine specialist at identifying remains (especially those that have been burned), and is in demand whenever there is a problem of this nature to be solved. He has done much original research in burned bone in both green (in the flesh) and dry condition. Furthermore, Dr. Baby was readily available, since he was on the staff of Ohio State University, the faculty of the Department of Anthropology, and the staff of the Ohio Historical Society. John was to find out a little later that Dr. Baby's availability was a bit overstated.

However, John had no way of knowing his renowned anthropologist was not just sitting in Columbus waiting for a call, so he was completely elated with this find. Not only had he come up with a top authority to identify the Saipan bones, but he had an entry through their mutual friendship with Dr. Brudzinski to shorten introductions and eliminate the necessity of establishing integrity—something that would most certainly have to be checked before a matter this serious progressed very far. John could hardly wait to get everyone together that evening and tell them the good news and get their approval to call Dr. Baby. He knew this was a formality and they would all say, "Why didn't you call him?" However, the protocol was to have a meeting before making any serious moves. This certainly was a serious move.

That evening the five gathered, and after listening to John, said in unison, "Why didn't you call Dr. Baby and get the show on the road?" John had spent more time thinking about the realities. He said, "Now do we just turn all of this precious evidence over to Dr. Baby or do we go down to Columbus with film and tape to make a permanent record?"

Don thoughtfully replied, "You are right, John. Here we have spent months of hardship and thousands of dollars to get this far with this project. We certainly should get this portion on film and tape regardless of how it turns out."

They were all thinking now and Ken added, "John, you call Dr. Baby and make an appointment. We will all go down together." He turned to Marty and asked if he could get away to film this meeting with Dr. Baby. Ken knew wild horses could not have kept Marty away. It was not that he needed more picture-taking experience. He was the only one who had any previous archeological experience and here was an opportunity to meet a big man in that field. He could explain the digging operation to a professional who would understand.

Marty lighted up like a pinball machine at the very thought of this impending experience. All eyes were turned on him, awaiting an answer.

He started out by saying, "I don't want to hurt you guys' feelings." After the laughter died down, he was permitted to go on. This group was so used to cutting each other up without the slightest hint of an apology that such an opening remark just had to be the laugh of the day. Marty took this all in stride and remained dead serious as he explained that a great many things came to his attention while they were excavating that only a real professional would be able to analyze. For instance, it was obvious the grave had

The lower portion of the large forked breadfruit tree that was a landmark for Anna to find the gravesite. Both Billy Burks and Everett Henson remember it be-ing nearby.

Anna Diaz Magoofna demonstrating the somauri executions she saw coming home from school.

been dug into prior to their excavation. He knew this because he observed the depth of the 30-caliber shells and other debris not likely to have been in the area prior to the invasion.

They all listened with fascination and agreed that these would be good points for him to discuss with Dr. Baby.

At 2 a.m. they left John's lovely handcrafted den and headed home to get a few hours sleep. Tomorrow would just be another working day for them. John could hardly wait to call Dr. Baby and see what he would be like. He wanted to tell him as little as possible to get a more accurate answer, in the event Dr. Baby might be swayed in his thinking if he knew where the bones came from. John felt it would be best not to mention who was supposed to be buried in the grave until the bones were identified as white or oriental.

John would soon discover his worries were completely unfounded. A man does not reach the top in any endeavor without extreme dedication and unquestioned ability to make an accurate diagnosis based on facts and stick to that decision.

The next morning John called Dr. Baby's office at the Ohio State Museum. The secretary told John that Dr. Baby was on a field trip excavating a prehistoric Indian burial mound and would not be back for several weeks. John left word for Dr. Baby to call him when he returned and went back to work with a real let-down feeling. However, there was nothing to do but wait for Dr. Baby's call.

Late in June, Dr. Baby returned the call and arrangements were made to visit him as soon as he could get organized with his great backlog of work. He explained that being away let everything pile up and there was always a lot of classifying of remains and artifacts after one of these working expeditions. While most businessmen are near a telephone if they are away from their offices, such is not the case on an archeological expedition. The locations are about as far removed from civilization as one can get, with no way to make contact with the office.

The great day finally arrived, and the group arrived at Dr. Baby's office. After formal introductions, Dr. Baby had given permission for them to tape and film the interview and Marty set up his equipment.

When they began telling Dr. Baby the story, he listened very politely, but seemed totally unimpressed. When they finished telling him about the trip to Saipan, he said in true professional style, "Put you evidence on the table." It was painfully obvious to all of them that this man would not be swayed by anthing they told him if there was no supporting evidence.

The contents of the tie boxes were dumped on the table. Dr. Baby looked at the bones while the group watched his reactions. Don admits now that he did not have any idea whether they had pork chop bones, chicken bones or any other kind and was prepared for the worst. Ken felt sure they were human bones, but admits he did not know why he thought so. John kept whatever thoughts he may have had to himself, but had seen more human bones in his police work than the others. Marty was much too busy filming to think or talk at the moment. He was a perfectionist with a camera. When he was taking pictures, his only concern was that the lighting be right and the subjects placed and good pictures would be proper testimonial to his ability.

After looking at the bones a few moments, Dr. Baby's interest intensified markedly. He picked up a bone and said he could make an educated guess it was a female, from the edge of the bone being sharp. This was an overwhelming surprise! They were pretty sure, if the bones were human, they had to be those of Fred Noonan. Anna Diaz Magofna had seen both Fred and Amelia at the gravesite, but only saw Fred beheaded and actually kicked into the grave this group had dug up. They surmised Amelia might be in the same grave since Anna said Amelia was forced to help with the digging of it. In any event, they were certain they had come to the right place to get some honest answers. Could they have Amelia's body and not Fred's? They were in a state of shock.

John asked, "Do you have enough bones to make an analogy? Maybe they are oriental. If so, how did they get in that grave?"

Dr. Baby studied the bones for several minutes before he started to answer John's questions by saying, "I will express an opinion based on my experience and my training. Any reference relative to age will be anatomical age and not chronological age." Knowing he had lost them by the puzzled expression on their faces, Dr. Baby explained that some people age faster than others. Their skeletons will reflect this aging by additional bone being deposited around joint margin. These differences can cause a slight degree of error in determining actual age of the individual in years. The aging process could make them appear a few years older or a few years younger.

They all expressed their gratitude for his considerate explanation and were eager for him to proceed. Dr. Baby went on, "The reduction is due to cremation, and perhaps due to others' digging attempting to remove remains from the same place. This is very common in our work. Often someone has been there ahead of us. We can draw some very definite conclusions relating to the fragments that I would be able to restore. This will require a great deal of study and comparison with some known standards. If you can leave these bones with me, I will do my best to retrieve as much informa-

Anna Diaz Magoofna helping the group locate the grave in the jungle.

A Japanese firebrick from the crematorium that was originally about 10 paces from where the remains were excavated. Anna used it as a reference point.

tion as they present." He picked up another piece. "This appears to be male."

They could hardly restrain themselves and all tried to talk at once. Dr. Baby calmly said, "It is best that I get to work."

The drive back to Cleveland was a very happy one because they felt everything was starting to shape around and they had really accomplished a lot today. Bit by bit they re-hashed the days' events as the miles flew by (with John driving, they do fly). Marty was sure he had gotten some good movies of the conservative Dr. Baby in action and was thrilled to have had the opportunity to discuss this expedition with a noted authority. He had confirmed a point he tried to make at the site on Saipan—that much more care should have been taken with the excavation and more material should have been brought back. The rest of the group accepted this with good grace and made Marty feel better by saying, "You were right and we should have listened to your advice."

To maintain the check and balance system that had been so effective in keeping this friendship progressive and without undue restraints, Ken quickly flashed an obviously devilish smile and said, "Any concessions we are making about listening to your advice apply only to *that* situation on Saipan."

Marty had to counter with, "I am just happy to know that you guys concede that I am right now and again. You, also, admit that we have some beautiful movies, but it was an uphill fight all the way—what a bunch of movie stars you would make!"

At this point, John couldn't resist saying, "Some of those other great movie stars are pretty temperamental, too, so you will just have to put up with us."

Don was enjoying the foolishness, but wondered out loud, "How long do you think it will take Dr. Baby to piece the parts together and give us an answer?"

They all agreed the suspense would be terrible. Dr. Baby had implied they had parts of two bodies. He was fairly certain they had both male and female. This caused John to remark, "Anna was right. She did see both of them at the gravesite even though she did not tell us what happened to the woman."

Marty spoke up, "She was a young girl at the time and the shock of seeing the beheading probably either sent her running away or so terrified her she could not look at any more brutality."

Don added, "She was no doubt paralyzed with fright. She knew they would kill her if they saw her."

John said, "We should have asked her specifically if she saw any more, but you all remember we had accepted the same assumption of many of those we talked to about Amelia. Most of them thought she had died of dysentery. Now we realize they had seen her very ill with the disease and when they saw her no more, just assumed she had succumbed to that malady. No one actually saw her dead or being buried. Now we find she was cremated and buried in the same grave that Anna saw Amelia and Fred digging, and where she saw Noonan beheaded. The crematorium was only ten yards away from that grave. That spot was probably selected so they could cremate her. This was the Japanese custom with anyone who had recently been ill prior to departure. They just hastened her departure, thus taking care of both of them at the same time." The others agreed that in light of today's findings, this just about had to be the case. There was very little chance that any other woman would have been buried in the same grave. They would just have to wait and see if Dr. Baby could determine if the bones were those of a white woman, as he strongly suspected. If this turned out to be the case, they had proof beyond their wildest dreams. Nothing to do but wait.

They had made the first trip to see Dr. Baby on June 25th. Every day seemed like an eternity to them while waiting to hear more about his findings. Finally, on July 9th, they just could not stand the agony any longer. Florence placed a call to Dr. Baby. He assured them that he was studying the bones, but did not have any new information to give them at this time. He told them he would write a full report when he had completed the study. He would not be pinned down as to how long he thought it might take, but he did leave the impression that he would be very thorough and this inspired more confidence. With this pleasant feeling of knowing everything was in good hands they all went about their daily living until late in August.

At a cookie and coffee session held at Don Kothera's August 25th they decided to call and see if Dr. Baby had found something more exciting to do and forgotten about them. He quickly dispelled all of their fears about putting them in the backgroud. He had been to Cleveland to confer with the late Prof. Sassaman about the dental bridge and one foot bone. There was a difference of opinion on this bridge as to whether it was upper right or lower left. Dr. Baby explained he had tremendous respect for Professor William H. Sassaman and that he must find a way to prove his belief that the bridge was indeed lower left (which later Prof. Sassaman conceded to be correct). After the entire group had talked to Dr. Baby, their efforts were concentrated on the teeth.

Florence was appointed as a committee of one to find Amelia's former dentist who might have put in that gold filling. Dr. Baby had told them that it was part of the cremated body so it had to be Amelia Earhart's. Florence accepted the assignment with pledges from everyone else that they would help all they could. She was

The grave-site in the jungle where the remains were found. Typhoon Jean stripped leaves from the trees.

The gravesite showing the small area excavated due to Anna's perfect location.

soon to find out that even with all their help, this was to be a maximum effort that would bring some very interesting people and leads into their lives and add more drama to their experience.

Florence first called Dr. James Scott in Palm Springs. He had been Fred Noonan's dentist. He was not much help as he had never done any work for Amelia Earhart.

Florence found out that a Dr. Horace Cartee had extracted a tooth for Amelia when she landed in Miami at the beginning of the ill-fated trip. After a great deal of detective work, Florence was able to get in contact with Dr. Cartee. He was very gracious and told her that he extracted an upper right molar. He could not remember any bridgework in the area of the extraction. He said he would try to locate the dental records. At this writing, the records have not been located.

At this point, Marty was sent to see Dr. John Clark, who is with the Western Reserve Dental School. Dr. Clark examined the gold bridge and confirmed that it was the type of dentistry used in the thirties and was now outdated.

While Marty was visiting Dr. Clark at Western Reserve, Florence was calling Massachusetts General Hospital. Mrs. Albert Morrissey had told them that Amelia had been there for a sinus operation. Florence found out two things from the call. 1. That the hospital kept no dental records, and 2. that a Dr. Wilmore B. Finerman had performed the operation. Mrs. Morrisseey then wrote a letter to Florence giving her permission to get a release on the operation. This was done on the slim chance that any x-rays taken before or after the operation might show the bridgework. This turned out to be another time-consuming effort. Dr. Finerman wrote back that there were no x-rays involved in the operation. So it went. Day after day of thinking, digging, trying to find someone who might come up with the dental charts of Amelia's left jaw.

Up to now, all that could be proven was that the bridge was from the lower left of a female with a large jutting "horse-jaw". Coming from a grave out in the jungle half-way around the world which had been pointed out by an eye-witness should have been good enough evidence for most anyone. However, it was not good enough for Florence and this group of die-hards. They wanted to be absolutely positive and were determined to leave no stones un-turned to get all of the facts that were humanly possible to obtain.

Before anyone realized it, September was nearly half gone. Not having had any word from Dr. Baby and with some additional infor-mation about their activities was excuse or reason enough to call him. This call was made September 14, 1968. He told them that he had completed most of his investigative study and should have a report for them by the end of the following week. They were all very excited about the final report of his findings. The group decided to call Dr. Baby back on the 23rd and make arrangements to go to Columbus to see the report and ask any questions they might have after going over his complete findings.

The appointment had to be delayed until October 26, 1968 to accommodate everyone. Marty set up his photography equipment and John took charge of the recorder. Then for the benfit of film and tapes, Dr. Baby showed how the bones matched up. He ex-plained how some of the bones had been only partially burned, which he referred to as "smoked"; i.e., not all of the organic ma-terial had been destroyed in the burning. The reduction was slight.

John, Ken, and Don were completely fascinated by the way Dr. Baby explained how he arrived at his conclusions. This could have gone on for hours, if not days, but Dr. Baby suggested they get down to a detailed report that will be reported verbatim:

"I will give you my conclusions. I am going to state again as I did earlier that any remarks or conclusions drawn from my analysis of the cremated human skeletal remains submitted to me in June of this year, I will be expressing an opinion based on my experience and my training. And secondly, another important factor should enter in here—any reference to age, or assessment of age, or what I think the age of the individual is at the time of death is an *anatomical* age and not necessarily *chronological* ages. The cremated remains consist of 188 pieces, highly fragmented, ranging in length from 2 to 50 mm; the largest being a portion of the ulna or the forearm bone. The reduction of these pieces is due to: 1) the burning or cremation and 2) the recent excavation by yourself and others prior to yourself digging in this area attempting to remove remains from the grave which you excavated on Saipan. So you have here a reduction, and with this reduction and the incompleteness of the total skeleton, one is, in a sense, literally going out on a limb, but I think we can draw some very definite conclusions. Let's talk about the fragments being burnt. I would say 99.9% of them are completely incinerated. They range in color from blue-gray to gray. They are twisted, warped with transverse and diagonal fracturing, which clearly indicates the burning of green bone or burning in the flesh in contrast to burning of dry bone which splinters or shatters in a different fashion. Secondly, there are a few smoked parts that are incompletely incinerated at the time the fire was extinguished or the time when the remains were taken out of the fire. Not all of the organic material in the bone was completely burned. Thus we talk about it being "smoked". I noticed this particularly on the arm. Also, there are two pieces of the skull, and they are in an area of the temporal muscle, where that muscle which raises the jaw is attached and this usually provides good protection for that boney

Singing nuns on Saipan that said they would rebuild their wrecked convent. The hat is improvised from a piece of cardboard.

Father Sylvan spent much time observing the excavation.

Father Sylvan and Ken watch John struggle through the mass of roots that made digging very difficult.

John sifting dirt with a make-shift piece of equipment made from a refrigerator fan cover and a dresser drawer.

part; so the fact that these are smoked lead to the identification as to what part of the skull they are from. Those are the general remarks we should make at this time. Now we can be a little more specific, which will lead us to the conclusion that I will give you very shortly. I should say that all parts of the bony skeleton are represented and are a very small part of the total skeleton. Let's start with the bone we looked at a little bit earlier. This is part of the ulna. It is the upper part of the shaft and just below the head of the ulna and by virtue of weak muscle markings and the sharp lateral edge clearly indicates this is a female individual. Also, metric dimensions or thickness dimensions taken at this site against the normal white female bone is almost identical in spite of the fact that there is burning and slight reduction; I am going to say probably white. There is much work to be done, of course, on race studies or configuration of bones and their differences among the various populations. We do have some information, and we do have some colored bones in this case and we have been able to check against them, but at least we have here in this one bone obviously a female, probably white... However, I think from the bone texture along, which the burning has not destoryed, I would say you have an adult individual. So just from this one bone, we can say: female, probably white, and certainly an adult individual."

One by one, Dr. Baby went through the bones with such composure and scientific reasoning that by the time he had finished, the entire group sat in an open-mouthed trance. He concluded with a formal presentation of his written report. While this report is fairly technical, it is included here as a part of the record to substantiate our conclusion. After seeing this report on bones brought out of the jungles of Saipan from a 6' X 6' grave that was pointed out by a woman who saw the white man and woman digging the grave, and

Jack and Ken screen dirt as they excavate the gravesite.

Ken found a gold bridge that convinced them they had human remains.

A gold cap and bridge found with the cremated remains. Dr. Baby identified as lower left.

saw the white man beheaded and kicked into that grave, one can only conclude that it has to be the bodies of Amelia Earhart and Fred Noonan.

Even though it was now an acceptable opinion that they had recovered the remains of Amelia Earhart, the group decided more effort should be put into finding the dental charts, or someone who would have known about Amelia's bridge-work. Her sister, Muriel Morrissey, supplied what Dr. Baby regarded as a substantial clue, when she said she did remember Amelia coming home one time and showing her some dental work of which she was very proud. Florence, with her unremitting drive, came up with a thousand dollar dental bill that Amelia had paid. Today that would not mean too much, but during the thirties when the whole country was in a depression, a thousand dollars would buy an awful lot of dental work. The bridge in question is gold leaf overlay and not a casting. This type of work is no longer done, but it was a good job at that time.

Dr. Baby asked about Mrs. Morrissey's teeth, explaining that environment and heredity have a great deal to do with similarities in tooth problems in families. She, too, had more than the usual amount of dental work and is a good example of the popularity of gold fillings and overlays of that time.

Mrs. Morrissey tried to be of further help by trying to remember Amelia's dentist in Boston. She could not quite remember his name, but did remember that it started with an "S" and she thought his office was on Beacon Street. With this bit of information, Florence got back into action. She first called the Bell Telephone Company to get the yellow pages for Boston to look up all of the dentists who could possibly fit her clues. When these failed to turn up the wanted dentist, she had to assume the dentist had died, retired, or sold his practice to someone else. Her next approach was to con-

Don and Ken leaving the Navy plane that took them to Guam after typhoon Jean stranded everyone.

John making a point with Guam chief of Police, Quintanilla, while Ken and Don observe.

tact several dental supply houses hoping one of them could supply a clue as to who she was looking for and what had happened to him. None of those contacted remembered a dentist on Beacon Street who would fit her description. One of them did suggest she contact the Massachusetts Dental Society. Joseph G. DiStasio, D.M.D., the executive secretary was very gracious and suggested their plea be published in their journal.

This effort brought some positive results and another disappointment. Dr. Clarence G. Severy wrote to say he probably was the dentist they were looking for and would be glad to help if he could. Dr. Severy was vacationing in Florida at the time and Don had planned to fly down with the bridge, but his tile business became too demanding. None of the others could get away for that long of a trip at the time, so they sent Dr. Severy some photographs of the bridge to see if he could identify it as his work. Then came the disappointment. He could definitely identify it as *not* a piece of his work. However, he could not say whether it may have been something done before he started doing Amelia's dental work.

There was one possibility left. They had obtained the name of a Dr. Harold Duey by corresponding with some of Amelia's personal friends. Dr. Duey had done Amelia's work after she went to California, other than just cleaning which was done by Dr. H. M. Barnhart. Florence placed a call to Dr. Duey and found that he had died in 1955, but she did have a nice visit with Mrs. Duey. Amelia had stayed at her home just prior to leaving on her ill-fated flight. This last effort had to go into the failure file along with the rest. A number of libraries were written to for information that might have been given to them. Their thoroughness is evidenced by a letter than went to Paoli's Old Library, 951 Clement Street, San Francisco, California 94118. Neither Florence nor any of the others can recall how they came up with this, unless "Old Library" sounded like a place to look for historical material. Mrs. Paoli eliminated it as a possibility by telling them "Old Library" is a restaurant and not a book depository.

Even though that piece of gold bridge would only establish more firmly what the group already knows, the search goes on to find someone that could identify it positively. Dr. Severy said it was not a piece of his work, but said he would like to have seen it to see if it would have fit the type of "horse-jaw" Amelia had. Dr. Baby, the anthropologist had already determined that this was exactly the type of jaw it was made to fit.

Temporarily, anyway, all leads regarding the teeth had been exhausted so the group's efforts turned to finding an author to put the world at ease as to the mystery of Amelia Earhart and Fred Noonan. This would seem to be a logical conclusion to a great adventure, but such is far removed from the facts of the situation. They knew from Anna, just what had happened to Fred Noonan, but they only had one piece of what they believe to be his remains. They could not rest until they got the truth about what happened to the rest of his body.

AMELIA CO. PHOTO BY MARTY FIORILLO

Jack presented the Guam Rotary Club with his Club's emblem.

256

Guam Chief of Police, Quintanilla and Joseph Gervais, who has done a great deal of research into the Amelia Earhart mystery.

Don, John and Ken pass the time aboard a jet on the return trip home.

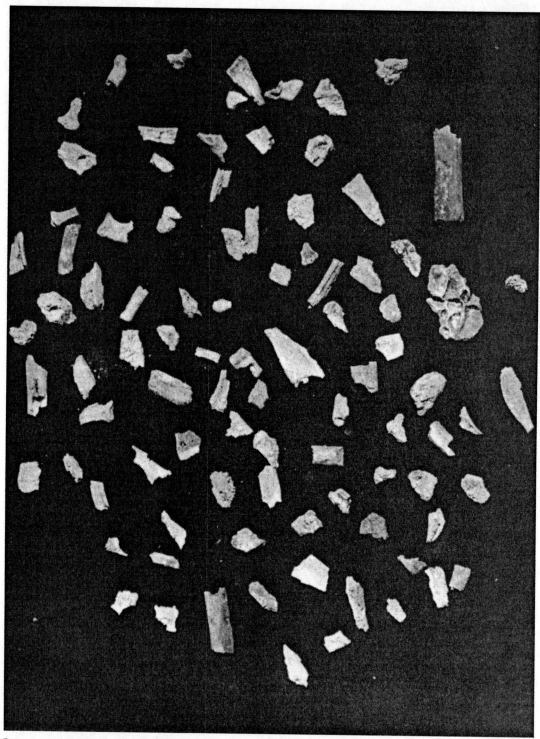

Some of the larger bone fragments.

CREMATED REMAINS

The cremated human skeletal material submitted for analysis consists of 188 small fragments ranging in length from 2.0mm to the largest piece, 50.0mm. The remains have been greatly reduced by burning and then disinterment. Ninety-eight percent of the fragments, ranging in color from light grey to blue-grey, are completely burnt with the exception of two small portions of skull and a portion of ulna that are "smoked" (Baby, 1954). Deep checking, diagonal and transverse fracturing, and warping are characteristic of burning in the flesh or "green" bone (Baby, 1954).

The fragments were sorted into anatomical groups and carefully examined. Sixty-five percent of the total number of parts were identified, representing approximately 1% of the axial and apprendicular skeleton. Pieces making contact with each other made possible the restoration of a few bony segments.

SKULL

The vault is represented by two fragments. One is a portion of the anterior inferior parietal bone; the second is probably a segment of frontal bone. Both are "smoked" or incompletely incinerated. The former is thin and female-like. Bits of charred periosteum are adhering to its outer surface. A small segment of the lateral margin of the right (?) bony orbit is moderately sharp and female-like.

The left condyle of the mandible and a portion of the ascending ramus are present and completely incinerated. The condyle is small and most certainly associated with a female individual. Slight bony "lipping" along the inferior articular surface is indicative of the beginning of the aging period—40 to 45 years.

The completely incinerated tip of a third (?) molar tooth

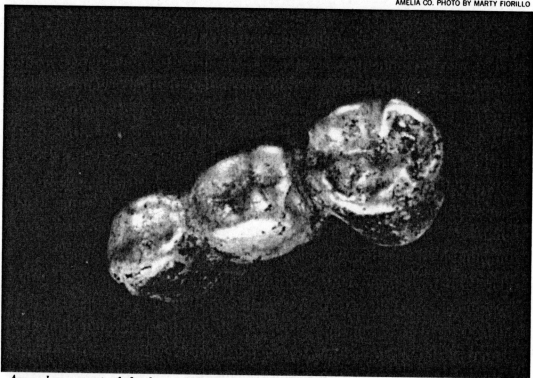

An enlargement of the lower left gold bridge that was darkened by the cremation. Dr. Baby confirmed this with the late Prof. Sassaman, who thought originally it was upper right.

Distal view of the gold bridge showing one tooth was missing. Dr. Baby was certain this and the amalgam filling proved the remains were from a white person.

is small and female-like. The closed root end is evidence of an adult individual.

A gold bridge between the first permanent pre-molar (Pm1) and the first permanent molar (M1) to replace an extracted permanent second pre-molar (Pm2), is 30.0mm in length. Incineration is manifest by ashen black stain and cracking of the anterior lingual surface. The small size of the caps or crowns (Pm1 lenght, 8.0mm., width, 5.0mm.; M1 lenght, 11.0mm., width, 9.5mm.) are within the range of a female individual. Wear on the labial surfaces of the bridge, the spacing, and the slight curvature are associated with the teeth of the lower left jaw. Professor William H. Sassaman (personal communication, October 13, 1968) "guessed" upper right.

A small, irregular metallic mass appears to be an amalgam filling (s?). The irregularity is the result of incineration.

RIBS AND VERTEBRAE:

Four rib fragments are small, delicate, and female-like

Bodies of vertebrae are represented by three fragments. One segment of a cervicle vertebra shows slight lipping along the edge confirming age change between the ages of 40-45. Three vertebral articular processes also exhibit slight lipping and bony exostosis. All fragments appear small and female-like.

EXTREMITIES:

Bones of the upper and lower extremities are represented by some 19 fragments. Perhaps the most significant fragment of the group is that of an upper shaft of the left ulna, 50mm in lenght. Muscular markings are weak and the lateral edge is sharp indicating a female. The metric dimensions (anterio-posterior and transverse diameters) correspond to those of a typical white female.

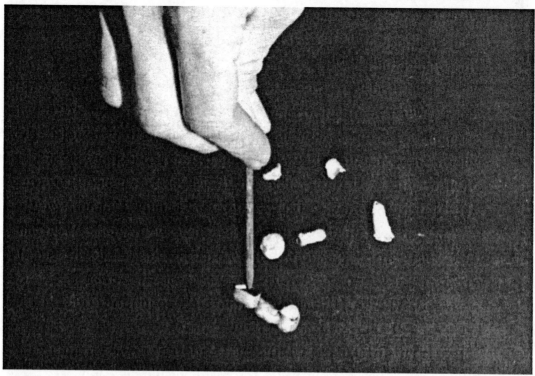

Under side of the gold bridge and amalgam fillings.

A close-up of some of the cremated remains that Dr. Baby says are from a 40 year old white female.

A midsection of the right fibula exhibits the morphic characters of a female individual.

Sections of the femora appear small and female-like. In spite of incineration, the bone texture is that of an adult individual.

Bones of the hands and feet are present in the total series. Two *complete* terminal phalanges clearly indicate age change ("aging") by slight bony deposits on the articular margins. This is consistant with the other bones mentioned above.

"NORMAL" BONE

A "normal" or unburnt bone fragment is present in the collection. It measures 26.0mm by 45.5mm. One surface is smooth and the reverse side exhibits irregular bony cells. This fragment is associated with the frontal bone which forms the upper margin of the bony orbit and frontal sinus. The thickness and ruggedness suggests a male individual, and certainly not a part of the cremated remains.

It is our opinion that the cremated remains are those of a female, probably white individual between the anatomical ages of 40-42 years is probably more correct. A single unburnt bone is not a part of or associated with cremated remains, but the remains of a second individual, a male.

Associate Professor of Anthropology

RAYMOND S. BABY, D.SC.
Curator of Archaeology
Associate Professor of Anthropology
The Ohio Historical Society—The Ohio
State University and

MARTHA A. POTTER, M.A.
Associate Curator of Archaeology
The Ohio Historical Society

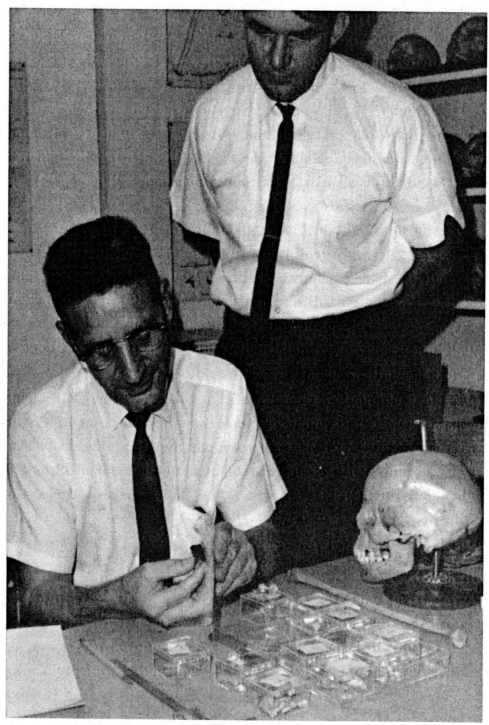

Dr. Baby making comparisons with known bones.

CHAPTER X

TO LET THE WHOLE WORLD KNOW

John Gacek was appointed to make a concentrated effort to find an author who could piece their story together from information they had collected on the two trips to Saipan. This included airplane parts, 10,000 feet of 16mm film, hundreds of still photos, 50 hours of tapes, voluminous files of letters and newspaper clippings, and the Saipan remains that no reasonable person could question were the remains of Amelia Earhart and Fred Noonan. John knew he would have no difficulty in selling the idea if he could find the right person. Fate, who had played such a part in their entire adventure, stepped in again.

Joe Dranek's Astorhurst is a lovely restaurant on the left bank of Tinkers Creek where many of the suburban businessmen go for lunch. It was John's day off and he decided to drive out to this lovely spot for lunch and ask congenial Joe Dranek, who made it his business to become well acquainted with everyone who frequented his place, if he knew anyone that could write a book.

John took a seat next to Joe Dranek's office—which was the end barstool in the back room where most of the businessmen preferred to eat and drink. John ordered a beer. While it was being fished out of the cooler by the bartender, Joe Dranek came in and greeted John:

"How is everything in Garfield Heights and what brings you out in the country, John?"

John got right to the point, "Everything is fine at the police department. We now have positive identification on our bones from Saipan and now we need someone who can write. Who do you know that could write a book, Joe?"

While he was thinking about that, this maladjusted veterinarian walked in for lunch.

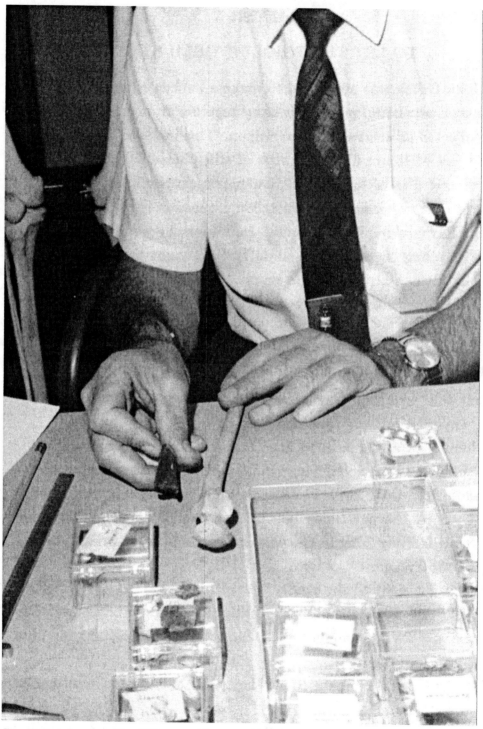

Dr. Baby showing the difference between incinerated bone and normal bone.

Joe Dranek turned full face and said, "Hi, Doc, you could not have walked in at a better time. Meet John Gacek, Lt. John Gacek of the Garfield Police Department. John, this is Dr. Joe Davidson who wrote that book, "All Horseraces Are Fixed.""

John picked up the cue, "Yes, I read that book and I like the way it is written—you know, it's written so everyone can understand it."

"Thank you, I enjoy writing." Turning to Joe Dranek, "Why is it such a great time for me to walk in; what have I done now?"

Joe started to explain, "John is one of those five fellows that went to Saipan to search for Amelia Earhart's airplane. They went back and now tells me they are sure they have her body. You read about it in the paper, didn't you, Doc?"

I had to confess that I travel most of the time all over Michigan and Ohio and was not aware of any such trip.

John picked it up there and filled me in on their adventure, and that now they were ready to put it into book form if they could find someone to write the book.

John was very direct with the next question. "How would you like to write a book about Amelia Earhart with our information?"

I countered with, 'That is a little out of my line. I write horse books. My only venture out of that field was a teen-age book called, "How To Be A Swinger" and frankly, I have not gotten up courage enough yet to publish that one. The main reason I write is to give me something to do in the evenings at the motels around the country."

John was already sure it was fate that had brought us together and insisted that he had read "All Horse Races Are Fixed" and he knew I could do justice to their story.

I was not so sure. However, before lunch was over, John's winning ways had convinced me that it would be worthwhile to meet with the rest of his group.

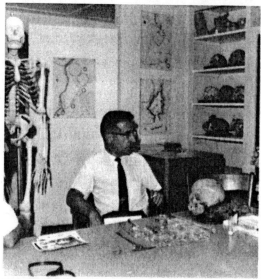

Dr. Baby being briefed on the digging operation.

Dr. Baby explains to Don how exact measurements enables him to determine between male and female.

Dr. Baby explaining the remains found on Saipan to Don and John.

We arranged to meet at the Gaslite Inn on Broadway in Bedford, Ohio, after five o'clock to discuss the possibilities. This was my first exposure to Don Kothera, Jack Geschke, Ken Matonis, and their lawyer, Dick Senn. Marty Fiorillo could not be there, but they had talked to him and he said he would go along with the group on whatever they decided at this meeting.

In less than an hour, I was convinced that these fellows were sincere and had a real adventure story to tell. Further, they had come up with tangible evidence to solve the Amelia Earhart mystery, where everyone else had failed. This was a bit puzzling at the time because I did not know their bulldogged tenacity for doing things they believed to be right. In retrospect, I am glad that I agreed to write this book or we might still be sitting at the Gaslite, as they had determined by the time they arrived that I was the one to write it.

It took a lot of evenings of listening to tapes and a lot of Saturdays and Sundays of personal interviews to get caught up. I wanted to relive as much of their adventure as I could through their tapes and pictures and meet as many of the people as possible who had figured in the adventure.

This involved a trip to Columbus March 2, 1969, to see Dr. Baby. You have read his conclusions on the remains. This man is pure scientist and one of the most fascinating people I have ever talked to. He has handled some 38 medico-legal cases that could fill an entire book. The first was a homicide, with the victim being put in a church furnace. He helped solve the case with a box of reduced bones and ashes. This trip convinced me completely that this group had recovered Amelia Earhart's remains and a small part of Fred Noonan's. It now became important to try to find the rest of his body if possible.

There were two possible sources to discover where his body was. There was no doubt it had been dug up by Billy Burks and Everett

Henson under the direction of Captain Griswold. There was no doubt that these bones had been turned over to Captain Griswold. From this point on, many doubts crop up at every turn. There is not much doubt that the U. S. government knows what happened to those bones, but so far they are not talking. This left Captain Griswold as the last resort, so it was decided to pursue this possibility.

Consideration was given to the possibility that there might be some good reason why Captain Griswold was not allowed to reveal what had happened to the bones that were turned over to him. He was to be approached on this basis: that if there was some reason why he could not tell, i.e. if he had been sworn to secrecy, then he could tell us that and this would end the story.

John made an appointment to meet with Captain Griswold through a mutual friend. The meeting was to take place at their club in Erie.

John, Don, and I drove over to Erie one rainy day to keep the appointment. After a very pleasant lunch, John explained to Mr. Griswold how he and Marty had visited Billy Burks and Everett Henson. Both had picked him out of a lineup of 10 pictures almost without any hesitation. He seemed a little surprised and asked, "Where did you get that picture?", when he saw the picture of himself taken in the forties. This was about his only show of emotion during the entire interview. He listened to me explain that we were only after facts, that we did not want to write anything that was not 100% correct, nor anything that he would not want us to write. Further, that if there was any logical reason why he should not tell us what had happened to the bones turned over to him on Saipan, we would accept his explanation.

With the stage thus set, we waited for his answer to the question, "Could you or would you tell us where we might find those bones so we can see if the part Dr. Baby is holding would match?" We figured there could only be two possible replies. He either had to say he was not allowed to tell or he would tell us. After all, he was being presented with proof that he had been there and was the man that Burks and Henson said they turned the bones over to.

We were wrong! He did not choose either of those alternatives. He simply looked at his attorney friend who was sitting directly across the table and said, "I do not remember going on any grave digging detail."

I am sure the same thought flashed through all of our minds at the same time; how do you make someone remember? Again, John asked, "Is it that you don't remember or has someone, perhaps higher up in Intelligence, insisted that you not tell?"

By way of explanation, Mr. Griswold said he was in charge of operations, he had a lot of things on his mind, and he could have been at the grave with Burks and Henson and not have remembered. We talked for several minutes about the invasion of Saipan. He remembered a great many details about being on Saipan and what took place. The hope was that by recalling as many incidents as possible, his memory would be refreshed on the excavation detail. He remembered a great many things, but was unshakable concerning the gravesite or anything related to it.

We finally gave up and came home completely bewildered. The only clue we got from Mr. Griswold was, "Have you checked the National Morgue? You might be surprised what you would find there." So someone had to check this out.

Florence had been the workhorse secretary, motivator, arbitrator, hostess and never-say-die inspiration throughout this entire adventure. They all felt they owed her a debt of gratitude and a couple of days vacation so they sent her on a working vacation to Washington, D. C. with an assignment to check into the National Morgue. This had been

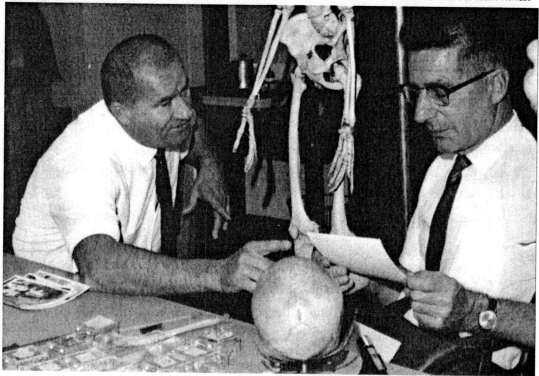

Dr. Baby being shown pictures of the expedition after making his report.

John talking to Billy Burks in Dallas, Texas. Billy helped Everett Henson and Captain Griswold excavate the same gravesite in 1944.

Mr. Griswold's only clue. When she was unable to locate any such place per se, another call was placed to Mr. Griswold for better directions. He suggested she check the National Archives.

Several days prior to leaving, she had written her Congressman, Charles Vanik soliciting any help his office might be able to provide. It was time to go to the Rayburn Building and check in for some directions. She was greeted by Bill Vaughn at Congressman Vanick's office. He gave her an official greeting and welcome to Washington that made her feel like a visiting dignitary. He listened to every word of her story and offered every possible kind of official and personal assistance. She assured him she would take advantage of his good nature and asked if he could get her an appointment with someone at the National Archives. This was no sooner requested than done. Mr. Vaughn talked to Miss Johnson who made an appointment with Mr. Harry Swartz.

Florence arrived at the National Archives and told Mr. Swartz about her interest in Amelia Earhart. She asked to see anything he might have regarding her last flight and especially any information following the flight. Mr. Swartz produced a file about the size of an unabridged dictionary. She looked through the contents which was mostly correspondence in response to official and private inquiries. When she turned up nothing about disinterment she was referred to Captain Loomis at the Office of Naval History. He threw up his hands in a gesture that suggested to her two things: 1. That he must get a lot of request for information about Amelia Earhart indicating that there was a lot of interest in what happened to her and Fred Noonan and 2. that if everyone had this fellow's attitude, it was not likely the truth would ever be known. He was well grounded in political buck-passing, however, so told her that he had no information and sent her to the Navy Yards to see Dr. Dean Allard.

It was an entirely different story here. Dr. Allard was very nice and most cooperative. He quickly provided another oversized file on Amelia Earhart, but nothing about the Marines, Griswold, Burks, and Henson or anything about any excavation.

She was a little surprised to find there had been personal investigations made on several people that had looked into the Amelia mystery. She was getting nowhere fast in obtaining any information about the remains or even a word about the excavation on Saipan in 1944.

Florence had planned to go to the Japanese Embassy while in Washington to see if they would give her any information at all about Amelia Earhart. She was greeted by a young Japanese that she was sure had not been born many years before 1937 and was doubtful that he would even know who Amelia Earhart was, but she was there and must try. She asked if he was familiar with a flyer named Amelia.

He said, "You mean the one that went down in the Pacific."

"Yes, that Amelia."

"I have no information on her."

Florence insisted that was a long time ago and that she could not see that it would matter now for the Japaneses to admit what had happened.

He said, "She was an American citizen, of course it would matter." He became quite upset.

It may have just been a case of very bad timing since it was announced just this last week that the Japanese were demanding that Okinawa be returned and he felt she was an envoy to throw a block in this pending action. After all a lot of good men died for that little piece of real estate at the hands of the Japanese. It could well be that it is in our best interest to return some of the islands to them to maintain harmony, but it is a delicate situation at best.

It would have caused Florence to have stood there with even

more mixed emotions if she had realized how horrible war really is and at the same time known or realized that our relations with Japan had progressed to the point that at that very moment part of this book was being written on a typewriter made in Japan, being taken off a tape that was manufactured for General Electric Company in Japan and listened to from a recorder made by Norelco in Holland powered by batteries brought from Japan. True, she was a little perturbed at the Japanese State Department, but not nearly as perturbed as she was going to be shortly at our State Department. Which causes one to wonder why we don't build huge coliseums, appoint gladiators to the State Departments, and let them put on the show when they let things deteriorate to the point that we need to have another war.

Anyway, the Japanese Embassy official asked Florence if she had gone to her State Department before coming there. When she said she had not, he quickly suggested she had better see Richard Finn at the Bureau of Pacific and Asian Affairs. She had taken along the pictures taken of our adventurers helping the Japanese reclaim their war dead on Saipan and asked him if he would like to see them. He assured her that he did not and practically pushed her out the door aiming her at the United States State Department Bureau of Pacific and Asian Affairs.

Florence arrived at the State Department to find Richard Finn had been replaced by Richard Herndon, who is in charge now. After listening to her story, he admitted they had a file on Amelia.

This caused Florence to say, "Good, could I see it?" It had bugged her a long time because no investigation had made any mention of what the Japanese might have to say about the events surrounding Amelia that were well known on Saipan. She assumed we had won the war and surely the Japanese had been asked at some time what they knew about Amelia and Fred.

Everett Henson studies a map of Saipan while John adjusts the tape recorder.

Everett Henson shows John a picture of a Japanese admiral taken from a building where he, Billy Burks and Captain Griswold stopped on their way to excavate the grave in 1944.

Mr. Herndon answered her with, "No."

"Why, because it isn't here or because it is classified?"

"Because it is classified."

Florence protested, "I understood that enought time had gone by that all of her files had been declassified. We have a letter to that effect and that was my understanding from my Congressman." When he offered no explanation, she said, "What can we do to get it declassified."

He replied, "It would take at least two weeks."

"Where are the files?"

"In this office."

With typical feminine logic, Florence said, "Can't you call the person who is responsible and get permission for me to see them? I had not really planned to be here two weeks."

That merited a, "No", without further comment.

She said, "I am going to write you a letter to bring you up to date on what this group has done with a request for material from that file so you can get it declassified."

He allowed it would be alright to make the request and she left with a feeling that would take the best diplomat in that State Department to put in acceptable words. One more State Department and she would have gone to the showers voluntarily. In fact, she did that anyway. She went back to the hotel and called Bill Vaughn to be sure she had not misunderstood about material concerning Amelia being declassified. She had not misunderstood. It was good to talk to someone again that seemed to be on her side. Mr. Vaughn said he thought the files should not be classified and that he would most certainly look into that. Further, he told her that he had talked to the Library of Congress and they were going to do some investigating to see what they can learn about the previous excavation and what would normal-

A close-up of the Japanese Admiral's picture and a Shinto Shrine he brought from Saipan.

Left to right, Everett Henson, Mrs. Henson's mother, Mrs. Henson and John Gacek having an early morning snack at their California home.

ly have happened to any remains that might have been recovered under such circumstances. This was good news to Florence because she could not find anyone who could even hazard a guess about such things. He told her to call back the next day after he had time to contact Mr. Herndon.

She called to get the report and was told that all he got was some stammering double-talk without any direct answers. Mr. Vaughn told him he would expect an answer in two weeks (that seems to be the standard time it takes for anything to happen in the State Department or maybe they have determined that in this busy world nearly everyone forgets what they wanted in two weeks). This book may go to press while Florence waits, but it is my guess that she will not forget and hopefully she will inspire someone else to do some looking into what goes on. She is thoroughly convinced that whole libraries of interesting information could be brought to light about what goes on in government by anyone with the time and inclination to pursue any given topic. Intentionally or otherwise the various governmental agencies are real masters at confusion. This caused her to recall a sign she had seen saying, "If you can keep your head when all of those about you are losing theirs, chances are you do not know what the issue is." She is certain of one thing. There are not too many people in Washington that know or care what anyone is doing except where they work. She quickly found out sneakers are far superior to high heels for any investigation; that you would be well advised to change the sneakers to track shoes just before 4:30 to keep from being run over by government employees leaving their labor of love and if you are exceptionally fast you will be towards the front of the line and only have to wait an hour or so for a taxi. So went the days.

The next stop was to be the office of the Chief of Naval Intelligence. Florence called to make an appointment. The girl that answered referred her to R. A. Halfinger. He told her there were absolutely no records regarding Amelia in his department. He referred her to a Mr. Paschal. He said he had no records about Amelia. He referred her to Major Ringler, who is in the Navy Annex Department that includes a lot of Marine Corps activities. He referred her to Ralph Donnley who was very nice and helpful. There she found out that there had been several inquiries about Tracy Griswold. The government writes him. He always answers that he does not remember. Florence commented, "That must be true, he told us the same thing."

She was now looking for two things: 1. Any mention of the excavation or the remains dug up by the three Marines in 1944. She found nothing; 2. Any correspondence between the Japanese and the American government related to Amelia Earhart. She found one line in a letter in this huge report which caused Florence to exhibit symptoms bordering on combat fatigue. She exclaimed, "Didn't we win the war! Where is all of the information from Japan? They did the executing of Noonan and we know they keep excellent records. Speaking of Noonan, I have asked every place for his file. No files on Noonan. Everyone else seems to have been asked about Amelia and Fred except them. Why not ask the Japanese and expect some answers? Americans have been asked to furnish all of the answers. It just strikes me that we have been talking to the wrong people." Then she remembered all of the letters that different members of the group had sent to Japan. None of them had any trouble getting answers until Amelia was mentioned. There never was a reply to a letter that mentioned her name. Who was doing the censoring? Our government? The Japanese government? Why? She walked to the nearest telephone and called to say she would take the next flight back to Cleveland. She had learned a lot in three days. Mostly she had learned that more people need to be concerned and get involved in things that affect their lives the way government does. When the people within the system do not know what is going on, it is time for those outside to find out. If we ever lose our democracy, it will be because of public apathy.

When Florence reported to the group, none of them were surprised that she was unable to find anything regarding the remains. They thanked her for the excellent try and were glad to get all of the other information. Tracy Griswold still was the key to unlock the mystery now about where Noonan's remains are or at least what he did with them on Saipan. Hopefully someday, he will remember so the entire episode can be brought to a close.

Until someone in the government decides to talk or until Mr. Griswold can remember, that missing piece of cranial bone will remain in Dr. Baby's care so that positive identification can be made if and when the rest of the body turns up.

In the meantime, the remains of Amelia Earhart have been laid to rest back in the United States from where she started her last trip thirty-two years ago. That last leg of the journey took a long time and a *lot of doing*.